A GIRL CALLED ANDIE

Her name was Andrea Stevenson, but she asked Joe Bradlee to call her Andie when he found himself sitting next to her on the flight to Paris. That wasn't all she asked him to do, as they moved to more convenient quarters.

By the time the plane landed, they were more than casual acquaintances, and Paris was waiting to more than live up to its reputation as the city of love. Andie was every man's dream come true in warm flesh and hot blood—even in the nightmare of sudden savagery and bewildering betrayal that closed in around Joe when he did all too good a job of posing as a target for an unknown assassin.

The French had a phrase for it: *Cherchez la femme.* Hunt for the woman.

Joe had found Andie—and he began to suspect as corpse piled upon corpse, that with a lover like Andie, he didn't need enemies.

DOUBLE IDENTITY

PRAISE FOR STEVE ZETTLER'S
THE SECOND MAN:

"Well worth reading. Good characters and relationships and a fast pace put this well-written thriller on an above-average level."
—*Affaire de Coeur*

"Suspenseful. An entertaining thriller."
—*Pinellas News* (St. Petersburg)

"A fast-paced, elegant thriller."
—*Seven Arts Magazine*

DOUBLE IDENTITY

Steve Zettler

AN ONYX BOOK

ONYX
Published by the Penguin Group
Penguin Books USA Inc., 375 Hudson Street,
New York, New York 10014, U.S.A.
Penguin Putnam Ltd, 27 Wrights Lane,
London W8 5TZ, England
Penguin Books Australia Ltd, Ringwood,
Victoria, Australia
Penguin Books Canada Ltd, 10 Alcorn Avenue,
Toronto, Ontario, Canada M4V 3B2
Penguin Books (N.Z.) Ltd, 182–190 Wairau Road,
Auckland 10, New Zealand

Penguin Books Ltd, Registered Offices:
Harmondsworth, Middlesex, England

First published by Onyx, an imprint of Dutton Signet,
a member of Penguin Putnam Inc.

First Printing, December, 1997
10 9 8 7 6 5 4 3 2 1

Printed in the United States of America

PUBLISHER'S NOTE
This is a work of fiction. Names, characters, places, and incidents either are the product of the author's imagination or are used fictitiously, and any resemblance to actual persons, living or dead, events, or locales is entirely coincidental.

Alan Nevins . . . Evermore thanks,
the exchequer of the poor.

Sex can only be a by-product of love and passion.
Sex without love is like gardening:
Plant your seeds, get a ham and cheese,
and go watch the Giants' game.

—Nina Lake

One

It's not always easy to tell the good guys from the bad guys. Unless, of course, you're playing baseball. If life was as easy as a baseball game, things would sure as shit be a hell of a lot simpler—the bad guys would be the clods wearing the blue hats. Oddly enough, Joe Bradlee was daydreaming about his long-gone baseball days, and not the more obvious, not the reality—a year out of his life wasted and gone—a year with the NYPD.

Babe Ruth ball. That's all it had been. It'd also been more than a few years ago. He'd been a center fielder for the Bushwick Cardinals—the guys with the *red* hats. So when Joe let his eyes fall open, on this disgustingly hot and humid New York August morning, and scoped out the Sixth Precinct's briefing room, it struck him as somewhat strange that each and every one of his compadres were either holding or wearing a *blue* hat. Cops were the good guys.

All this aside, the painful drone of authority remained the same. No matter how much time had slipped through your fingers. Pep talks hadn't changed much in the past fifteen, twenty, or ninety years. And the old cops, or old coaches, who stood up to give these pep talks remained pretty much the same as well: Fifty-eight, crew cut, beer gut, and half-smoked, cold and dying cigar butt hanging from the right corner of their liver-colored mouths; counting their days until retirement and—ya-hoo, yippy-doo—Florida, The goddamn Sunshine State. Old cops and old ball players . . . You can pick 'em off the trees like grapefruit down there.

Joe's mind played with the limerick possibilities of coaches and roaches, police and grease, as the captain rolled on, "Look, I know it's tough out there. Believe me when I say: I've been there myself, I've seen it all. We've all been down before and we've always bounced back"—this is where the Bronx-Irish accent jumped in to work a little overtime—"Let me tell you, this isn't the first time we've had our backs to the wall and we're not about to let a bunch of punks from Queens knock the socks off us this time. I want you men to go out there, behave like the true-blue winners you are, and show them who's in charge." And then as an afterthought, "Goddamn it."

Joe felt a nearly uncontrollable desire to stand and point out to Captain McGuire that he had missed a fabulous chance to use three of the all-time classic, bullshit, coach clichés. Joe didn't rise though. He knew the odds were at least fifty-fifty that McGuire would squeeze these clichés into his next pep talk. Plus, Joe was already on thin ice with New York's Finest and Captain McGuire—Joe Bradlee had developed a bad attitude and bad reputation for doing things his own way.

The punks Captain McGuire had made reference to, were a group of sixteen- and seventeen-year-olds from the borough of Queens who had been spending their weekends in Manhattan's West Village, home of the Sixth Precinct. As a form of entertainment, these young *hooligans*—McGuire's word—had been going on small rampages and terrorizing the local homosexuals—men and women alike. The boys had decided that a good way to keep these *queers*—again McGuire's word—from holding hands was to break the index fingers of the offenders. Both of them. Right and left. In the last month, the orthopedic surgeons at St. Vincent's emergency room had set forty-three index fingers. One of the *offenders* had been missing her left arm, thus accounting for the odd number of fingers.

A few of the men sitting in the briefing room with Joe, the men with the *blue* hats, had decided that a quick and efficient way to put an end to these fun-and-games was to send some of the lads from Queens over to St. Vincent's emergency room as well, with a few broken index fingers of their own. It would have worked like a goddamn charm, except that one of the fathers of these youths happened to be a lawyer of the worst type, and the man was now in the process of bringing legal action against the City of New York, Mayor Gould, and the NYPD for the brutality the officers had mercilessly inflicted on his innocent child.

Naturally the newspapers had gotten into the act and had run a front-page photo. A photo of Joe, surprisingly enough, coming out of the station-house door on Tenth Street, his dark hair, T-shirt, and shades making him look more like the ball player of his youth than the city employee he was. Actually, he hadn't had a damn thing to do with this particular *operation;* in fact, he'd been on vacation in St. Lucia when the whole thing went down, but that hadn't stopped him from flipping the bird to a *Newsday* photographer. Then, when questioned about his obvious hostility for the fourth estate, he'd said, "I learned how to do that from the late-great Nelson Rockefeller, dick-head . . . You guys remind me of maggots," fondly remembering his years with the Secret Service and the only politician who knew how to tell a joke and make it come out remotely funny.

At this point the entire Sixth Precinct fiasco had become known as "The West Village Finger Bowl." Odds makers were actually making book on whose digit would be next to be featured on the cover of the *New York Post* or *Daily News*. The *New York Times* had yet to get into the spirit of the situation. Mayor Gould, who had an annoying habit of pointing his middle finger at nearly everyone he came in contact with, hadn't taken his hands out of his pockets in over a week.

And Captain McGuire droned on. "I know these youths are still hanging out on the street corners and making wisecracks, I've seen them myself. But let's not forget that we're all professional police officers here, except for maybe Bradlee over there . . . Mr. Secret Service . . . Retired, isn't that right, Joe?"

McGuire's little joke. He was the only one to laugh. He may have been the only one who was actually listening.

"So . . . What I want is exactly what I *don't* want. I *don't* want anything else to appear in any goddamn newspapers; anything that might reflect badly on this department. Okay? That's it . . . Any questions?"

Joe Bradlee raised his left hand.

For some unexplained reason, Captain McGuire

didn't seem to notice him. "All right, dismissed. You all have your assignments."

"I have a question, Captain."

"Forget it, Bradlee. I don't want to hear your goddamn question. Dismissed."

McGuire walked through the side door, out of the briefing room, and back into his glass-paneled office, where he lit a match in a feeble attempt to return the glow to his cigar.

Joe remained with his arm raised while the other officers exchanged complaints and paraded out of the briefing room. Three of them slapped Joe's hand as they passed by. After a minute he brought his arm down. He sat alone, as if he half expected McGuire to reappear. Joe then let his head fall backward. His eyes closed once more.

His mind then took him to Washington, D.C. It'd been two years. They'd just slipped away. Evaporated. He'd walked away from the Secret Service as though it'd never been a part of his life.

Nina had saved him. She'd latched on and given him a life, then vanished as quickly as she'd appeared.

His career flew through his head like a tick trapped in a tornado—the ex-marine, decorated from Vietnam, who'd shone as a young Secret Service agent. The early counterfeiting ops. Cross-agency drug busts and crime sweeps. The stakeouts. The eternal stakeouts. Standing tall before visiting dignitaries; Presidents and Vice-Presidents. How many had there been. . . ? Always ready to take the big one for God and Country. The good times, the bad times. Panama, Hong Kong, Bogotá, Cairo, London, Moscow, Venice.

The good agents, the not-so-good agents. The good politicians, the good candidates, the others.

It was the others who'd burned Joe out.

They'd sapped him. Nearly broken him. The sleazy dictators, the politicians bought and paid for by any number of special-interest groups, the U.N. representatives sampling every whore Twelfth Avenue had to offer, the ambassadors who were nothing more than diplomatically immune drug couriers—every one of them afforded Secret Service protection. They weren't what Joe had signed on for. So he'd moved on. Requested the advance work. Became a Roadrunner. Clear the way for these clowns but never see them in action. Sweep the path in front. Make it safe and keep moving. Don't look back.

And then Nina. She'd dropped into his life like a gift from the gods. She'd picked him up and dusted him off and they were married on Independence Day.

Joe reopened his eyes.

He studied a half-dozen flies scrounging for tidbits on the peeling asbestos of the briefing-room ceiling and began to chew over, for the millionth time, the void left in his gut after his new wife had been lost—killed in an insane burst of violence by a man whose wires had snapped. And her son, Eubie; both gone in an instant. Left in a pile of blood. Joe wanted to go back. He wanted his family back. He wanted to erase the last year of his life and change the events. Go back to a happier time.

He sat in silence.

After another two minutes a broad-shouldered man with a dark beard eased himself into the chair next to Joe. He wore an olive-drab military-type field jacket, blue jeans, and high-top basketball sneakers. A torn T-shirt covered his chest. He was a few years younger than Joe, and much to this man's dismay, he was beginning to lose his dark curly hair. He was African-American and spoke with a pronounced Baltimore accent.

"You're Joe Bradlee, right?"

"Sí, sí, señor." Joe pointed to the ceiling. "I was just wondering if those flies were at all concerned about getting cancer from the asbestos . . . Fuck it, they seem to be enjoying themselves. Might as well go out with a smile on your face. Careful they don't shit on you." He then lowered his gaze and looked over the man's outfit. "I think we've got the same tailor. Nice shoes."

"My name's Jack Harper. I'm with the FBI."

Harper presented his ID.

"Who would have guessed? Welcome to New York," Joe said.

"Oh, I know New York, I've worked Chinatown for over six years."

Joe again eyed the agent from head to foot.

"Plainclothes?" he said.

"Sometimes."

"Now, you see, a field jacket in August would send up a flag to me . . . especially if I was Chinese. I'd say to myself, 'That black guy over there sure must be hot.' "

"I like the pockets."

"And the accent . . . ? People don't say, 'Where the fuck you from, homey?' "

"You should talk."

"Manhattan accents are a dying breed. Besides, I like people to know where I'm from. Like you. What the hell. It's a melting pot, right? Why shouldn't a guy from Baltimore live in New York? In Chinatown? I met a guy from Pakistan the other day, can you believe it? Pakistan. Right here in New York City. He was driving a cab of all things."

"You got a few minutes? I'd like to talk to you."

"Shoot."

"Not here. How 'bout I buy you a cup of coffee?"

"It's your buck . . ." Joe stretched his arms out to the side, placed them behind his head, and glanced once more at the flies. "I assume this little get-together has Captain McGuire's blessings?" he said, acting bored, but somewhat intrigued with this Harper person. There was something about him that said he could handle himself.

"We'll discuss McGuire's blessings."

"Benny's?"

"How's the coffee?"

"You'd prefer cappuccino? Espresso? Some Italian pastry? Star-fucking-Bucks? You want to spend three dollars a cup, we can go to the Upper West Side."

"Benny's is fine."

The two men stood and walked together, silently, until they reached the heavy glass doors that opened onto Tenth Street. And although the *Finger Story* was now well over a week old, two photographers still lurked between the parked cars.

"Try to behave yourself," Harper said with a smile as he held the door open for Joe. "I'll meet you at Benny's in ten minutes."

Joe stepped out and both photographers banged on the shutters of their motor-drive Nikons. Each rattled off five or six shots, the shorter of the two men called out:

"Hey Bradlee, anything for us?"

Joe held up two fingers on his left hand to form a V.

"Victory? Victory for the men in blue?" the photographer said and squeezed off three more shots.

"Peace, asshole . . . You fucking guys are like overgrown fruit bats. Don't you have caves somewhere? Families?"

Two

Jack Harper waited inside the police station while Joe walked off to the west. Toward Hudson Street. Away from the parasitic photographers. He then exited the station house and walked down Tenth Street. In the opposite direction. Off toward Fourth Street. Joe was tempted to yell back at the agent: "See you at Benny's in ten, Jack," but thought better of it. Harper was only doing his job. Obviously trying to lay low for some obscure reason. And Joe calculated the reason would become apparent soon enough.

Joe crossed over Hudson Street and headed uptown. After five blocks he reached Benny's Bus Stop Cafe. Nearly half the people he'd passed on the sidewalk said hello, along with two cab drivers. All called him by his first name. When he walked into Benny's he was again greeted by smiling faces and a small chorus of "Hey, Joe, what's up?" Miraculously, Harper had already arrived and found his way to a small booth at the rear of Benny's, by the men's room. Although the agent sat with his back to the rest of the patrons, Joe had no trouble recognizing him by the glistening bald spot on the back of his head. He slid into the opposite side of the booth. Faced Harper, and smiled.

"If you didn't want to be seen with me, this was a dumb fucking place to meet. Everyone in here knows who the hell I've been working for lately." Joe looked up to the waitress who'd followed him over to the table. He'd known her since he was fourteen. "I guess we're both having coffee, Liz."

"Okey-dokey, Joey," Liz said. And as always, Joe winced noticeably when she used *Joey*.

"It's just a thing I have," Harper said without looking directly at Joe, more checking out the faded print of the Statue of Liberty on the wall. "I don't like being seen on the street with a New York City cop. I don't like city cops, any city, doesn't make any difference to me. The less people associate my face with the NYPD the happier I am. Talking to a cop in a restaurant is a hell of a lot better than walking down the street with one, or spending too much time in a precinct building."

"Well, I'm not what you'd call a real cop. I look at my position with these Boys in Blue as temporary at best. Kind of a loaner situation. No telling when I'll move on. But still, it hurts me deeply to know you don't have a soft spot for the NYPD."

Joe's sarcasm was mostly ignored by Harper.

"Don't take it personally. Something tells me I might like you. I can't think you're a happy man here. But . . . A couple of your new playmates have gotten in my way in past joint ops. Made my life difficult. So . . . Let's just say I prefer to keep clear of New York's Finest."

"Buying them coffee doesn't seem like a brainy way to keep clear."

"Tell me about it . . . But like you said; you're not a real cop." Harper drummed his fingers on the Formica tabletop and glanced back to see how Liz was coming with the coffee. ". . . So, fill me in a little. I mean, what's your story, Bradlee? I've been doing a lot of reading up on you over the last week, but there's holes. Your file's only black and white."

"What do you want to know?"

"Let's start with, you flush down the toilet, what some would call a brilliant career with the Secret Service and end up going plainclothes with NYPD . . . Mostly busting chess hustlers in Washington Square from what I can tell. You're still a young guy by Service standards. What gives? It looks to me like you're going backward instead of forward?"

"I grew up in the village. I like people. It's where I want to work. I like the city . . . What's this all about?" Joe said in an almost deadpan set.

"I'll get to it. I like to know who I'm working with, that's all."

Joe cleared his throat and laughed, only slightly. "You're working with me?"

"No. *You're* the one who's working with *me*. Actually, to be more precise, you're working *for* me."

Liz arrived with the coffee.

Joe gave her a smile. Said, "Thanks."

"You got any Sweet'n Low, Liz?" Harper said.

Joe added, "My friend Jack here is trying to lose some weight . . . I think he looks fine, but he thinks he's fat. Becoming a blimp. A real fatso. What do you think, Liz? Stand up for her, Jack, let her take a look.

Show her both sides. You know, some women like a little beef on their men."

Harper didn't stand.

"I'll get the Sweet'n Low," Liz said and moved off.

"Thanks, partner."

"Well, Jack, what do you say we talk a little more about this partner business. How about *you* fill *me* in a little?"

Harper took a long moment. Liz placed three packets of Sweet'n Low on the table and left. Harper picked up two of the packets, tore them, and dumped the sweetener into his cup. He swirled the coffee with a thin stainless-steel spoon as he talked.

"You ever hear of a guy named Arthur Preston?"

"Does he live on Carmine Street?"

"No."

"Then I never heard of him. And even if I had, something tells me, the chances are pretty good that I wouldn't give a shit about him."

"How can you live in New York City and not know who the hell Arthur Preston is?"

"Obviously it's not that hard."

"Arthur Preston is the charity schmuck who misappropriated a cool forty million from a few of the less fortunate people in our society."

"Okay?"

"Shared Charities of the United Martyrs?"

"You mean the ponzi guy . . . ?"

"He's a slippery, slimy, fuck."

"I would guess so. I read about him."

"Anyway, we've got a good case against the bastard but it's not foolproof . . . This is where you come in."

"I give to the United Way. Sorry."

"There's a crucial witness."

"Right . . . Let me guess. You can't find him, and you suspect he's holed up somewhere on Carmine Street?"

"We know right where he is. We have him. Our problem is; getting him to New York."

"Rent a car. I don't own one."

"You're a real smartass, aren't you, Bradlee?" Harper pulled Joe's FBI file from a ragged backpack, having taken enough shit. He opened it and read. "Joseph Otis Bradlee. Interesting military record . . . Marine, natch, thus the attitude. What was it, the uniform? The recruiter sold you on that leatherneck crap, right?"

Joe made like he hadn't heard it. Harper went on.

". . . Two meritorious promotions . . . Decent set of medals . . . Goes on to become a kick-ass Secret Service agent." Harper put his own sarcastic twist on *kick-ass*. "And then, all of a sudden, he starts taking the advance work . . . Roadrunner, right? Begins to put a lot of space between himself and the politicos. Next thing you know, his partner gets himself killed in Venice, Italy, and our Agent Bradlee's out. He chucks it all. Takes a leave." Harper continued to flip through the file. "He gets married, goofs off in Manhattan for a year, loses wife and kid, then pulls some strings with his father's old friends and gets himself put on the NYPD Bunko Squad and spends his days busting petty thieves in the West Village. You think your pop'd be proud, this last year of yours? The famous, or should I say infamous, Buster Bradlee? How'd your old man get a nickname like that . . . ? Buster?"

"You tell me."

"Well, we've all heard the stories, haven't we?

Makes a guy feel better about having grown up in Baltimore. Especially a black guy."

"Look, I didn't know my old man. I kept my distance. As far as I know he was a good cop. Subject closed."

"Your mother's dead, too, right?"

"I'm sure you've got it all right there," Joe said as he flicked at Harper's file with his index finger.

"Yeah. Shot in a cross fire at the Feast of San Gennaro by some piss-ant from the Bronx. They should've fried the little fucker . . . But he gets away with twenty-five years. Shit, he'll be out before you know it."

"He's already been out. Not for long, though. He pulled the same fucking stunt down on Delancey eight months ago. So now he's whacked two people and the judicial system still can't seem to give him life in the can."

"Life? Fuck life. Like I said, they should've fried the cocksucker when they had the chance." Harper flipped through some more papers. "Let's see . . . How old were you when your old lady got it?"

"Eighteen," Joe answered before the agent could find the information. "Listen, this is all bullshit. It doesn't have a damn thing to do with anything. It's my history, not yours. What're you trying to prove?"

"Nothing. I just wanted to see if you had any buttons that could be pushed."

"Right." Joe called to the waitress. "Liz, can I get one of those chocolate donuts. None for Jack here. He's trying to trim down."

"How about your wife?" Harper continued. "How's that sitting with you?"

"Well, Jack, now you've found yourself a *button*.

And, if you know what's good for you, if you don't want me to come across this table at you, I suggest you don't go anywhere near it—let alone push it. Okay?"

"Okay. We all read about it. If it means anything, I feel bad for you. But take sagely advice from a younger guy; get over it. You weren't the only one it happened to. There was over a dozen people on that train. The fucker hosed them all. Nobody walked. Either join the dead or move forward . . . Life goes on."

"Obla-dee . . ."

Harper looked long and hard at Joe and then slowly closed his file and stuffed it back into his backpack. "What I'm trying to get at here is, word's out you've been doing some heavy drinking since she died. You've been sliding . . ."

"Nothing I can't handle."

"And the sleeping around . . . ?"

"This is getting a little old. I don't need a new mother. What's it all about?" Joe looked at his watch. "I've got a chess match at ten."

"Okay, here's the deal." Harper pulled a Polaroid photograph from his pocket and slid it across the table to Joe. "That's our witness—Billy Barton. He was Arthur Preston's right-hand man and he's the only one who can put the scumbag in the can for eternity . . . Look familiar?"

Joe picked up the Polaroid and analyzed it for a long time. He held it sideways for a second, half expecting the miniature image of Billy Barton to tumble out. He then set it down on the table, raised up his coffee cup, and took a slow sip. He glanced back down at the picture and swallowed. He had nothing to say.

After a minute, Liz showed up with Joe's donut. She set it beside his coffee cup and picked up the photograph of Billy Barton. She then looked at Joe.

"Nice shot, Joey. You look good in a coat and tie. I didn't think you owned one anymore."

Three

Benny's Bus Stop Cafe was beginning to empty out. People had to get to work. It was Tuesday. It was almost nine o'clock. Joe glanced at his watch. He picked up the Polaroid one more time. He then looked across the table to Agent Jack Harper.

"So what are you saying? Billy Barton is my long-lost twin brother?"

"You should've kept your mug out of the papers. Otherwise, we would've never found you," Harper said with a laugh. He took a pull from his now stone-cold coffee. "As you can see, you've become very useful to us."

"Actually, I don't think I do see."

"Arthur Preston needs to keep Billy-boy out of court. He's fucked royally if Billy testifies. We've got strong reason to think Preston's going to set up a hit on Billy before we can get him back to New York. . . ."

"Hold on. Preston's a charity broker, for Christ's sake. Sometimes you FBI guys amaze me. Go take a peek at the people in Saint Luke's thrift shop down the street. I don't think I'd call them killers."

"They're also not in Preston's league. This goes beyond the cheesy ponzi scheme the papers've been talking about. This guy's pyramid stretched all the way to South America and Africa. From coke to diamonds. The bastard pulled nickles out of the hands of people in Oklahoma, Texas, Utah, wherever, and supplemented it with laundered drug money. Then pumped it straight back to the Cali cartel nice and clean. As far as we can tell, not a cent was passed onto anything charitable. Worse yet he had legit organizations investing in the ponzi bit. And you don't think he's dumb enough to skim his forty mil from some neck-slicing Colombian, do you? Fuck, no, his share came from the old ladies. Your friends at the Saint Luke's thrift shop."

Harper stopped to take a breath. He was on a roll.

"Look, Billy's got all the goddamn numbers on this—how much went where, and when. How much Preston's siphoned off. He hasn't paid a fucking nickel in taxes in the last three years and if we can pull this off, if we can lock this bastard up and toss the key, he's going to start coughing up some names. He's scared, but not scared enough. I want him sharing a cell with a three-hundred-pound gorilla named Tiny for a month. I want his ass in a vise."

Joe picked at the chocolate donut, glanced out the window, and said. "Done?"

"No. Fuck no. Not by a long shot. We've got the son of a bitch in a cell on Rikers Island, no bail set, he's sixty-seven fucking years old, and if Billy makes it into Manhattan to testify, old Arthur never sees the light of day again. He's in for the duration, or he gives us what we want. Plus, there's too much goddamn money at stake—forty million is conservative. Don't tell me he's no killer. Don't tell me Saint Luke's thrift shop. He'll do whatever he has to do to keep from getting fifteen to twenty."

"And you think he has the wherewithal to set up a hit?"

"Money talks."

"I still don't think some charity bozo's going to operate that way."

"Fuck charity."

"I don't buy it."

"Well, but this: Billy was all set to testify. Five days before he's due in court for the hearing, his wife is found raped and sexually mutilated in front of an ATM machine in Westport, Connecticut. The next day her lily-white Mercedes is found in the parking lot of the New London Mall, down on its axles, with all the windows smashed out, blood all over the place, and Billy's sitting in my director's office in Washington, D.C., crying: 'Get me out of the country.' He doesn't even stick around for his wife's funeral. Arthur Preston doesn't play games, my friend."

"It's redundant."

"What?"

"The 'M' in ATM? It stands for machine. You can't say 'ATM machine,' It's redundant."

"Thank you."

"You want the rest of this donut?" It was a peace offering on Joe's part as much as anything.

"No thanks."

Joe finished it, looked into his empty coffee cup, and debated the benefit of a second round.

"So where do I fit in?" he said.

"It's simple. We bring you into New York first. Lots of press. Lots of front-page photos. We publish the travel route. The works. Preston has no idea where Billy is, and if the old man's going to make a move, he'll do it when we bring Billy in. It's his only shot. And we'll be more than ready. You'll be armed to the teeth and I'll be right there with you. Any shithead of a hit man will have a real surprise coming to him."

"I hope you're planning to wear nicer clothes. You look like a fucking bum."

"I'll find something . . . You should talk, my friend."

"Well, *my friend,* aren't you forgetting that my photo's already been on page one?"

"We're not bringing Billy back for over a month. The city will have forgotten you by then. It's New York."

"Where's Billy now?"

"Paris."

"Texas?"

"France."

"Jesus, why France? You couldn't find anywhere closer? Like Nepal, maybe?"

"It was Barton's choice. It was the only place he felt safe."

"Safe? Paris? I hope he took out some fucking bomb insurance. You think the word *Algeria* means anything to him?"

"It was his call. We're making him happy. We don't want to lose him . . . And we won't."

"What if I refuse?"

"You actually don't have a choice. It's all been cleared with your department. Up top. And McGuire's very happy to get rid of you for a while. I'm sure that doesn't surprise you too much."

"You know, the thought has occurred to me, that if I

were to be greased, gunned down in some fucking French airport, it'd make it that much easier for you to bring Billy in. Preston would just assume the schmo was dead."

"That's the scenario McGuire's hoping for." Harper smiled. "Hey, chances are nothing will happen and you'll get yourself a month or two in France."

"When do we have to go?"

"You leave tomorrow. We'd like to keep your mug out of the New York papers, and it seems the only way to do that is to remove you from the country." It was Harper's turn to stare into his empty coffee cup. His left eye twitched slightly and he continued, "You'll lay low in Paris for a while. In two or three weeks I'll pick you up, we'll coordinate the press and TV coverage, and then move you back to New York."

"Can I take a friend?"

"A friend?"

"A friend? A lady I met in Saint Lucia. Can she come to Paris with me?"

"I don't think so, Bradlee. This isn't a goddman vacation."

"Easy. I just don't want to get bored. I'm also deathly afraid of sleeping alone."

"Bored in Paris? How can you get bored in Paris?"

"I don't speak French as well as I'd like. She does . . . very nicely."

"You'll have to get by without her. In fact, you'll have to stay away from all women while you're there. I want you to stay away from anyone you don't know . . . And also any of your old Federal associates."

"That covers just about everybody, wouldn't you say?"

"You'll have no backup until I get there. All of our manpower is on Billy. This has to be done my way and it has to be played very close."

"What if I run into Billy?"

"We've got him tucked away. He's not stupid enough to go walking around the streets of Paris—alone."

"But I am . . . ?"

"Christ, Bradlee, you're a cop. Almost. You'll have a gun. It's been cleared with the French police. What do you want?"

"I want a guarantee that in two months I'll be back on Carmine Street in one piece."

"Okay." Harper thought for a moment. "You've got it. You've got my personal guarantee."

"Thanks, Jack, that makes me feel a hell of a lot better."

"Any time, partner."

Four

Inside his cell on Rikers Island, Arthur Preston reclined on a poorly padded bunk and listened to the Yankees game on a small portable radio that doubled as an alarm clock. His shockingly white hair was neatly parted on the left side, and his prison clothing somehow appeared as if it had just come from the dry cleaners. This, put together with his neatly trimmed snow white mustache, made it seem as though the authorities had wrongly arrested the little guy from the Monopoly board.

It was now two-thirty in the afternoon. The Yankees had just returned to the Bronx from a seventeen-game road trip where they had gone thirteen and four. For the first time in a number of years they were actually making a run for the pennant. The Blue Jays were in town. It was also the first time in ten years that Arthur Preston hadn't been in his box at Yankee Stadium and the television cameras had already zoomed in three times on his empty seat while the announcers made inane comments about his absence. The radio announcers had mentioned it as well.

". . . Well, Frank, it just doesn't seem the same out at

the stadium without seeing Arthur Preston in his box. Let's just hope it doesn't throw the Pinstripers off. A lot of these ballplayers can get very superstitious over the littlest things. It has been known to hurt their timing. And as we move further into August, it promises to be a crucial series for the Bronx Bombers. Why, I remember when I was with the A's back in . . ."

Actually Arthur was somewhat enjoying having his lieutenants locked out. Not that he wanted to spend the rest of his life on Rikers Island, or even in a country club prison, but this was the first time he'd been alone in more years than he could count. It seemed kind of nice. Of course he'd been kept far away from the fifteen-thousand Rikers's regulars, and he found himself wondering what all the complaints were about. So what if the food wasn't so good? Look at all the reading a person could get in.

With one out, in the bottom half of the second inning, and two strikes on Cecil Fielder, Arthur was disturbed by the guard. "Mr. Preston, ya got a visitor."

"My goodness, I wonder who that could be?" he said in a voice that cracked with sarcasm and too many years of Scotch and cigarettes.

"Your lawyer, sir."

"It was a joke, young man."

After Fielder struck out, Arthur was escorted out of his cell, down the corridor, through a double set of sliding steel doors, up two flights of stairs, and into a small room. The room was furnished only with a table and two chairs. The window was barred. As Arthur entered, the roar of a Delta jetliner taking off from La

Guardia Airport created a barrier that made it almost impossible for him to hear his lawyer's greeting.

What Sam Zuckerman had said, as he stood, was, "Good to see you, Arthur. You're looking well."

Arthur's response was, "I thought you were going to be here before the Yankees' game started?"

"There was quite a bit of traffic on the BQE, and they gave me a hell of a time at the gate. One delay after another. They're not making this easy for us, Arthur."

"Take it into consideration next time. Be on time or don't come . . . What have you found out with regards to bail?"

"We're trying everything we can. Judge Whitestone considers you a very high flight risk."

Another plane took off from La Guardia. The window glass behind the bars shook with the vibration.

"Good God, Sam, I thought this airport had noise abatement procedures," Arthur complained. "This is worse than suffering through a Mets' game."

"This *is* the noise abatement. They send the planes out over Rikers Island and Shea Stadium, avoiding the neighborhoods."

"I want out of here, you weasel. I don't care what it takes, but you get me out of here. . . . What's going on with the *Star Witness* Billy-boy Barton? Have you found that fruitcake yet?"

"We're working on it."

"You're working on it . . . Marvelous."

"The FBI has him. We know that for sure. We just haven't nailed down where yet."

The two men sat in silence for a minute. Arthur with

a scowl on his face and Sam with his hands in his lap. Arthur was the first to resume the conversation.

"Is this room bugged?"

"Well . . . Technically, no. It would certainly be unconstitutional. Remember the O.J./Rosie Greer fiasco? And that thing with the priest? Of course that doesn't mean they don't do it . . . Though nothing they taped could ever be used as evidence in a court of law. So there would be very little point in doing it, except to get some information. A lead or something like that . . . But then if they got caught, they'd pretty much have to let everyone in here out . . . Lord, I love the Constitution." Zuckerman chuckled at his little joke and continued, "I've never heard of any real abuses, now that I think more on it."

"Good God Almighty. Speak in English, will you? Is this room bugged? Yes or no?" Preston was now shouting, both out of anger and necessity. It was the only way to be heard over the roar of the next departing jetliner. This time it was USAir.

"No, but I should advise you to keep your voice down. Remember the O.J. mess."

"This may come as a huge surprise to you, Sam, but I care very little about O.J."

Arthur then leaned into Zuckerman and spat his words through his teeth in a harsh loud whisper. "I want you to find that turncoat Billy Barton. I want you to carve him up like a piece of calve's liver. You understand me? If that worm gets anywhere near a courtroom, your wife's going to be the next one to have a date with my good friend Nestor. You follow me on that?"

"There's no need to make threats, Arthur. I have a man who can take care of our problem. He assures me everything is under control."

"It better be."

"Now," Zuckerman braced himself, half expecting Preston to leap across the table and tear his head off when he heard his next bit of news, "They're trying to push our court date back to September twenty-seventh." Zuckerman flinched overtly when he said this, but the old man seemed to have calmed down somewhat. Zuckerman pushed on. "That should give us a month to solve this Billy Barton problem. Right now there's more pressing financial concerns. You're still holding a sizable amount of property that can legally be seized by the government. If you," he cleared his throat nervously, "*we,* lose this case . . . Property that can, and will, be sold to pay back the Shared Charities of the United Martyrs debt. I've drawn up some papers that places the property in question—into your wife's name."

Preston began a slow laugh. By the time he was finished he'd nearly fallen off his chair.

"My wife?" he was finally able to mutter. "I'd rather see it go back to the crippled children. At least they might know what in blazes to do with it. Although I doubt it."

"It's either her or your son, Arthur."

"My God, you're full of laughs today. My son. The golfer. Do you know what he does? With his time, that is? With his life?"

"Actually . . . No."

"He plays golf, for God's sake. That's it. That's all he does. He plays golf. With those little white balls. It makes me sick just to think of it. Always muttering about his graphite shafts."

". . . Transfer of the property in question to any other individual or corporation would involve a sure thirty-two to thirty-eight percent tax bite. I don't think you want that."

"Which properties are we talking about?"

"Your home in Palm Springs, all six of the condos in Aspen, the Congregational complex in Mobile, the diamonds, if they know about them, the house in Palm Beach, and the yacht. I think your ranch in Ontario will be safe. It's Canada."

"Is it really?"

Zuckerman wasn't sure if he should've answered but he said, "Yes," anyway.

". . . He plays golf . . ."

Preston said this in a low whisper, and the noise from the next La Guardia jetliner again made it impossible for Zuckerman to hear a thing. But he'd seen Preston's lips move.

"I'm sorry, Arthur, I didn't hear you."

"Put them in Arthur Junior's name. But not until I talk to him. See that he's here before noon tomorrow. I have a thought."

"I believe he's in the South of Spain." Zuckerman cleared his throat again. "Marbella I think." He cleared his throat once more. "Playing golf."

"By noon tomorrow or he gets nothing."

"I'll do my best."

"God knows that's all I could hope for. You people depress me beyond belief. You be on time tomorrow, too. And if the Yankees get into the World Series and

I'm still in here? You're a dead man. You and that entire sleazy firm of yours." Preston stood, walked to the door, and knocked for the guard. He then turned and looked back at Zuckerman and said, "Who's this person you have working on our little Billy Barton problem?"

"I've found someone at the FBI. I think he can be trusted. He likes money. His name is Jack Harper."

Five

At seven p.m. on Wednesday evening Joe Bradlee found himself sitting on a fiberglass bench in the American Airlines terminal at John F. Kennedy International Airport. Three screws were loose and a fourth one dug into his left buttock. Sitting right beside him was FBI Agent Jack Harper. According to Jack Harper, everything was ready.

Joe'd been furnished a brown leather attaché case from Mark Cross. Inside the case was a one-way, coach-class ticket to Paris's Orly Airport and two passports; one imprinted with the name Joseph Otis Bradlee, the other with William Erskine Barton. The passport photographs were identical. Also in the case was a Paris guidebook containing a map of the city and a Métro plan, a Berlitz 'New, Revised!' French phrase book, five thousand dollars in American Express travelers' checks, four thousand French francs, and a key to a small one-bedroom apartment at number 6 Rue Racine just off the Boulevard St. Michel in Paris's Sixth Arrondissement.

Earlier that day Jack Harper had taken Joe on a small shopping spree at Barney's on Seventh Avenue. The FBI had bought Joe two suits, two sports jackets, three pairs of slacks, six dress shirts, five neckties, three pairs of shoes, two belts, and a raincoat. All of which had been placed in a Mark Cross suitcase and had been checked in at curbside with the American Airlines skycap, only fifteen minutes earlier.

"You'll use your own passport when they ask you for it tonight, and again at Orly tomorrow morning when you arrive," Harper said without looking at Joe. "After that, get rid of it. Burn it. We'll supply you with a new one when you get back to the States."

"I somehow feel like I'm forgetting something."

"There'll be a weapon waiting for you in the apartment. Bottom drawer of the dresser. Under the extra blanket." Harper looked at his watch. "You've got a couple hours. You want to grab a beer?"

"You don't have to stick around. I know how to get on an airplane."

"I like to see things through."

"You'd like to see that I don't get shitfaced, is what you mean."

"I like to see things through."

Joe shrugged. "So let's get a beer . . . You buying?"

"Jesus. You've got close to six thousand dollars in that case, and you want me to buy the fucking beer?"

"Okay, okay, I'll buy the beer. Jesus. The same people are paying for it no matter how you slice it."

They stood, walked past the ticket counter, and entered the lounge. It was a fairly large room. It seemed to be doing a booming business. A lot of nervous air travelers hoping to get a little buzz on, before they had to endure their nine- and ten-hour flights across the Atlantic Ocean. Jack and Joe sat at the bar and Harper ordered.

"Two Kronenborgs," he said to the girl behind the bar. Then he looked at Joe. "Get you started off with some decent French beer."

After she'd poured the beer, Joe took a sip, looked at the label, and said, "This stuff's French? It doesn't look it."

"Fools you, doesn't it? Just shows you not everything's what it appears to be. I don't know what its history is, but it's French. Says so somewhere on the label, if you don't trust me."

"I trust you like a brother, Jack."

"Say, are you two guys cops?"

This came from a small, round man with glasses now standing directly behind Harper. They both turned to face him. Joe looked down at him and said, "What?"

"Are you guys cops? Every time I see a black guy and a white guy together, I figure they're cops. Especially in a bar. That's the way it always is in South Bend. See . . . I've got a little bet going with my friend over there." He pointed to the corner of the room. His friend, another short, round guy, waved and smiled. "I say you're cops, he says you aren't . . . So, who's right?"

Harper answered. "You're half right. I'm a cop." He showed the man his FBI identification and then pointed his thumb at Joe. "And this fucker's a murderer . . . Little girls, mostly. I'm taking him back to Los Angeles for execution. The son of a bitch escaped two days before we were going to gas him last year. Can you believe that shit? I'm sure you read about it. Lefty the Mule? It was all over the papers?"

"Uh, no, we're from Indiana . . . Shouldn't he be handcuffed?"

"Nah. He promised me he wouldn't try anything funny. You don't see any little girls, do you? Twelve-year-olds? I figured there wouldn't be any in here. It being a bar and all."

Harper scanned the area for effect.

"He likes them flat chested . . . More like little boys when you think about it."

The short, fat man glanced at his friend and then back. "You're foolin' with me, right?"

"Nope." Harper looked at Joe and said, "Go ahead, Lefty, it's okay, show him your dick." He then looked back to the short, round man. "Murderers always have huge dicks. I'll bet you didn't know that. Cops have little dicks. You want to go to the men's room with him and look at his dick? He won't try anything."

". . . Uh, no, that's okay."

"Maybe your friend wants to look at his dick. Why don't you go ask him? It's as big as a fucking milk carton. That's why they call him the Mule."

"No, that's okay. Look, I'm sorry I bothered you." And the man rolled back to his table.

"I liked that," Joe said after the man from Indiana left. "Is that a standard piece of Baltimore charm, or did the FBI teach it to you?"

"I made it up. Some people rub me the wrong way."

"So I see . . ."

Joe grabbed a handful of peanuts and slid the dish over to Harper.

"What do you do for two or three weeks, while I'm laying low in Paris?"

"I get everything set up here so it runs smoothly

when we bring you back in. I know it doesn't sound like fun, but ideally we'd like to let someone get close enough to you so they can make a move, and we can pick him up. And then make the direct connection with Preston. The most important thing is, we take whoever makes the move, alive. And I'd be lying to you if I told you you weren't expendable. I'm sorry, but I'm sure you figured that part out awhile ago."

"Yep."

"Look, Bradlee, if it makes any difference, I think you're a good man. I've read your record backward and forward. You've had some tough breaks in the last few years . . ." Harper sipped his beer. "I think the world would be a shittier place without you and your type. You watch your ass until I get over there. After I'm there, I guarantee you're home free."

"Thanks, Dad . . . Just out of curiosity, what exactly is my *type*."

"Oh, you know . . . white guys."

Joe choked and nearly spit his last sip of beer out his nose. Then put a twenty on the bar, and ordered two more.

"I'd definitely feel a hell of a lot better if this *white guy* had a safe phone number. If I contact any of my old Parisian friends, the wrong people are bound to find out that I'm in France. I know you don't want that."

Harper took another minute to finish his beer. He then reached over the bar and picked up a dry cocktail napkin. He took out a pen and scratched a phone number on the piece of paper. He spoke as he wrote. "By all rights, I shouldn't be doing this. I still can't give you any number here in New York. It's just too damn risky. Preston has his fingers everywhere. I'm not altogether sure the Bureau's even safe. A few months ago another agent used my name to pull some of Preston's files. I got it straightened out, but we never found out who the agent was."

Harper slid the napkin over to Joe.

"That number's in Paris. Her name is Danielle. If anyone else answers the phone, hang up. Only talk to Danielle. If a man answers, don't call a second time. She works for no one. Not us, not the French police. She's just good people. Maybe she can help you if you're in a jam. She's done it before. Tell her you're a friend of mine."

The bar girl brought two more Kronenborgs and picked up Joe's twenty.

"Is this for both rounds?" she said.

"Yeah."

"I need eight more dollars."

"What for?"

"It's seven dollars a beer."

"What . . . ? What if we'd ordered Buds?"

"Six-fifty. You're better off with the Kronies."

"Jesus," Joe said as he placed another twenty on the bar and looked to Harper. "No wonder you didn't want to buy me a goddamn beer."

"I've spent a lot of time in airports. I've researched this thoroughly."

Joe looked at the cocktail napkin and tucked it into his shirt pocket. "I'd still like something more official."

"I'm trying to be as subtle as I can here, Bradlee. Preston's tentacles may stretch a lot farther than any of us suspect. I'm trying to tell you that you're pretty much on your own. You can trust no one."

"Including you?"

"I'm probably the only one you can trust."

"Uh-huh."

"I'll tell you one thing . . . If someone calls you up and says he's Jack Harper, you'd better be damn sure you recognize the voice."

The rest of their conversation consisted mostly of Harper filling Joe in on what current museum shows not to miss, and a rundown on some of his favorite Parisian watering holes. After two more rounds, Joe and his brand-new Mark Cross attaché case were strolling down the gangway and onto the American Airlines MD-11.

Harper stayed and watched until the large plane pulled away from the gate. He then walked over to a bank of telephones and placed five phone calls. One to his apartment in West New York, New Jersey, to check for messages, two to Paris, one to Westport, Connecticut, and one to FBI headquarters in lower Manhattan. All of this took him less than eight minutes. Harper then exited the terminal, picked up his sedan, and headed back toward the lights of Manhattan.

Six

"I know you!!!"

Joe's eyelids shot open as though they'd been connected to a pair of overstretched rubber bands in the back of his head. And the sight he saw before him seemed more out of a horror show than anything he could imagine. Through the dimmed airline cabin lights, he could just make out the figure of a short, wiry woman, maybe seventy years old. She had one of those pageboy haircuts that had gone out of style in the forties, beady little black eyes, and a face like an ancient toad. She wore a pale blue sack dress that gave her a strange ghostly appearance and she was backlit by the in-flight movie. The effect made it seem as if Bruce Willis was doing a small jig on her left shoulder. Joe hadn't sprung the four dollars for the headphones so he couldn't hear a word Bruce Willis was saying, but Bruce did seem to be trying to warn Joe to be wary of something. He seemed to be saying, "Keep your fucking head down, José."

The woman repeated herself.

"I know you!!! You're that policeman who was on the cover of *Newsday* last week."

"Jesus, lady, I was sound asleep. What time is it?"

"We're halfway between New York and Paris. Time doesn't make any difference. You'll have jet lag for six days no matter what. It's one day for each hour . . . I know quite a bit about these things. I worked a number of years as a reporter. I was a very influential writer. I could have won a Pulitzer prize if I had put my mind to it. Of course I was much younger . . . Why did you give *Newsday* the finger?"

"What are you talking about?"

"You're the cop. I recognize you."

"Lady, Jesus, I'm no cop . . . I'm from . . . Indiana." It was the first place to pop into Joe's mind for some reason. He squinted to focus on her, "Leave me alone, will you?"

"You're not from Indiana. Not with that accent. You're that cop. What'd they do? Fire you? They should have. The press people are only doing their job. They deserve respect."

"Lady, I've had a long day. I'm no cop. You've got me mixed up with someone else." Joe tried to roll over in his seat.

"Well, you look just like him. He was in the *Post* again today. It wasn't the front page, though. It was in the back somewhere; just before the sports section. He gave a photographer the peace sign this time, but he still had some foulmouthed comment. I don't know where some of these policemen get off . . . Stay right here. The man sitting next to me brought the *Post* on board. I'll go see if he'll let me borrow it. Well, maybe I shouldn't wake him up . . . Oh, I'm sure he won't mind . . . I'll be right back."

Joe rolled back to face the Toad Lady.

"Lady, you're waking up the whole damn plane.

I really don't care about this policeman. I've got an important business meeting tomorrow morning and—"

"Why aren't you in business class?"

"What?"

"Well, if you're going to Europe on business, if you're a businessman like you say, the least your company could do would be to purchase you a business-class ticket. When I worked for Birdseye, you know, the peas and carrots people? They always sent me *first*-class. But that was years ago, too. After I was a reporter, though. Things just seem to be going downhill every minute . . . What's the name of your company? I'd be happy to write a letter to them on your behalf. I write very effective letters. I almost always get a response. I know, give me one of your business cards. I'll do it as soon as I get back to Floral Park. That's where I live, Floral Park. It's on Long Island, just across the line from Queens. Have you ever been there?"

"Lady, I'm from Indiana, and I'm tired. I know this may sound rude, but I can't talk to you and I can't listen to you. Go have another nightcap and call it a day."

"You are that cop. You're all the same. You have no respect for anyone. I'm probably twice your age and you can't even stand up when I'm talking to you. You can go to hell for all I care . . . The idea. Suggesting I would drink some alcohol. You don't even know me. A nightcap, he says . . . I'm going to talk to the captain." She spun and walked up the aisle.

It took the Toad Lady close to fifteen minutes to muster reinforcements. Joe had almost managed to doze off again, but he could hear them coming. This time he opened his eyes more slowly.

"That's him," she said defiantly as she pointed to Joe.

She had with her the captain, and her seat-mate, the man with the *Post*. Both men appeared even more groggy than Joe.

The captain approached Joe and said, "Excuse me, sir, I wonder if I could have a word with you?"

"Sure," Joe said with an exhausted sigh. He stood up.

The man with the *Post* opened it, looked at Joe, and then to the Toad Lady and said, "It's not the same man, lady. This guy in the paper's much shorter." He then turned and staggered back to his seat.

The captain walked Joe to the rear of the plane. He spoke slowly and with an Arkansas drawl. "I'm sorry about this little disturbance. The flight attendant informs me that this woman has managed to consume five Scotches, two splits of wine, and a brandy. I'm surprised she can walk. We do have an empty seat in the business section, and if you like, I can move you up. This way we can keep her from bothering you further."

"Thank you."

They walked back to Joe's seat where he picked up his attaché case. The captain perched himself on the armrest, which had the effect of bringing his face down to the Toad Lady's level.

"Ma'am, I'm going to take this passenger up to the business section. That way I'll be able to keep a closer eye on him. I'm sure he won't disturb you for the remainder of the flight."

"Thank you, Captain. I don't know why they allow

such people on airplanes. It certainly seems like a security breach if you ask me. It most definitely never happened in my day."

"Yes, ma'am."

She made a feeble attempt to kick Joe as he passed her in the aisle, but he sidestepped her nicely, and followed the captain up to business class.

Joe said, "Thank you," to the captain and lowered himself into the wide seat. He lifted the collar of his shirt, adjusted the pillow, and leaned his head to the left. Seated beside him was a woman in her late twenties. She had long auburn hair and also had her collar turned up. As Joe settled, she opened her eyes, lifted her head slightly, and smiled.

"I know you!!!" she said.

Seven

"You know me?"

"Yes . . . Billy Barton, right?"

"No . . . No . . . I'm . . . Jesus, I'm from Indiana."

Joe squinted at the auburn-haired woman. Despite the fact that she had just awakened from what was obviously a very deep sleep, she was radiant. Her smile seemed to illuminate her small corner of the darkened cabin. Joe smiled back and said, "Wait, hold on, I'm not from Indiana. I've just had a horrible experience with a Toad Lady back in the tourist section and the pilot was nice enough to move me up here . . . I'm sorry I woke you."

"That's okay. It's good to see you again. I guess it's been two years now. What were you doing sitting in the tourist section?"

". . . Sleeping?"

By the look on her face, Joe knew he wasn't going to get away with that answer. He was right.

"Surely Billy Barton hasn't been reduced to traveling tourist?"

"Listen, I know this was a stupid thing to do, but before I got on the plane I had a few drinks and then popped a couple of those damn sleeping pills doctors hand out to forty-year-old first-time mothers? Then I got attacked by this Toad Lady. I think Bruce Willis was in on it somehow." Joe rubbed his eyes for effect. "Everything's just a little fuzzy. . . . Has it really been two years?"

"I know, it's hard to believe, isn't it?"

She looked him square in the eyes for a long moment and Joe had the sensation that she was about to lean over and kiss him. He rubbed his eyes once more.

"Oh, Billy, you're so sweet."

She put her hand to his cheek.

"You don't remember me, do you?" She waited for a reply, but Joe sat paralyzed.

"I can see it in your eyes. You're trying desperately . . . It's nice of you."

"No . . . No . . . It's coming to me. I'm sorry. I'll get it." He started to laugh. "Two years ago, right? Give me a minute."

"That's okay. I'm not hurt . . ."

It was the truth, she didn't seem in the least bit hurt.

"It was Labor Day Weekend in Newport . . . at the Rutherford estate?" She laughed. "Listen, I'm not surprised you don't remember me. You and that Lazlo character were so wigged out on cocaine, it's amazing you even remember your own name, let alone mine."

"You're right about that . . . I'm sorry. That whole weekend was a mess. A big, out-of-focus mess. Bruce Willis wasn't there, was he?"

It still looked to Joe as though she were about to kiss him. She glowed for some reason. He pressed on, "Jesus, I barely even remember Lazlo."

"Yeah . . . that's a shame what happened to him."

"Yeah . . ."

A small bead of sweat formed at Joe's hairline. She put her hand on his forearm.

"I'm sorry. It probably wasn't easy for you."

"What makes you say that?"

"Weren't you two . . . Well, you know . . . an item?"

"What. . . ? Are you nuts? Me and Lazlo. . . ? Where'd you ever get an idea like that? Jesus. Lazlo?"

The man across the aisle from Joe stirred and said, *"S'il vous plaît, monsieur. Je suis très fatiguè."* He glanced at his watch and added, "Would you mind holding it down a little, monsieur?" in a heavy French accent.

"Je suis désolé," Joe said.

The auburn-haired woman leaned into Joe and whispered, "You mean you're not gay?"

"Are you crazy? Me. . . ? Joe," Joe stammered."I mean Jeez, Jooz, for God's sake. For crying out loud . . . Wait. Christ. What the hell am I thinking of? I was married for a while there. I had a wife, you know? How could I be gay if I had a wife? Answer me that."

"You make me laugh. You always did." And she did—she laughed. She squeezed his arm. Joe started to laugh, too.

"You've got a great laugh," he said.

"I'm sorry . . . I always assumed your marriage was one of those *marriage of convenience* deals."

"That's not how I looked at it," Joe said with mock indignation. "We tried very hard to have children . . . nearly every night."

The man across the aisle grunted. Joe moved back into a whisper.

"I feel really bad about this, but you're going to have tell me your name . . . one more time."

"Andrea Stevenson."

"Andie. . . ?" he said very tenuously.

"Andie."

Joe breathed a sigh of relief. "Well, at least I remembered something from that weekend. At any rate, I've straightened myself out. I haven't touched any blow since Newport. It's a real one-way street. Actually, it's been almost two years . . . now that I think back on it."

"Well, that's why I couldn't hang out with you and Lazlo. You probably thought I was pretty rude."

"Hey, I don't remember a thing, remember?"

She locked her eyes onto his once more.

"You're different, Billy."

"You think so? How?"

Again Joe felt a nervous sweat forming.

"You've grown up . . ."

"You can tell that, this quick? After three minutes?"

"Yes, I can. Your eyes have changed. You've come a long way, and it's very becoming on you. Maybe it's because you've dumped the coke. You're not still working for that sleazy-eyed son of a bitch Arthur Preston, are you?" She turned and looked out into the blackness that hung above the Atlantic Ocean. "I'm sorry. That wasn't a fair thing to say. Let me rephrase it . . . Are you still working for Arthur Preston?"

"Not Arthur Preston the sleazy-eyed son of a bitch? That Arthur Preston? If I was still working for him, do you think I'd be sitting back in the tourist section?"

"Thank God. They should hang that bastard from the highest tree they can find. By his balls . . . if he has any."

"Jesus, it sounds as though you've given all your money to Shared Charities of the United Martyrs."

"No, but a lot of people did. I have no use for people like Preston. Stealing from the disadvantaged. They should all be drawn and quartered. Butchered like the pigs they are . . . and then fed to the crows."

"Remind me not to get on your bad side."

"It just pisses me off, that's all."

"All right." After a minute Joe said, "Why are you off to Paris?"

"Don't try to change the subject."

"All right."

They sat quietly for ten or fifteen minutes and just as Joe was about to drift off, Andie said, "It's a fashion show."

Joe let his eyes open slowly.

"Pardon me?"

"It's a fashion show. I'm going to Paris for a fashion show."

"I see."

"How about you?"

"Sure."

"What?"

"Sure."

"What do you mean, 'Sure'?"

"I've never been to one, but why not? There's a first time for everything."

She started laughing again, and then finally said, "What are you talking about?"

"I've never been to a fashion show . . . Weren't you inviting me to go to a fashion show with you?"

"No."

"Oh, sorry, I thought you were. I thought you were suggesting we spend some time together. Since we're obviously going to be in Paris at the same time. And we're obviously going to have to entertain ourselves . . . somehow."

Joe closed his eyes again.

"I was asking you why you were going to Paris in the first place?"

Joe opened his eyes again. He silently cursed Harper. The agent's last words had been, "Don't worry, you won't run into anyone you know. Your old cronies wouldn't come anywhere near the Left Bank." And Joe had felt confident Harper was right. But now, he was barely out of United States airspace, and he'd already been fingered by two strangers.

"Vacation," he said.

"Who are you working for now?"

"Nobody, I just needed to get out of New York for a while."

"You're not ducking prosecution, are you?"

"Jesus, you're nosy."

"Well?"

"I left Preston long before that Shared Charities of the United Martyrs stuff. I was more involved with his S & L ventures."

"I thought I read somewhere that you were in on the charities thing, too. Or had the dirt, or something?"

"Listen, Andie, I can't talk about the charity business. But I can tell you I'm going to do everything I can to see that Arthur Preston spends the rest of his life in jail. And that's the truth. How's that? Okay?"

Andie leaned over the wide seat divider and kissed Joe square on the lips.

"My hero," she said with another beaming smile that eventually broke into a laugh.

Joe was left stuttering.

"Well . . . Yeah . . . I mean . . . What else could I do . . . the guy's a bastard . . . I'm not about to let him get away with screwing all those kids. All those people looking for a little help. I mean . . . Jerry Lewis wouldn't behave like that."

"Where are you staying? I think we *should* get together this week."

"I have an apartment."

"You have an apartment? In Paris? And you weren't in on Preston's scam?"

"No. No. It's a loaner. The apartment. It belongs to a friend. Believe me, if I had any money, I'd be riding up here in business class with you."

"Thank you, I'm flattered."

"Well, it's the seats, really. Free drinks. Free headsets. I'd be a better informed person. Right now I'd know what the hell Bruce Willis was saying."

"Thanks a lot . . ."

"Does Bruce look more dense without the sound, or is it my imagination?"

Andie looked to the screen. "I don't think it makes any difference with Bruce. So, where's the apartment?"

"Have you always been this nosy? I don't remember you being this nosy before."

"What's nosy? I'm making conversation. Besides, you don't remember me, remember?"

"Right."

"Where's the apartment?"

Joe pulled his attaché case to his lap, opened it, and took out his Paris map. He spread the map out on the case. In the center of it, just below the blue curvy line that represented the river Seine, was a red X. It had been placed there by Agent Harper a few hours earlier. Joe pointed to the X and said, "It's right here."

"How are you getting in?"

"I have a key."

"Jesus. No." She laughed again. "How are you getting into the city, from the airport?"

"Cab?" Joe's answer again was very tenuous.

"Do you always take a cab?"

"Always?" he said, thinking that every other time he'd come in from Orly he'd been on a Secret Service detail, riding in a limousine, with either the President or Vice-President of the United States of America.

"When you come in from Orly? Do you always take a cab?"

"Obviously you have a better idea."

"There's an Air France bus. But now that I think about it, it may work out the same if we split a cab." She looked up to the overhead bin, rolled her eyes, and did some quick math. "The bus is still cheaper by a long shot. We'll take the bus in."

"We?"

"I'm staying at l'Hôtel Salomé. It's very close to you. We can split a cab from Montparnasse."

"Montparnasse?"

"The train station?"

"Right. The station. Jesus, I'm really whipped. I'm not focusing on a damn thing. I should probably try to doze off."

Joe closed his eyes once more. All was quiet for another five minutes. He didn't, however, doze off. He had the distinct feeling that Andie had been watching him for the entire time.

"I've been watching you," she said. "You're not dozing off."

Joe opened his eyes.

"I was trying."

"No you weren't."

"Yes, I was."

"Well, I won't argue with you, but you weren't. You were thinking."

She gave him a very straightforward look and continued.

"I have to be serious for a minute. I have to ask you a very serious question."

"Okay. I may not be able to answer it, but shoot."

"Are you awake?"

"That's the question?"

"No, but I want to make sure you're awake. It's important."

"I'm wide awake. I've been thinking, remember."

He smiled at her. She put her hand on his arm again.

"Jesus, you're attractive," she said.

"Thanks. So are you."

"Do you think so?"

"Is that the question?"

"Sort of."

"It is?"

"Well, not really. I was just sort of pondering . . . Well . . . What I mean is . . . I've never had sex on a plane. I know it may sound strange, but if you're attracted to me as much as I am to you . . . Well, this would be the perfect opportunity, don't you think? It may never come up again."

"You're joking?"

"No. If you're not interested . . ."

"No. No. I didn't say I wasn't interested. I've never done it, either. I mean, I'm just a little shocked, that's all."

She pulled Joe toward her and planted a long passionate kiss on his lips. After he came up for air he said, "This sounds like it could be very interesting. How do you think we should go about it?"

She stood and pulled her skirt high above her knees, straddled Joe's legs, and sat down on his lap, facing him. Again she kissed him deeply and after the next break she said, "Give me three minutes in the lavatory, then join me. Knock four short knocks so I know it's you."

Andie lifted herself off of Joe and into the aisle. She bent down and kissed him once more. As she did, she placed her right hand directly between his legs.

"Seems like you're all ready . . . I know I am."

Eight

By the time Joe and Andie had cleared customs it was almost nine a.m. and neither one was in the least bit rested. When all was said and done they had spent nearly an hour in the MD-11 lavatory and had tried virtually every sexual position the space would allow. They'd then returned to their seats and ended up yacking for another two hours. Finally they'd drifted off; but only an hour and a half remained of the flight. They both had been rocketed awake when the plane's fat tires smacked down hard on the Orly tarmac.

After perusing Joe's documents, the French passport agent had said, *"Souhaiter la bienvenue à Paris, Monsieur Bradlee,"* and Joe had coughed a loud sort of bark when he'd sensed that the man was about to call him by name. Fortunately Andie had stepped far enough through the line. Joe guessed she hadn't heard a word. He was still on safe ground.

But as they now stood waiting for the Air France bus, Joe had an unbelievably strong desire to fill Andie in on his entire story. To begin with, he hated the name Billy. It was a fucking little boy's name. Billy, Jesus. He wanted Andie to be calling him Joe, not Billy. He did, however, recognize all this as some sort of deep-rooted macho homophobic bullshit, but also he didn't particularly care. The name just stuck in his throat. Billy.

The only thing that kept Joe from spilling the beans right then, at the bus stop, was that somewhere in the back of his brain he had this tiny image of Jack Harper saying, "Don't trust anyone. Especially in France." Then there was the other thing Harper had said about staying away from women while he was in Paris. But Joe wasn't actually in Paris . . . The city limits . . . Officially . . . Yet.

Within a few minutes a huge white bus with red trim and the Air France logo painted in blue appeared from behind the terminal building. It sparkled in the morning sun and seemed to dwarf the other city and local buses. It angled head first into a diagonal spot directly in front of Joe and Andie.

"It's too bad," she said with an overly bawdy smile, "but I don't think these buses have bathrooms in them." Then gave Joe a slow seductive wink.

"Don't tell me you've never had sex on a bus, either? Christ, didn't you go to high school? I'll bet money you were a cheerleader at one point. I can almost see you in a pleated skirt making life difficult for center fielders."

"Shortstops."

A Moroccan porter gave them a broad smile, opened the luggage bay, and tossed their bags into the empty cavern beneath the bus. After a minute the driver stepped down and out of the idling beast. He lit a cigarette. A small group of passengers began to arrive. They all waited patiently for the driver to finish his smoke.

Finally he crushed the butt into the pavement with his heel and motioned for the passengers to follow him onto the bus. Joe pulled a wad of francs from his pocket. He looked at them as though they were a collection of Chinese movie tickets.

"What do you think the fare's up to these days?" he mumbled to Andie.

"Thirty-two francs, monsieur," the driver answered.

"Thanks. *Merci bien.* So, *pour deux* . . . it would be *soixant-quatre*?"

"Oui."

Joe fumbled through his cash while the travelers behind him sighed loudly. The driver finally pulled a bill from Joe's grasp, gave him some change, and handed him two tickets. Andie did her best to make believe she didn't know him.

"How big is this apartment you're borrowing?" she said after they found seats.

"Small, I think. One bedroom. Why?"

"Nothing . . . Maybe we should go there first. Just to make sure you can get in."

"No. It's all set. I won't have any trouble."

The ride into Montparnasse station was a quiet one. The two of them were drained. They might have been sleeping most of the way. Neither knew.

After exiting the station they jumped into a taxi and Andie told the driver, in fluent French, to take them to l'Hôtel Salomé. She insisted on paying for the cab, after all, Joe had paid for the bus.

The cab rolled to a smooth stop in front of the hotel's gate and as the bellboy took Andie's bags, she ran into the hotel and returned with a pack of matches.

"Here."

She put the matches into Joe's shirt pocket. She then gave him another long kiss and told the driver to take him to number 6 Rue Racine. It was only five blocks away, but Joe was in no condition to walk it.

"Give me a call when you're rested," she said, "I want to see more of you."

"I don't think there's all that much more of me to see," he groaned.

Nine

Arthur Preston Junior's flight from Madrid to New York City actually came within 150 miles of Joe Bradlee's flight to Paris. This happened somewhere over the Atlantic Ocean at about two a.m. in some uninhabited time zone at thirty-five thousand feet. Neither man knew the other man existed. Neither man cared. They both had more important things on their mind. Joe was having the sexual romp of a lifetime and Arthur Junior was on his way to being twenty-four hours late to a very important meeting with his father. In a holding pen. On Rikers Island.

Arthur Junior had good reason for being late. Two days earlier he had been on the twelfth green of the Marbella Country Club when an afternoon thunderstorm forced his foursome to head for the clubhouse and vodka martinis. It was here that he'd received the urgent message from his father's lawyer, Sam Zuckerman: Return to New York at once . . . Blah, Blah, Blah.

Arthur Junior's problem had been this: He'd had fifty thousand dollars riding on this little golf match, and if he'd left the club immediately, he'd have to forfeit his bet. And really, how important could one day be? If you're sitting in a jail cell? That had been Arthur

Junior's reasoning. The weather had cleared as predicted and he'd gone on to win the bet. Hands down. Before noon the next morning.

He'd guessed his father would be pleased to hear that he'd won, but hardly surprised. Arthur Preston Junior hadn't lost a golf bet since he was eight years old and it was how he'd supported himself for the last six.

As the sun came up on John F. Kennedy Airport a car waited patiently for Arthur Junior at the international arrivals building. The car was driven by a man in his early thirties. He was dark skinned. A lean, swarthy Cuban who usually went by the name of Nestor. Arthur Junior stepped out of the terminal, was greeted politely by this Nestor, escorted directly to a limousine, and then onto his father's apartment on the twenty-second floor of the Sherry Netherland Hotel, overlooking Manhattan's Fifth Avenue and lower Central Park. The trip lasted one hour and five minutes.

Arthur ordered up some eggs and bacon from room service. Took a shower and then a two-hour nap. By eleven o'clock he was back in his father's gunmetal gray limousine with Nestor at the wheel. On his way to Rikers Island. Their entire conversation consisted of the following nineteen words:

"Did the Yankees win last night, Nestor?"

"Nah."

"Oh, Jesus . . . What was the score?"

"Thirteen to two."

"Oh, Jesus."

Upon arrival at the Rikers's front gate Arthur Junior was greeted by a weary, and overly stressed, Sam Zuckerman.

"I'll walk you through this maze," the lawyer said. "Hopefully it will go a little quicker. They should recognize me by now. The delays at this place can be unbelievable at times."

After being passed through two sets of steel gates, Sam approached the duty officer. She was sitting behind what appeared to be an eight-inch-thick piece of bulletproof glass. He spoke to her by way of a cabled microphone that twisted obscenely out from the wall to the left of the guard's window. Sam spoke slowly, as though the woman spoke no English and had received only a second-grade education.

"My name is Samuel Zuckerman. I am a lawyer. I am here to see my client. Arthur Preston."

"Have a seat."

"I was expected at noon . . . at twelve o'clock." Sam looked at his watch and pointed. "That would be in five minutes."

"You're on the clock, Mr. Lawyer. Have a seat."

"Excuse me?" It was Arthur Junior, and as he spoke he slid two crisp one-hundred-dollar bills through the woman's paperwork slot. "I'm Mr. Preston's son. I was wondering if you could see that this goes to your union's Christmas fund."

"Certainly, Mr. Preston."

"Thank you, Rita."

Arthur Junior then moved to the far wall and eased himself down onto a wooden bench. He was followed closely by Sam Zuckerman.

"Arthur, gratuities are out of line here, and it's poor form to call these people by their first names."

"Why do they give them name tags, then?"

"Well, maybe you might call them officer so-and-so, but that's it. Nothing more. No first names."

"DeNunzio. Her name was DeNunzio, Sam. It wasn't so-and-so. And, don't lecture me. Jesus, sometimes you're such a fucking—"

"Excuse me, Mr. Preston?"

"Yes, Rita."

"We have a room ready for you. It's this way. Your father will be up shortly."

Rita had come out from behind her protective glass, and was now holding the heavily barred door open for the two men. She had a very nice figure.

"Thank you, Rita."

"No problem, Mr. Preston."

"Call me Arthur. We may be seeing a lot of each other in the next month or so."

"Okay. Arthur." Rita had a very nice smile as well.

They were picked up by another guard. He stood about six foot seven and had bright orange hair curling out from beneath his dark blue cap. This giant led them down an endless corridor. The floor, walls, and ceiling were all painted the same color of hospital green. Everything else was polished stainless steel and vaguely resembled leftover parts from a 1957 Volkswagen. Sam spoke under his breath.

"Well, I guess they're finally beginning to recognize me. This is the fastest I've ever passed through that woman. She can be a real sloth when she wants."

"Right, Sam," was all Arthur Junior said.

They were taken into the same room that Sam and Arthur Senior had used countless times before, however three chairs had now been arranged around the table. Arthur Junior sat and moved his feet up and onto a spot on the table, where in the past, Sam had been very fond of placing his attaché case. Sam put his case on the floor, sighed a pathetic sigh, and walked to the window. Delta flight 1123 had been cleared for landing. Its engine noise rattled the window and bounced around the room's airspace like an electrically charged superball.

"I don't know whether to congratulate you for being on time, or to be justifiably annoyed with you for being a day late." Arthur Senior nearly had to scream this to be heard over the Delta jet.

The younger Arthur stood and said, "It's good to see you again, Father." Although he didn't mean it for a second.

Sam simply said, "Arthur," and bobbed his head congenially. He knew all too well that his function at this meeting would be that of witness and nothing more. Arthur Preston never spoke to his son without another body in the room. It was as if the old man feared Arthur Junior would attempt a palace coup, or steal the car keys, or maybe his Rolex. Or worse yet, say something impertinent. Having a solid backup in tow was the only way to keep the young one in line. In place. Arthur Junior, surprisingly enough, was the only person within miles who didn't need Preston's money, and the old man hated the reminder.

"Sam says you couldn't leave your precious golf game?"

"Match. It's not a game to me . . . I had fifty thousand on it."

"Peanuts."

"He was a Greek. I couldn't walk away. I needed

the money, he needed to lose it. It's in his blood. I think it made his day."

"I make more than that in ten minutes . . . and there's no gamble involved. I take it."

Arthur Junior only shrugged. Facetiously thinking, there's something to be proud of.

"Sam's put some property in your name. He has papers for you to sign. Sign them. But under no circumstances are you to involve yourself with the manipulation of these holdings. If I hear that you've meddled in any way, there'll be hell to pay. You'll find yourself in a very sorry position."

"A tough lie, as it were."

"Don't get impertinent with me. This isn't a golf *game*." The old man smacked the word *game* as though he were driving home a railroad spike. "There's a lot at stake here. If I don't roll out of this place as free as a bird, you, your mother, the whole lot of you bloodsuckers, end up penniless. It's something to keep in mind . . . whether you want it or not. But I want you to stay away from those properties. Don't go snooping around. Sticking your nose where it doesn't belong. Go to Canada. Go to Ontario. See your mother. But stay away from the other places. Especially the boat. I will not allow you to take the boat out. Clear?"

He didn't wait for an answer. Only lit a cigarette. Zuckerman produced a portable ashtray from his attaché case. Arthur Junior slid his chair back to avoid the billows of smoke that were intentionally being snorted in his direction.

"Is there anything else?"

"Yes . . . Sit down."

"I'm down. I never got up."

"We need to find someone . . ."

He took a drag from his cigarette.

His son waited.

"Billy Barton."

He sucked down another drag. Then let his used smoke pollute the room.

"You've met him, right?"

"At your office. Maybe three years ago."

"He seems to hang out with your crowd. The fruity country-club set. I don't suppose you've heard where he might be?"

"Nope."

"He's got a bonus coming and we're having a little trouble locating him. If he pops up anywhere, if you hear about him, if you see him in your travels . . ."

"I'll tell him you're looking for him."

"No. Listen for a change, will you? Just pass Billy's whereabouts onto Sam . . . Sam will handle it. Sam will contact him. I don't want him contacting Sam . . . it makes a difference."

There was a long empty space of time where no one spoke. The two younger men watched the older one finish his cigarette and crush out the red ember.

"That's it?" Arthur Junior said.

"That's it."

"I can leave?"

"You can leave."

But Arthur Junior wasn't about to leave empty-handed. Or without jousting back.

"Say, Dad, nobody's using the box at the stadium tonight, are they?"

Zuckerman made a feeble attempt to crawl into his attaché case while the younger Mr. Preston continued,

"The Blue Jays are hot from what I understand. Nestor says they kicked ass last night. What was it? Thirteen to two? Jesus, what an ass-kicking. I don't suppose you want to put something on tonight's game? I'm willing to give you odds."

"No."

"But I can use the box . . . ? I mean, what the hell, you can't use it, right? You're going to be here, right? No point in letting it rot. What do you say?"

"Okay."

It was said to make his son shut up more than anything else. And although Arthur Senior merely mumbled his answer, and although an approaching jetliner once again shook the room hard, Arthur Junior heard his father loud and clear.

"Sorry, Dad, I didn't hear what you said. The jets. They make a lot of noise, don't you think. Have you noticed that?"

"Yes," the old man shouted. "Use the blessed box. How many times do I have to say it?"

"Great. I'll tell you what, I'll spot the Yankees three runs. What do you say? Twenty bucks?"

"I don't gamble. How long are you going to stay in New York?"

"I don't know . . . couple of nights. I hate this town. I feel like I'm in prison every time I come here. The sooner I split, the better. Four runs. That's my last offer."

"I don't gamble . . . Where can we find you? In case you have to sign something else."

"Two to one. My twenty to your ten, and I still give you the four runs? Paris."

"France?"

"Oui."

"It's a bet . . . I want you to keep in touch with Sam."

"Sure."

"And I want five runs."

"Jesus . . . you're a hard man, Arthur Preston Senior. I often wish I could be more like you."

"Five runs or no bet."

"You're on."

On his way out, Arthur Junior stopped to ask Rita if she would like to see the Yankees' game that evening.

"I have a box," he said.

"Yes," she said.

Ten

Joe Bradlee stood at the curb and watched as the driver retrieved the Mark Cross suitcase from the trunk.

"Merci bien."

"De rien."

Nothing else was said. No money changed hands. The driver smiled anyway.

Joe watched as the man and taxi, with its French diesel clicking methodically, eased their way slowly up the Rue Racine and off toward the massive Odéon theater. He turned and focused on the wooden Rue Racine door, and the number. Six. Somehow he was surprised to see that the number appeared the same in French as it would have in English or Italian. It had been painted a black-blue and vaguely resembled the 6 on Roger Maris's uniform. Joe shook his head. His mind went back to a day at Yankee Stadium. The day he'd asked his father what it meant when Roger held his middle finger up to the stadium as the fans booed him for striking out. And the thought of his father's feeble explanation made him smile.

Joe opened the heavy door and checked the buzzers

on the wall. Twenty-four—Nichols. He glanced at his key. Twenty-four—Nichols.

"Son of a bitch," he said under his breath. Somewhat surprised that the damn place actually existed.

He unlocked the inner door, hefted his bag, and walked up one flight of stairs. Number 24 was the rear apartment on the first floor. There was also a front apartment, number 21, and two apartments on either side of the central stairway numbered 22 and 23.

But something didn't check. Something was definitely off with the setup. And it made the air thick.

From his vantage point on the stairway Joe could see a sharp beam of light racing from the slightly ajar door of what was to be his new abode. Somebody was home. He slowly placed his suitcase and attaché case down on the polished poplar of the hallway floor. He instinctively reached under his right arm for his nine millimeter. Nothing doing. The nine millimeter was in New York in a dresser drawer on Carmine Street. He silently cursed Harper.

The walls and the darkness of the hallway now began to close in on Joe. He'd been here before. Not this building, but one just like it. Some domestic violence crap in Manhattan. Some bozo smacking his wife around. Always the same shit. Christ. The cops were the ones who ended up taking a piece of lead. Not the goddamn wife or husband. They'd kiss and make up, fuck all night long, and be back at it a week later.

Joe shook his head once more. Clearing it some. This had to be one of the worst places to get himself stuck—standing out in a apartment house hallway with his pants down. Not one goddman place to hide. Especially if some lunatic decides to take a few potshots.

Joe considered his options. He started to slowly work his way along the wainscoted wall. Toward the open door of apartment 24. If worse came to worse, he could always jump over the railing and be back down on the first floor—a sure way to break at least one ankle. He tried to fine-tune his hearing. Home it in on the situation. But his lack of sleep and jet lag were working hard against him.

Someone in apartment 22 was watching the morning news on a television set. It was all in French, but the mellifluous tones of the newscaster needed no translation. Joe assumed the man came to his viewers with a huge toothy smile slapped on a well-tanned face as he reported on the arrest of some space cadet devoted to the decapitation of house cats. There actually were cat meows coming from the apartment, and Joe found himself wondering if his fabricated scenario was accurate or if the apartment was just full of fucking cats.

When he reached the door to 24 he was presented with two options: ease the damn thing open, or knock. He could hear a faint sound of movement coming from the other side. He waited for a minute. Listening for voices. Checking the odds. Anything. Anything that would help. He waited a moment longer. He found himself wondering how he was going to confront a Parisian crook. French wasn't Joe's forte. It was okay, not great. And the only words he was feeling comfortable with at this point, were: *"S'il vous plaît"* and *"Merci."* Joe then found himself pantomiming,

"S'il vous plaît, monsieur!" and attempting a put-on indignant expression. An indignant *French* expression.

He eased back down the hall and snatched up his attaché case. It would be his only weapon. It would be his only shield. Again he practiced his French indignations. Except for the mustache, Joe felt he was beginning to look a tremendous amount like Peter Sellars in the worst of the Pink Panther movies. Perhaps if he jumped into apartment 24, swinging his Mark Cross attaché case over his head, and screaming made-up French obscenities, the crook, or crooks, might pass out laughing. Or possibly he could jump them as they wet their pants. Then, he wouldn't have to converse with them at all.

And that's pretty much what Joe opted for, minus the French obscenities and mustache. He kicked the door wide open, held his attaché case to his chest, quickly stepped inside, and said, "What the fuck's going on here?"

No answer.

Joe heard a scramble coming from the bedroom. Off to his right. Then the unmistakable sound of someone chambering a round into a semiautomatic pistol. Not solid enough for a .45. Most likely a .38 or .32. Either way, the Mark Cross attaché case, two passports, a few maps, and five thousand dollars in American Express travelers' checks, weren't about to stop a slug no matter how big. With pantherlike movements he threw the case onto the couch, yanked the bedroom door closed, and stepped off to the side of the door frame. The instant he cleared the frame, three .32-caliber slugs, one right after the other, splintered their way through the door at chest level. They lodged themselves in the far wall, just to the right of the kitchen clock.

"Missed me, you fuck. You've got five seconds to put that fucking gun on the floor and walk the fuck out of there, or we're coming in—all of us—and it's not going to be a pretty picture. You hear me? You understand what the fuck I'm telling you?"

No reply.

"Shit . . ."

Nothing.

"You speak English, you fucking dickhead?"

Nothing.

Joe looked around the room, as if searching for his fictitious reinforcements. He decided to give this French crook another chance.

"Okay . . . I'll tell you what we'll do . . . Put the gun down on the dresser, then leave by the window. When I hear the window close I'll give you two minutes to get lost. Otherwise we come in shooting. You've got three seconds."

Joe heard a shuffling from the bedroom and then the window slide shut. He sprang over to the living room's French doors. There he caught sight of an eighteen-year-old girl scrambling down the fire escape. Once down, she darted through the garden, over a short fence, and out on to the street. She had long flowing black hair, paler than pale white skin, and was as skinny as a rail. Joe thought, not the type to blow three slugs at someone she didn't even know.

He eased his way back over to the splintered door. There was a damn good chance that someone else had remained in the room.

"Okay, Jacques, you and Pierre, stay here. Marcel? You and de Gaulle come with me. We're going in . . . I'm going to waste this fucker right where he stands."

If Joe could have thought of some extra French names he would have boosted his team up with three or four more monsieurs.

He stepped back and kicked with his right foot. The door flew open. He lunged into the room, dropping to the floor and rolled over twice.

Nothing.

The room was empty. The girl had been the only one. Joe stood.

Like the living room, the bedroom had been thoroughly searched. The dresser drawers had all been dragged open. The mattress had been thrown off the bed. The rug lifted. In the bathroom the medicine cabinet door was ajar. Pill bottles all opened.

"What a stupid bastard," Joe said as he walked over to the dresser and picked up the .32-caliber automatic. He removed the ammunition clip and the shell in the chamber. Three rounds fired. Six remained. His first thought was, Where the fuck do you buy bullets in Paris?

"Monsieur?"

Joe turned. Standing in the doorway was an elderly woman with two cats prowling between her legs. She glanced at the holes in the door. And Joe stammered.

"I'm sorry . . . I don't speak French . . . not today, anyway." He looked down at the gun in his hand. "I thought it was a toy . . . Jeezo . . . Well, what do you know . . . ? Went off by accident . . . what a mess. Do you speak English?"

"Yes."

"Well . . . Great . . . Well . . . Thank you for your concern. Everything seems to be under control, now. I guess I should be getting some sleep. My name is J-J-J-J . . . Billy Barton. I'll be in Mr. Harper's apartment for a month or so . . . vacation. Looking to get a little R and R . . . you know how it is . . ."

"Nichols."

"Pardon me?"

"It's Mr. Nichols's apartment."

"Yes, of course it is. I'm not thinking. Mr. Harper is Mr. Nichols's partner. Business partner, that is. An associate. Every now and then I get them confused. They look like brothers don't you think?"

"Mr. Harper is black."

"Well, right, yes . . . other than the black part. Listen, I should get a little sleep." Joe walked the old woman to the door. The cats followed. "I came in on the overnight flight. I'm exhausted. Thank you very much. What would your name be?"

"I'm Mrs. Meighan."

"And you're not French at all?"

"No, I was raised in Pittsburgh."

"Pittsburgh. No kidding? Well . . . that's nice. I would have guessed Indiana."

She was now well out of the apartment. Joe stepped out with her and looked up and down the hallway. He gritted his teeth and shook his head twice.

"Problems, Mr. Barton?" she said.

"Well, you might say that, Mrs. Meighan . . . You didn't happen to see anyone leaving the building with a good-size Mark Cross suitcase, did you?"

Eleven

Jack Harper exited the FBI offices at 26 Federal Plaza in lower Manhattan stride for stride with another man. A man in a dark suit. Harper also wore a suit. He'd shaved. Cut his hair. He now bore little resemblance to the person who'd shown a Polaroid photograph of Billy Barton to Joe Bradlee a few days earlier at Benny's Bus Stop Cafe in Greenwich Village. Jack Harper was no longer plainclothes.

Harper had joined the FBI eleven years earlier. The government had recruited him the day he'd entered law school. In fact, they'd paid for most of it. They knew a good catch when they saw one. But Harper wasn't so sure. Not a week went by when Jack Harper hadn't questioned his decision to take up government work. His Johns Hopkins classmates were now making ten times what he earned. They were professionals. Driving very nice cars. They had families. They had homes. They had lives. Harper thought, There's got to be a better goddamn way.

The two agents ambled down the granite steps and sat on one of the circular concrete planters that rested in the open space on the west side of 26 Federal Plaza. Nichols had just arrived from Paris. He was short, well built, almost completely bald. Hard as nails—his own opinion. He spoke first.

"It's a sad fucking day when you can't even speak freely in your own goddamn office building."

"I think it's best we keep as many people guessing as we can," Harper said. "Right now, besides the Director, we're the only ones who know exactly what's going on with Bradlee. I'd like to keep it that way . . . at least for as long as we can. He's our responsibility in Paris. Until we move him, nobody else needs to know anything. He's the ace."

"Ace? Jesus, he's a lush according to the paperwork I've been reading. If he doesn't royally fuck this whole thing up, I'll be real goddamn surprised."

"He's what we've got. Or have you found another look-alike for me?"

Nichols remained silent. Staring straight ahead.

Harper asked, "How's Billy Boy holding up?"

Nichols smiled and shook his head, "There's another winner. I think he's actually glad someone waxed his wife. Keeps moaning about missing the great social life Paris has to offer because we've got his ass locked up. It wouldn't break my heart in the least if Preston got to the bastard."

"It may not break your heart, but you'll be looking for a new line of work if he does." Harper looked at his watch. "Bradlee's got to be in the apartment by now. You left a piece for him?"

"Yep. Thirty-two."

Harper stood. He put his back to the building. As though he expected someone inside to be reading his lips. "You're all set to go back Friday, right?"

"Right."

"We've got to find a way to keep—"

"Hold on . . . Westfall's coming this way."

They both watched as the man approached. Westfall's suits were notorious for fitting too tightly. His trousers were always too short, he'd worn a flattop haircut since 1973 as homage to his boyhood idol, Johnny Unitas, and sported black horn-rimmed glasses. All this had the effect of making him appear more like an indemnity salesman than an FBI agent. He had a personality to match. But that was all just fine and dandy with the Bureau. He'd busted up more slimy insurance scams than any agent in the history of the FBI.

Westfall was all smiles as he advanced. "What's up, boys? What are you doing for lunch?"

"We're going to have to pass," Harper said.

"Hell, it wasn't a goddamn invitation, fella. I hate eating with government employees. Might as well be chowing down at the post office. Yuk-yuk. I was just going to tell you to check out that place by the river. The Dear's Inn. Good. Good. Good. I highly recommend it. A-one. Two thumbs up on the old Westfall rating system. Cheap, too. You won't leave hungry. You can count on it like an abacus."

"Thanks. We'll do that. You're not on commission there, are you?" Nichols said.

"Nah. Good chops, that's all . . . Once you get past the pretentious trendy fucks air-kissing each other." Westfall eyed Nichols. Then an idea seemed to flash into his fervid brain. He smashed his palms against his forehead for exaggerated effect. "Wait. Nichols. Jesus. Fuck. Damn. What the fuck am I thinking of? I thought you were in Paris on that hush-hush bullshit. Christ. Sometimes I think I should have my noggin examined." This time he tapped the top of his head working for a different effect. "Am I glad to see you, or what? What are you doing in New York, big guy?"

The term *big guy* always annoyed the hell out of Nichols, being only five-eight. He avoided eye contact with both Harper and Westfall as he spoke in almost a monotone.

"Back for a few days. Briefings. Getting caught up."

"Well, damn, man. You're just the person I've got to sit down with. I finish up with the Rodrigo crap in less than a month. Taking the wife to Pareee for a week. Prices drop like a motherfucker after the kiddies go back to school. You've got to fill me in on what to hit—what to miss in the old City of Lights. What do you say? You know, restaurants and that shit. No museums though. Once you've seen one guy on a cross, you've seen 'em all. That's what I say."

"Uh . . ."

"I know. Jesus. I'm not even fucking thinking here. Why don't you drop by for dinner tonight? The wife won't mind. She usually cooks too much crap anyway. We got language tapes already. So you don't have to teach us any of that *Parlez-vous* shit. Say six-thirty?"

"Uh . . . Jeez . . . No . . . Wait, Harper and I were supposed to be somewhere, weren't we, Jack?"

Harper smiled. "Nah, it was canceled. I've got a date. You're free. I meant to tell you."

"Great," Westfall said. "Sixty-two West 85th Street. Number 4B. Say six-thirty? This is bitchin'. Thanks, Nichols. I appreciate the hell out of this. Listen, big guy, I gotta run. See you at six-thirty. Thanks." And Westfall was off.

"You goddamn motherfucking son of a bitch,"

Nichols said to Harper. "You couldn't fucking save me there. You couldn't open your goddamn mouth? What date? You don't have a fucking date. You know Paris as well as I do. You go have dinner with the bastard. Christ."

"Believe it or not, I do have a date." Harper looked at his watch again. This time for no particular reason. "We've got to get a few things straight. There may not be another chance to talk before you split on Friday."

Again Nichols only looked straight forward.

"I want to keep Bradlee watched. But I also want him out in the open. I want him seen. We've got to make sure Preston finds him. I can drop some hints around New York, but it won't happen if Bradlee's hid out in some damn room somewhere watching French TV and boozing it up. We need someone to show him the city. Get him out and around. Museums. That shit. And it's a hell of a lot easier to have someone right by his side rather than tailing him. He'd pick up a shadow in a second."

"You mean like a woman?"

"It's the easiest way. But she's got to be good. He can't know he's being set up."

"Jesus, Jack, we've got to let him know what he's in for. He's got to be ready for something if it happens. He's a fucking sitting duck otherwise."

"Now all of a sudden you're worried about him? He knows all he needs to know. I'm afraid he'll start acting professional on us if he knows any more than he needs to. And if Preston's man is smart, he'll catch onto him in a second. The more he acts like Billy the better."

"I don't like it."

"When did you get so concerned about the welfare of ex-Secret Service agents?"

"I'm not. I just think we've got to give the bastard a fighting chance, that's all. I'd hate to think that I could be set up like that. I have nightmares about being poorly informed."

Harper laughed.

"It wasn't a goddamn joke, Jack."

"You haven't met Bradlee. He's smarter than he lets on. He's not about to get caught with his pants down . . ." Harper turned and studied the lunch crowd in the plaza. "So, who do we get to give him the grand Parisian tour?"

"Danielle?"

"I'm saving her for something else. Something more important."

"Well, that's about it for my long list of trusted Parisian women . . . Hold on." Nichols eyed a passing street vendor. "I'm starved . . . I'll be right back."

He walked over to the vendor and returned with two hot dogs smothered with onions and chili. Two diet Cokes. He handed a Coke and a dog to Harper.

"My treat. I'll find a date for Bradlee when I get back to France. There's got to be someone. Maybe the Gendarmes have a broad they like to use."

"You guys going to eat that shit?" Agent Stevenson said as he came up behind Harper and Nichols.

"Man, this fucking place is crawling with Feds. What do you care what we eat? You move over to the FDA?"

Stevenson ignored Harper and focused on Nichols, "What are you doing here? I thought you were in Paris keeping an eye on the worm, Billy Barton?"

"Jesus, this is the question of the hour. Maybe I should have taken out an ad in the goddamn *Times*. I'm here for briefing. Going back Friday. You want me to bring you some perfume or something? Duty-free condoms with little French flags on them?"

"How's it going?"

"What?"

"Billy."

"Fine. He's tucked away."

"Oh-oh," Stevenson said with mock surprise. "Do I detect a little hush-hush going on here? Information you don't want to share with your fellow agents?"

Harper looked at Nichols and they shrugged in unison.

"That's the kind of deal I need," Stevenson continued, "Paris. Jesus. They've got me in Queens on that bullshit bakery detail. The Great Italian Bakery/Mob's Got Their Fingers Into Everything Including the Cookie Mix Case. I'm beginning to feel like the Pillsbury fucking Dough Boy." He looked at the sky and added, "France . . . that's what I need. Actually, you know what? My sister's over in Paris now. Went over for a fashion show."

"I didn't know you had a sister," Harper said.

"Andrea."

"Andrea?"

"Andie."

"Andie?"

"Yeah. Everyone calls her Andie."

"Where's she staying over there? Decent place, I hope?" Nichols said. Now doing his best not to look at Harper or Stevenson. Concentrating more on his shoelaces.

"She goes over a lot. Stays at a place called the Hôtel Salomé."

"I'll look her up for you when I get back this weekend. Make sure she's okay. You never know. Paris is a big town. Gets rougher every year."

"Whoa, whoa, hold on there, big guy, she's okay. Back off. I don't want any of you bastards sniffing around my sister. That's the last thing she needs, is to be hooked up with some goddamn Federal agent. Ruin her life . . . especially one like you, Nichols."

Nichols glanced at Harper and said, "Jesus, you try to do a guy a little favor, and look what you get." And then to Stevenson, "Some gratitude, that's all I can say."

"Yeah. Right . . . I gotta make dough."

Stevenson began to move across the plaza, but after a few steps, he turned back and said, "I hope you bastards choke on your fucking hot dogs. If either one of you goes near my sister, I'll cut your balls off."

"Nice talk," Nichols called. "I won't touch her. You have Harper's word on it."

When Stevenson was well out of earshot, Harper again said, "I didn't know he had a sister. A looker?"

"I think she came down when we passed Quantico together. It was damn near ten years ago, but if that was his sister, yeah, she's a looker all right. Testarosa. Real hot."

"Andie?"

"That's what he said."

"The Hôtel Salomé?"

"That's what he said."

"I think your ex-Secret Service agent just got himself a date."

Twelve

As Joe Bradlee closed the door to apartment 24 at 6 Rue Racine he found two things extremely hard to believe. One, that Mrs. Meighan, the old lady from Pittsburgh with all the damn cats hadn't seen anyone leaving the building with his brand-new Mark Cross suitcase. And two, the old bat had apparently been the only person in the entire city of Paris to have heard the incredibly loud noise created when the pale skinny girl with the black hair fired three pieces of lead through Joe's newly acquired bedroom door. Were these people deaf, for Christ's sake? Or just as apathetic as everyone else in the world. He guessed the second to be the case.

Joe hefted the pistol in his left hand. Placed the loose bullet back into the magazine. Shoved it all back into the gun. Chambered a round. Engaged the safety. Then walked into the kitchen. Put the whole mess into the oven. He opened the refrigerator. Not a goddamn thing.

He considered going back out to the street. Search for his lost luggage. But he knew it would be a colossal waste of time. This was Paris. The suits were probably already being altered to fit their new owner. And what was the point? He hated all the crap Harper had picked out for him at Barney's. Made him look like a used-car salesman moved up to Wall Street exec. Or worse yet, vice versa. Joe had five thousand dollars in cash. He'd just do a little shopping. That's all. The only real annoyance was having lost his shaving stuff and underwear.

Joe took a moment to speculate who it might have been who'd taken three shots at him. And why. But it had all become an immense wad of fuzz rolling in his head. He was just too damn tired. He knew whatever explanation he came up with, in his present state of mind, would only seem moronic after he'd had some rest. And more than likely, the explanation would get lost somewhere deep in his sleep.

So, he began to straighten up the living room. In slow motion. It required no thought. He placed the cushions back on the sofa. Closed up the record cabinet. Record albums, he thought, the FBI hasn't even moved up to tapes, let alone CDs. He slid the drawers back in. He was moving like a zombie by the time he'd finished. He'd had it. He was beat. He dragged himself into the bedroom, put the mattress back on the bed, and collapsed with a vision of a scratched Patsy Cline album spinning in the recesses of his mind. He slept like a baby until the phone jolted him awake at nine that evening.

"Billy?"

"Huh?"

"C'est cinquante, vingt-quatre, soixant-trois, dix-neuf?"

"What?"

"Is this fifty, twenty-four, sixty-three, nineteen?"

Joe looked down to the dial of the telephone.

"Yeah."

"Is this Billy?"

Joe's head began to clear—slightly.

"Yes. Right. Yes, this is Billy."

"It's Andie. I thought you said you were going to call me?"

"Did I say that?"

"Well, I gave you my phone number. I thought we could have some dinner. I can be there in ten minutes. You haven't eaten yet, have you?"

"Ah, no. I just woke up."

"Me too. I'm starved."

"Umm . . . Listen . . . Don't think I'm being impolite here . . . just mildly curious, that's all. But how did you get this phone number?"

"So you don't want to have dinner, then?"

"I didn't say that. Dinner sounds great. Come on over. But how the hell did you get this number? I didn't even know what it was myself."

"Mrs. Meighan's from Pittsburgh."

"What?"

"The woman who lives in apartment twenty-three? Her name is Mrs. Meighan? She's from Pittsburgh. She's a friend of my mother's. She said she'd spoken with you."

"What are you talking about? Run through this for me, will you? Slowly."

Andie began to giggle like a child on the other end of the line. It had the effect of annoying Joe somewhat.

She continued, "Okay, try to pay attention. When you said you were staying at number six Rue Racine I knew the street sounded familiar. I went through my address book and lo and behold it turns out that's where Mrs. Meighan lives. This friend of my mother's? In fact, she knows all the Stevensons very well. We go way back. Anyway, I called her up. She said she'd talked with you. She happened to have the phone number for apartment twenty-four and she gave it to me."

"Sounds real fishy, if you ask me."

"She said your suitcase was stolen, and you'd been playing with a gun?"

"Yeah. Well, it was left here by someone. I thought it was a toy. It went off by accident."

"Have you called the police?"

"No."

"Okay, I'll do it for you."

"No. Jesus. Don't do that. It was my fault. I shouldn't have even picked the damn thing up in the first place."

"I mean for the suitcase. You should report it."

"Forget it. I'll get another one."

"You don't want your clothes back?"

"Hey, this is Paris. What a great excuse to buy some new stuff. You know what I think? To hell with the old junk. The police'll never find it and it's mostly worn out. You can take me shopping. If you have the time?"

"Maybe . . . Who's Danielle?"

"What?"

"Who's Danielle?"

"Beats me. Who *is* Danielle?"

"You've got her phone number written on a cocktail napkin in your shirt pocket. I figure you must know who she is."

Joe reached into the wrinkled shirt he'd been wearing for the last twenty-four hours. He pulled out the cocktail napkin Harper had written Danielle's name and number on, and the Hôtel Salomé matches Andie had placed there. "Ahh . . . that Danielle. What are you? Some sort of private detective or something?"

"It fell out at thirty thousand feet. I think I'm jealous already."

"Yeah . . . well . . . she's just some friend of the guy who owns this place. He told me to call her up if I got lonely."

"Lonely?"

"Well, you know, Jesus, bored. You know what I mean."

"*Bored?* I don't think I do know what you mean."

There was a tremendous pause. Neither said a word for almost thirty seconds. Finally Joe said, "I guess it's my turn to say something, isn't it?"

"It is if you want to have dinner with me tonight."

"Here. Look. Bingo-bang. I just threw the damn cocktail napkin in the toilet. Are you happy?"

"Bingo-bang?"

"Jeez, you should see it. The ink's running like crazy. Can't even read the numbers anymore."

"I don't believe you."

"I won't flush it till you come over. How's that?"

"You've got a phone in the bathroom? Not hardly . . . Maybe I shouldn't have called."

"Listen. On your way, do me a favor, will you?"

"What?"

"Pick me up a razor, some shaving cream, some aftershave, some deodorant. Nothing too fruity, if you don't mind?"

"What does 'fruity' mean?"

"'Like peaches. You know, don't get me anything that'll make me smell like an overripe peach."

"I didn't say I was coming over."

"Sure you did. It was the first thing you said. Maybe a new shirt, too. I'll pay you back. And some socks."

". . . Underwear?"

"Yeah. That would be great. Thirty-fours."

"I know."

"You do."

"Another piece of information I picked up at thirty thousand feet."

"Plain white cotton boxers are just fine. Don't get overimaginative. Don't get me anything with chuck wagons or Wiley Coyote on them. Or silk. I hate silk . . . And paisley, no paisley, okay?"

"It's against my better judgment, but I'll see you in twenty minutes."

Andie hung up.

Joe went into the bathroom, used the toilet, then flushed it. He went back out to the living room. He found a pen and paper in the desk and copied Danielle's phone number. He placed the paper in his wallet, went back to the bathroom, threw the cocktail napkin into the john, and waited for the ink to run. He then stripped, stepped into the shower, and remained there until he heard the buzzer from the downstairs door. Twenty-seven minutes had passed. He dried himself slightly. Wrapped a towel around his waist. Then pressed the button to open the front door.

Joe stepped into the hallway and watched as Andie climbed the steps. She carried a shopping bag marked in bold letters with the name, *Marcel Lassance*. She was beautiful. She could wear clothes like no other woman

Joe had ever known. The yellow overhead hallway light made her auburn hair go to an almost fiery orange. Her lips had been painted a dark Chinese red. Joe felt the towel around his waist begin to unfold.

Andie came straight up to him. They engaged in a long deep kiss that lasted until the latch on Mrs. Meighan's door began to stir. They moved into Joe's apartment just before the old lady stepped out.

"You're going to get wet," Joe said.

"Do you think so?" Andie said. Then lifted her tongue to her top lip.

"Come here. I've got something to show you."

Joe took her hand and led her into the bathroom. He pointed to the open toilet and the now disintegrating cocktail napkin.

"There," he said.

"You're such a romantic."

"I just wanted you to know I was telling the truth earlier."

"I never doubted you for a minute."

Andie slipped the fingers of her left hand inside Joe's towel at the waist. She then stepped backward toward the bedroom, pulling him along with her. Her green eyes fixed on his the entire time. Joe had no trouble reading her mind.

"I thought you said you were hungry?" he whispered.

She peeled the towel from his waist and shoved him onto the bed.

"I'm starved," she said and was down on him before he had time to put up any kind of decent resistance.

Thirteen

Arthur Junior had won his bet with the old man hands down. The Blue Jays had creamed the Yankees one more time and had taken over first place. But Arthur didn't bother to make another trip out to Rikers Island. To collect his ten bucks. Rita DeNunzio, the guard with the cheery smile and nice figure, had two days off coming her way and was very anxious to get as far away from Rikers Island as she could. So Arthur took her to Toronto. She'd never been there. He even taught her how to play golf. She had a very natural swing, but she was a New York girl in the end. They'd known that from the beginning. It was a great few days, but Rita had to get back to Rikers. And work. So Arthur shuffled onto American Airlines flight number 42 at seven o'clock Friday evening. Happy to be out of New York and on his way to Paris.

Arthur had boarded early. Along with a good deal of the other first-class passengers. He paid little attention to the short, wiry, bald man in the charcoal suit as the man passed through first class on his way to the business section. There was absolutely no reason Arthur should have noticed, recognized, or even cared about the man. They had never met.

But FBI Agent Nichols had seen enough photos of Arthur Junior in the last month to be sure of his identity. Plus, he didn't look all that much different from the old man. Younger—that's it.

After spying Arthur, Nichols walked through the business section. He crossed over at the galley to the opposite side of the aircraft. Then walked back down the right-side aisle and stepped back onto the jetway.

"Sir?" the flight attendant called.

"I left something in the terminal. I'll be right back."

"We'll be pushing back in four minutes."

"Right."

Nichols walked back to the ticket counter. The woman behind it was obviously from Brooklyn. The accent. She had a smile like a Cheshire cat and was almost nine inches taller than Nichols.

"Can I help you, sir?"

"Yes, Stacey. Flight forty-two? Anything left in first class?"

"Yes, sir, there is."

Nichols pulled out his FBI identification and his boarding pass.

"I need to be bumped up."

"Yes, sir . . . Anything the pilot needs to be alerted to?"

"No, I just have a lot of work to do, and I'm going to have to spread out some. Three-B would be fine if it's empty."

"Yes, sir, it is. But someone would be sitting right next to you in three-A."

Nichols resisted the temptation to say "No fucking shit."

She continued.

"I can give you the entire center section of row five. If you *really* want to spread out."

He didn't like the way she said really. He'd detected a fair amount of sarcasm. But ignored it. She wasn't bad looking at all.

"Too close to smoking. I'll move after we're airborne if I need to."

"Yes, sir." She punched a few buttons on her computer and handed him a new boarding pass. "There you are. Three-B. If you would just sign here."

He did.

"Thank you, sir. Have a pleasant flight."

"Thanks. You have a great smile there, Stacey. I'm almost sorry I'm leaving town."

"Why, thank you, sir."

Gotta love these tall women, he thought.

Nichols reentered the aircraft. Stopped when he came to row three. Looked down at Arthur's carry-on bag and sighed slightly. "I think I've got B," he said and pulled his new boarding pass from his pocket. "Yep. B. Sorry. I don't know why they have to jam us in like sardines when half the damn plane's empty."

"That's okay. Here, I'll move this," Arthur said. He hefted his bag from Nichols's seat and placed it on the floor in front of him. "You can probably move when we're airborne if you want."

"Right."

Agent Nichols extended his right hand.

"My name's Jack Harper," he said. Doing the quick name change as much to entertain himself as anything.

"Arthur Preston."

"Arthur Preston . . . ? Shared Charities of the United Martyrs? I somehow expected you to be a lot older."

"That's my father's mess."

"Yeah. That's right . . . they've got him in jail or something, don't they?"

"Right."

"Sorry. Guess it's something you'd rather not yak about."

"Actually it's something I can't *yak* about. I have no idea what the hell he did. Or does. He doesn't bring the family in on a great deal of anything and I'm happy to keep it that way."

"I haven't read too much about it, myself. But I always say a man's innocent till proven guilty."

"He's guilty."

Nichols gave Arthur a somewhat sideways glance.

Arthur continued, "I don't know what he's done or supposed to have done, but I'll tell you one thing, Mr. Harper, I know my father. He's guilty as hell."

"Call me Jack."

"Right. Jack."

The plane had been sealed almost immediately after Nichols had reboarded. It pushed back from the gangway and in a matter of minutes the pilot came on to say they were number one for takeoff. After five more minutes they were steadily climbing toward their cruising altitude of thirty-five thousand feet.

Nichols stuffed the in-flight magazine into its pouch and ordered a Johnie Walker Red from the stewardess. Arthur asked for some champagne.

Nichols cleared his throat and lifted his head as if he'd just remembered something. "You know, I think one of my old business partners left our firm to go to work for your father."

"Is that right?" Arthur said.

"Yeah . . . I'm sure it was United Martyrs. A guy named Billy Barton. Ever hear of him?"

"Sure. Billy was one of my father's right-hand men."

"Huh. How about that. Small world."

"As a matter of fact, my father's lawyer has been looking for him. Something to do with an overdue bonus or something. Funny you should bring his name up."

"Haven't seen Billy in years . . . Although, now that I think of it, he used to come over to Paris a lot. Stayed with a guy named . . . um . . . Nichols. If I remember correctly."

"I understand Billy's a little light in the loafers, so this Nichols character must be one of his paramours."

Nichols again cleared his throat. "I wouldn't know. I wouldn't want to jump to conclusions on that."

"I guess it would be only civil of me to look Nichols up . . . See if he can get a message to Billy. You ever meet Nichols?"

"Nope."

"Well, I suppose I should be prepared for the worst." Arthur chuckled. "What if Nichols turns out to be a drag queen. Wouldn't that be something?"

Nichols downed his Johnie Walker in one gulp and ordered a second.

"You have any idea where this fruitcake lives?" Arthur said.

Nichols was having a hard time with the direction of the conversation. He squinted at Arthur and his vocal quality bordered on indignant. "How do you know Nichols is gay?"

"Billy Barton comes to Paris to spend some *time*

with him? Come on . . . you can't be that naive. Who comes to Paris to spend *time* with another man unless they're going down on each other right and left?"

Nichols downed his second Scotch.

"Yeah. I guess I see what you mean. I suppose it's possible . . . Miss, can I get another Johnie Walker?"

"You better take it easy on the Scotch. I brought a girl over to Milan once and we drank champagne for damn near the entire trip. You don't really feel it until you land. Something to do with altitude and sugar content or something. They had to carry her off. It was embarrassing as hell, but she was worth it. Great tits."

"You know I think I have Nichols's address here somewhere."

Nichols pulled his attaché case to his lap.

"You do. . . ? You have Nichols's address?" Arthur eyed Nichols. Then slid over in the wide seat. Closer to the window. "Why do you have Nichols's address?"

"We had to do a lot of corresponding with Billy after he left our firm. Loose ends, you know."

"And you've still kept Nichols's address? Are you planning to visit with him? Spend some *time* with him? Because if you are, just tell Nichols to have Billy contact Sam Zuckerman. He's my father's lawyer."

"I've never met this Nichols. Honest. I'm just one of these guys who never throws shit out." Nichols fumbled with his address book. ". . . Ah. Here it is. Number six Rue Racine. I don't know the city that well. Have any idea where that is?"

"No . . . I'll look it up later. Thanks."

Arthur scribbled the address on a corner of the

emergency exit guide, ripped it off, and stuffed it into the side pocket of his flight bag.

"I hope Nichols doesn't try to put the make on me. These characters always seem to be attracted to me for some reason. You have anything you'd like me to tell Billy if I run into him?"

"No." Nichols looked down the aisle for his other Scotch. Then back to Arthur. "What's the movie?"

"Some piece of shit with Bruce Willis."

"Ahh, Christ . . . Wouldn't you know it. Just when the fucking headsets are free, too. I'm going to slide across the aisle and get some shut-eye. See you in Paris."

"Say, Jack, you don't play golf, do you?"

Fourteen

After settling into the palatial four-bedroom apartment in Paris's fashionable First Arrondissement that the FBI had set up for Agent Nichols, his two underlings, and Billy Barton, Nichols picked up the telephone. His first call went out to the Hôtel Salomé.

"Yes, good morning. Could you please connect me with Miss Stevenson's room."

"Oui, monsieur."

After two rings Andie came on the line.

"Miss Stevenson, my name is Nichols. I'm with the FBI. I work with your brother in New York."

"Oh my God. Is Drew okay?"

"Yes. Yes. I'm sorry. He's perfectly fine."

"Jesus, I hate it when you people call. I always expect the worst."

"I'm sorry. I wasn't thinking. Drew's fine. He suggested I give you a call."

"You're not the Nichols who owns Billy's apartment, are you?"

"Pardon me?"

"Um . . . never mind. I guess it must be someone else . . . Another Nichols."

"No. No. That's okay. What Billy? I do have an

apartment here in Paris. And I've loaned it to a guy named Billy."

"Billy Barton?"

"Yes. Do you know him?"

"We flew over on the same plane. I've known him for a few years. Is he in some sort of trouble?"

"No, not at all. Just the opposite. Billy's agreed to testify against Arthur Preston in this Shared Charities of the United Martyrs scandal, and we thought, or I should say, *he* thought it would be a little safer for him if he stayed here until the trial."

"He didn't tell me anything about all this. What do you mean safer?"

"Well, actually he's not in any danger. I guess safer wasn't quite the right word."

"What would the *right word* be?"

". . . Pleasant. It would be more pleasant for him to wait for the trial date here."

"I think it's been *pleasant* for him so far."

"Have you seen Billy since you got off the plane?"

"Yes. We did a little shopping together."

"Hey. Well, that's great. I've always liked Billy. He's a real gentleman."

"I don't know if gentleman is the right word, either. But he's fun. Are you with him in your apartment? Didn't he say anything about going shopping with me?"

"No. I'm staying elsewhere. I haven't checked in with Billy yet. I'm not sure he knows I'm here."

"Well, he's fine. Why did my brother want you to call me?" Andie said somewhat apprehensively.

"It's all related to Billy, actually. I was telling your brother how we had the poor guy over here, and how Billy had no friends, and how it was going to be a pretty miserable month for him. Your brother suggested I look you up and see if you'd be willing to show Billy some of the sights."

"You're joking?"

"No . . . Why?"

"Well, one, I know my brother, and I know he doesn't want any of you guys coming anywhere near me, and two, I don't think Billy would have trouble entertaining himself even if he was stuck on a cheetah preserve in Namibia."

Nichols clicked his tongue twice, "Sorry. You're right on both counts. But your brother did tell us you were over here, and we just wanted to keep an eye on Billy. For his own sake. We knew Billy wouldn't want to have an agent strolling around with him all the time, and we thought that maybe you could take him around a little . . . and keep in touch with me. So that we know he's okay. What do you say? It'd be a big help. I'm sure you've got to be as disgusted with Arthur Preston and this Shared Charities of the United Martyrs business as the rest of America is."

"What did you have in mind?"

"Not much, really. Just take him to a few museums. Dinner and whatnot. I'm not asking you to have an affair with him or anything . . . God no, nothing like that. Just keep me posted. That's all. Oh, and I think it's best you don't tell Billy we spoke. I don't want him to think there's any danger. Nothing could be further from the truth."

"I really don't like being dishonest with people."

"Well, I think it's best for everyone. I'm sure you'd like to see Arthur Preston hang as much as any red-blooded American. How long will you be in Paris?"

"A week."

"Well, I can arrange to have that extended to a month, if you'd like."

"All expenses paid?"

"Absolutely."

A month in Paris was too much for any patriotic American to turn down.

"Okay," she said, almost too quickly, "but I would like to tell Billy what we're doing. I don't see what harm it could do."

"Trust me. If he knows what you're up to he won't have anything to do with you, and we'd be back to square one. It's very important we get a conviction with regards to Arthur Preston."

Nichols held his breath. Waited for Andie to commit.

"Okay," she said finally. "But I'm not sure I like it."

"It's only for a month. Billy's not a bad guy. Once you get to know him a little better."

"Billy's not the part I don't like."

"Here. Take down my number. Got a pen?"

"Yes."

"07-13-28-30. Try to call me once or twice a day. There are two other agents here. You can talk to any one of us. And, of course, if you have any emergency at all, call us right away. We're here to help."

Andie still didn't like it. It put her relationship with Joe, or Billy as she knew him, on a completely different level, and it wasn't a level she was interested it. But she was stuck. She saw no other choice but to play along with Nichols. However, she knew better than to be completely up front with the FBI. She simply said, "Okay," and hung up the phone.

Nichols placed the receiver in its cradle and walked to the kitchen. Poured himself a cup of coffee. Billy Barton was playing solitaire with a deck of cards at the kitchen table. The other two agents were out getting breakfast.

"Coffee?" Nichols said to Billy.

"No thanks. So, this policeman/ex-Secret Service fellow looks just like me, huh?"

"Close enough to fool your friend Andie."

"Andy Day? How does he know Andy Day?"

"Who's Andy Day?"

"Andy Day's . . . Andy Day."

"Who the hell is *she*?"

"She. . . ? Andy Day's not a she, he's a he."

"Okay. Who the hell is *he*?"

"Just some guy in Manhattan. What Andy are you talking about?"

"This Andie isn't a guy. It's a woman. A broad. Andie Stevenson."

Billy thought for a minute. Then shrugged and said, "Never heard of her."

"She says she knows you. I was just on the phone with her."

"What's she look like?"

"Well, if she's who I think she is, she's got red hair and is a real knockout."

"Doesn't sound familiar. But I had a few years there of heavy coke and booze. I could have met the fucking Pope and I wouldn't remember. I guess it's not too wise of me to mention past substance abuse to an FBI agent."

"Talk about it all you want. We can only bust you for possession, and we can't even do that in France."

Nichols slipped some bread into the toaster.

"You're sure you don't know this woman? Her brother's an agent. I wouldn't think she'd lie to me . . ." He opened the cupboard. "Ah, shit, I thought we had some fucking jam around here?"

"It's in the refrigerator. Well, it wouldn't be the first time. I've forgotten people before. We could have met . . . somewhere, I guess."

Billy stood and looked out the kitchen window. Across the Rue de Rivoli and the immaculate park and gardens. Farther beyond sat the Seine. A colorful glass-enclosed barge, loaded with tourists was passing under the Pont Royal. "Too bad it wasn't Andy Day," he said.

"Why?"

"I liked him. It would have been nice to spend some time in Paris with him."

"Yeah, well, I'm afraid you're not going anywhere but the bathroom for the next month or so, Billy, so use your imagination."

"Speaking of that . . . What would you say if I asked you to pick up some films? I mean since there's no way I'm going to get the real thing while I'm locked up here."

"What do you mean, *films*?"

"For the VCR."

Nichols looked somewhat indignant. "You don't like the movies I've rented?"

"True Grit?"

"John Wayne won an Oscar for that. It was a great performance, for Christ's sake. Okay, sure, it loses something in French, but that was a great fucking performance."

"I was thinking something a little more sensual. Perhaps an adult film . . . all-male cast?"

"Whoa . . . Hold on . . . You want me to go into the video store and rent you a gay porno film?"

"It won't kill you."

"No way. Forget it. I'm not going into that section of the store. What if someone saw me?"

"Look at it as an educational experience. You might learn something."

"No way."

Nichols shook his head then moved off with his toast and jam for the living room and back to the telephone. Billy returned to his game of solitaire. Nichols dialed a memorized number. The phone was answered on the third ring.

"Oui."

"Joe?"

"Who should I say is calling?"

"Nichols."

"Yeah. This is Joe."

"Your French is getting very good. Do you know anything other than *'oui'*?"

"I've been taking lessons . . . Where's Harper?"

"He won't be here for a week or two."

"This fucking apartment of yours is a walking goddamn booby trap."

"Harper didn't warn you about the toilet? It's always kicked back up like that. Stand up before you flush it."

"I'm not talking about the fucking toilet. Some little twat tried to blow my goddamn head off when I walked in here."

"Just now?"

"No. When I got in from the airport. She was here. In the apartment. Tore the place apart looking for something. Then blew three shots at me and split through the window."

"Did you get a look at her?"

"Good enough."

"I left a piece for you. Did she get it?"

"I'm not detecting a shitload of surprise in your voice. Does this sort of crap happen a lot around here?"

"Probably just a junkie. It's happened before. We try not to leave anything of value there. Did she get the gun?"

"Junkies don't shoot at people they think are cops. There's a gonad differential involved. They may steal guns, but they don't fire them. They hock them."

"Jesus Christ. You didn't tell her you were a cop, did you?"

"No. I told her I was fucking Tinker Bell. If you bastards get my ass killed over here, I'm going to be one pissed off son of a bitch. So who the hell was she?"

"Look. If she wasn't a junkie then she was just a regular old thief."

"She wasn't old."

"Well, Christ, how do I know? I don't know why the fuck you had to tell her you were a cop. This could blow the whole deal. Did she get the gun?"

"Thirty-two?"

"Yeah."

"No. She left it for me. Along with three holes in the bedroom door. It'll be great next time you want to watch your roommates get laid."

"Well, I don't know. I don't know who she was. You

don't think Preston could be this quick in finding you, do you?"

"That's your department. But a little advance warning would be appreciated next time."

"We'll see what we can do. Listen, I called because there's a new development."

"Hot damn. New development. I love new developments. New developments are my favorites."

"I see why Harper didn't have nice things to say about you."

"Nobody has nice things to say about me. What's the, ta-daaa, new-fucking development?"

"Arthur Preston's here—"

"What . . . ? Who? How did he get out of the can?"

"Shit. Just listen, will you? Arthur Preston. Junior. The son. The old man's son. He's in Paris. He knows his father's looking for Billy Barton. Christ. Why do I feel like I'm talking to a fucking four-year-old here? Jesus . . . Anyway, Junior's been told where you are. He has your address. And he has two choices, the way I see it. He can either pass your whereabouts on to the old man, or come to see you with the message. He doesn't have the phone number."

"Speaking of phone numbers, what's yours? I'm feeling a little stranded out here."

"I don't think that's a good idea. I don't want the wrong people finding the right Billy."

"You guys fucking amaze me, honest to Christ. So . . . should I expect Arthur Junior to arrive strapped down with plastic explosives and an Uzi?"

"No. He's harmless. I don't think he's involved with United Martyrs, or any of the family business for that matter. I've got a feeling he hustles golf for a living.

He was only asked to tell Billy he has a bonus coming."

"Some bonus. What does Arthur Junior look like?"

"Just like the old man. Younger, naturally. The point is, Arthur's going to tell you to contact Sam Zuckerman, the old man's lawyer. Which, of course, we don't want you to do. It wouldn't make sense. Are you following me on this?"

"Yes, Dad." Joe let out an exaggerated sarcastic sigh. "I've got to find a way to have Arthur Junior tell Zuckerman where I am."

"Right . . . Well, what are you going to say to Arthur?"

"I'll work on it."

"Well, be prepared. He could show up at any time."

" 'Be Prepared' is my fucking motto."

Both men returned their receivers to their respective resting spots. Joe's telephone rang the instant the Nichols connection was lost. The chime rattled up through his fingers, hand, and arm. Made him flinch. It was the last thing he'd expected. Andie was on the other end.

"Can we get together for lunch?"

Fifteen

Paris was hot. It was August and Paris was hotter than hell. And humid. Joe walked the length of the Louvre. On the outside. With each forward step he thanked the slimy bastard who'd stolen his suitcase. Andie had outfitted him with some decent summer clothes. Ninety percent of the crap Harper had picked out from Barney's had been made of wool. "Wool is great in the summer," Harper had said defensively. "It breathes." Joe was glad to be rid of the shit.

The Seine rolled by on Joe's left. A damp mist hung above the river's surface. Barges, working and tourist alike, plowed their way through the low-lying fog. Condensation steamed the windows of each vessel. Hot time in the city. High noon. Ninety-five degrees. Ninety-five percent humidity. Just like New York. Except everyone was speaking French.

Joe passed the museum and headed into the park. The Jardin des Tuileries as Andie had called it—in her perfect French accent. It was a park. Not unlike Central Park but more resembling the Washington Mall in its layout. He passed the large fountain littered with reclining high-school students and thought of all the fountains he'd passed in his life. From Munich to

Hong Kong to Moscow to Rome to Buenos Aires and back to Washington. And beginning to feel a little sorry he was out of it all.

He continued down the wide gravel path toward the Champs Élysées and the Arc de Triomphe.

Joe had never been overly fond of the French or this city. When he'd passed through with the Secret Service, he'd always laid pretty low. There were a few night spots he liked to hit. Places where you could catch a good singer every now and then, but mostly he and his kind were treated like ugly Americans, so they stayed to themselves. However, the more he saw of Paris from this new casual viewpoint, the more he felt himself warming up to it. It had a character. He guessed there had to be more than a few rough-and-tumble neighborhoods. He vowed to find them before he left. Nothing was perfect.

After a short walk he came to the outdoor cafe Andie had selected. He sat at one of the small tables. A waiter approached and smiled.

"Oui, monsieur?"

"I'm waiting for someone."

"Ah . . . you are American?"

"Oui."

"Parlez vous Francais, monsieur?"

"Non . . . but I'm working on it," Joe said. Not giving much up.

"Very well, monsieur. Call if you need something."

"Merci bien."

Joe checked his watch. Andie wasn't due for another fifteen minutes. Off in the distance he could hear the brassy sound of a small band. A street clown paced back and forth. Up and down the wide path in front of him. Falling in behind passing businessmen. Then duplicating their walks. Joe hated clowns but this guy didn't miss a trick. Every now and then one of the men would turn and shout and wave his hands as though he were chasing a fly away. The clown would cower. Then assume a pose that said, "Please don't beat me anymore, Master."

After a while Joe spied Andie coming from the direction of the Louvre. It would have been impossible to miss her. Again she was radiant. The sunlight seemed to be illuminating her like a giant follow-spot. Her hair appeared electrically charged. The clown caught sight of her immediately. He raced up to her. Big feet flapping all the way. He stood directly in her route. Andie refused to go around. The clown pouted. They remained squared off for almost a minute. Nearly every other pedestrian stopped to watch the show. Finally the clown clutched his heart, rolled his eyes toward the sky, and fell into a heap on the ground. Andie looked down. Smiled. Stepped over him. Continued down the pathway toward the cafe.

The clown jumped to his feet. He raced to get in front of her. Then began throwing mock rose petals in her path. Joe was still laughing when she arrived at his table. He gave the clown a ten franc coin. A polite hat tip from the clown followed and he waddled off.

"Jesus, I hate clowns," Joe said after Andie was seated.

"Did you hire him to do that?"

"No. I'm sure you just inspired him. You look beautiful."

"Thanks. I hate clowns, too. They frightened me for some reason."

"You held your own."

"It wasn't easy. Who were you on the phone with?"

"What . . . ? Jesus, where did that come from?"

"This morning. When I called you. The phone was busy for ten minutes."

"Man, you're nosy."

"I was wondering if you'd gotten *bored* and found it necessary to call *Danielle*?" She put unusually strong emphasis on the words "bored" and "Danielle."

"I threw that number away. You saw me do it. You saw it disintegrate in the toilet. What more do you want?"

Danielle's disintegrating phone number had become a mild source of amusement for them by now.

"I took the phone off the hook," Joe lied. "I was in the shower. It's a good thing I like you so much. You could become a real nuisance."

She reached across the table and gave him a long kiss. She then called the waiter over and ordered lunch for them both.

After the waiter left, Joe said, "Thanks. What are we having? If you don't mind me asking. I missed a few of those words."

"Pâté. Bread. The pâté's a goose liver base, okay?"

"Sure. I'll eat anything."

Andie's cheeks turned nearly as red as her hair. She turned her face to the side and looked up into the trees.

"This gives me an idea," Joe said. "What's on your schedule for this afternoon?"

"Forget it. I know what your idea is. I've got work to do."

"Too bad . . . What work?"

"I have a few fashion houses to check out. New lines. You know."

"Like some company?"

"I don't think so, Billy. I need to concentrate."

Their lunch arrived along with a large bottle of mineral water. They were quiet as the waiter poured. The man placed the bottle on the table along with a small piece of paper. Then stood at Joe's side.

After a moment Andie said, "You have to pay him now."

"Right . . . I was concentrating on you."

Joe fished out some bills and paid.

"Merci beaucoup, monsieur."

"De rien."

"I have to admit your idea sounds very tempting," Andie said after the waiter moved off to greet another couple.

"You don't know what my idea was. Maybe I wanted to go to the Louvre or something."

"I wouldn't bet any money on that."

She brought her foot up to meet Joe's left calf. He jerked his leg back but not quick enough.

"What the hell is that?" Andie said.

"What?"

"That," she said and kicked the .32 automatic he'd strapped to the inside of his right leg.

"My wallet?"

"Jesus, Billy. Do you know how to use that thing?"

"Absolutely. Didn't you see those holes in the bedroom door? I was practicing. A very tight bullet grouping, didn't you think?"

"I'm serious. Why do you have that thing with you?

You almost killed yourself with it. Now you want to blow your foot off?"

"This is going to be a little tough to explain . . ."

"I'm all ears."

"Well . . . it makes me feel safe?"

"Safe from what . . . ? You know, the truth may be easier than you think. Maybe you should share it with me?"

Joe sat silently and watched her eyes. After a moment, Andie placed her elbows on the table. She moved closer.

"I've got a feeling you're going to testify against Arthur Preston . . . Aren't you?" Trying not to let her conversation with Nichols show on her face.

Joe searched Andie's features for some kind of sign. Something that would tell him what she knew. What she didn't know.

Their eyes dueled for a time but he found no clues.

"How did you know that?" he finally said.

"Just guessed."

She reached over and took his hand.

"I'm glad you're doing it, Billy, but I think carrying a gun is a big mistake. You don't know how to use it, and you're being paranoid if you think Arthur Preston would be so extreme that he'd want to hurt you."

"You're probably completely right. But it makes me feel better. I'm going to keep it. I think I've figured out how the damn thing works."

"This is stupid."

She pulled away from him.

"Is this going to be a fight?" he said. "It's shaping up like a fight. I've had fights with women before. I know how to recognize them in the early stages now."

She moved her chair sideways and gazed down the gravel path. "I don't think so." She let out a long sigh. "You do what you want."

"Oh, man . . . And I suppose now you're not going to eat your lunch?"

"I'm not hungry."

"Oh, man . . . Okay, suit yourself. Jesus."

Joe ate his pâté slowly. Savoring it. Occasionally stopping to take a drink of water or gnaw at the sharp pickles.

Andie sat in silence.

After five minutes Andie said, "I don't like to lose. Are you going to get rid of that gun or not?"

"Non, mademoiselle."

"Damn it. Damn it. Damn it."

She stomped her feet into the gravel. Joe laughed.

"You're nuts. You know that?" he said.

"I'm telling you, I don't like to lose."

"Well, you lost. Turn around and face it. You lost. And if you don't want what's on your plate, I'm going to eat it . . . Loser."

"You touch that plate and I'll kill you, you son of a bitch. Gun or no gun. I'll punch your lights out."

Andie slowly turned her chair back to the table. She smiled at Joe. Said, "You'd be so easy to hate."

"Thanks."

She spread some pâté on a crust of bread and took a bite.

"When do you have to go back for this trial?" she said.

"It's set for the twenty-seventh of September. I'm not sure when I'll fly back."

"And these Nichols people are letting you use their place for an entire month?"

Again Joe looked for information in Andie's face. But there was nothing unusual. Harper's warning to "trust no one" pounded into the back of his brain. But in the end, the truth did seem better than any lie he could come up with.

"Actually there are no 'Nichols people.' The apartment is rented by the U.S. government. That's who's putting me up until the trial."

"So they won't be too upset when they find out you shot it full of holes."

"At least it wasn't a post office."

Andie now seriously considered telling Billy what Agent Nichols had asked her to do. She wanted to put some of her information on the table. What difference could it make? Besides, there was an off chance it would bring them closer. But she didn't do it. She didn't do it because she trusted the FBI's instincts on this. She believed they were probably right. Billy would have nothing to do with her if he was aware she was reporting back to Nichols. And she needed to stay close. So she said nothing about the agent. She smiled at Billy and said, "I feel like something sweet."

And Joe motioned for the waiter.

Across the street. Across the wide Rue de Rivoli and up three stories, Agent Nichols stood before a set of opened French doors with a pair of binoculars pressed to his face. He scanned the park. He was looking for teenagers. Teenage girls with short-stretch skirts that barely covered their firm young bodies. And there were hundreds of them. High-school and college students on their summer break. Every time Nichols spotted one of these young lovelies, his jaw would go slack and he would mumble something like, "God-damn, baby. Move that thing," or "Come to Daddy, you sweet thing, you," or "Oh, man, talk about legs up to her ass."

He panned up from the Louvre's courtyard. Past the glass pyramid. Past the carousel. Up the gravel path that led to the Champs Élysées. Young girls were everywhere. He moved his gaze farther up the path. Past a clown busying himself by harassing passing businessmen. Until finally his binoculars came to rest on a couple having lunch in an outdoor cafe.

"Well, I'll be dipped in shit," he said. "She was able to pull it off. She brought him by so you could have a real good look-see . . . Come here, Billy. Here's something that will interest you. You want to see your new twin brother? Mr. Joe Bradlee?"

Sixteen

Billy Barton tossed his FBI playing cards onto the kitchen table. He ambled into the FBI's Parisian living room. Agent Nichols was holding his position at the French doors. He handed Billy the FBI binoculars and said, "Bradlee's at the outdoor cafe . . . Pan to the right . . . Past the carousel . . . You'll see a clown . . . Keep going . . . There's a guy sitting at a table. There's a broad with red hair with him . . . Find him . . . ?"

"Yep."

"What do you think?"

No question about it. Billy was stunned. Joe Bradlee truly was his identical twin.

"Wow . . . it's amazing," Billy said. He watched Joe for almost two more minutes and then added, "Have you ever wondered what it would be like to have sex with someone who looked exactly like you? I mean, think about it. Twins must do it all the time. Everyone believes that they themselves are the most beautiful person in the entire world. And the hottest. What could be better? It's got to be heaven . . . When this mess is all over, I'd like to get to know this Joe."

"You're a sick fuck, you know that?" Nichols said. "Give me those." He took his binoculars back.

"Me? You're the one who's been spending his entire morning watching all the underage snatch walk by."

"That's different."

"How so?"

"It just is . . . It's normal."

"You could probably get some legitimate arguments on that point."

"Yeah? From who?"

"Whom."

"Whom?"

"Just about anybody . . . Mostly psychiatrists, though."

"Buulll-shit," Nichols nearly shouted.

"Suit yourself."

Nichols opted to move on to a more relative subject, "What about the broad with the red hair? She's the one who says she's met you before. Look familiar?"

"I didn't spend any time looking at her. May I have the glasses back?"

"You didn't look at the broad? One of the best-looking bimbos in the whole fucking city, and you didn't look at her? You're a sick fuck, you know that? Here."

Nichols handed over the binoculars. Billy took another long minute to stare into the park.

"You're right. She's very good looking."

"*Very good looking* . . . Jesus. Well?"

"I don't know. She doesn't look familiar."

"Shit. Are you sure?"

"What can I say? I don't think I've ever met her. I could be wrong, though."

"Jesus Christ! You know Preston's attorneys are going to bring all this poor-memory-booze-and-cocaine shit up at the trial. You better be a little more clear about your facts, or the old man's going to fly like a goddamn bird."

"Don't worry. With what I have, Arthur's going nowhere. It's very solid stuff."

"I fucking hope so."

Nichols walked to the kitchen and poured himself some coffee. He opened the refrigerator and gritted his teeth.

"What happened to the milk?"

"I drank it," Billy said.

"You drank the fucking milk? It was for coffee, for Christ's sake. People don't *drink* milk."

"Your partners are getting some on their way back."

"They are?"

"I gave them a list."

"A list?" Nichols said. He was back in the living room by now.

"A shopping list. We ran out of just about everything while you were in New York."

"Fuck."

"And that's another thing," Billy said, "you can't let those two bozos buy wine from now on. Either let me out of here, or you pick up the wine. Your buddies have absolutely no discerning taste. None whatsoever."

He pulled an empty bottle out of the trash and handed it to Nichols.

"Look at this garbage. It's from Poland, for God's sake. I asked them why they bought it. They said: 'Because it was on sale.' Can you believe that? They're in Paris, they've got an open checkbook, and they buy what's on *sale*. Of course it's on *sale*. When do you think was the last time the store sold a bottle of that sludge? Nineteen sixty-eight?"

Nichols looked at the label. "The vintage is ninety-six."

"It was a rhetorical question."

"Well, Christ, I don't know. Did Austin buy this, or Petrie?"

"Who knows? I can never remember which one's which. What difference does it make who bought it. Would you buy a bottle of that junk?"

"I'll talk to them."

"No, no, no. Don't *talk* to them. You buy the wine from now on or I'll slip out through the window and do it myself."

"Right." Nichols dropped the bottle back into the trash can as if he expected to catch leprosy from it. He then picked the binoculars up and focused on Joe and Andie. They were engaged in a long kiss across the cafe table. "Christ, this guy doesn't waste any fucking time."

"What's he up to?"

"Nothing that would interest you. How well do you know Arthur Junior?"

"Him I remember meeting. Looks a lot like his father . . . Younger. Supports himself by hustling golf money out of people who have too much."

"He's here in Paris. Has a message for you from the old man . . . You have a bonus coming."

"Not likely."

"That's what I figured. How much does Junior know about what the old man was skimming from Shared Charities of the United Martyrs or the ponzi operation?"

"Nothing. He's always off with the golf. You have to respect him for keeping clean. Not going anywhere near Arthur Senior . . . or his money."

Nichols handed the binoculars to Billy and said, "There's two dick-smokers necking in the grass to the right of the fountain, but they haven't gotten into anything hard-core yet, if you're interested."

"Not really."

"So, Arthur Junior's clean? You're sure of that?"

"Absolutely. Although, I'm sure he could be implicated in some way or another. Only because he must have overheard at least one or two conversations along the way. But that's nothing I could swear to. He's actually a decent kid from what I can remember. You should lay off of him . . . He's not going to attack anyone."

"Lay off? I haven't gone near him."

"I'll bet. I'm beginning to see how you boys like to operate. A touch of honesty wouldn't hurt every now and then."

"You know better than that. I'll give you a little tip, Billy, don't count on anyone being honest. Watch out for number one."

Nichols moved back to the kitchen. Billy walked over to the long couch. It had been draped with a chintz slipcover. Pink roses with pale blue satinish ribbons on a light cream background. It matched the curtains. Billy put his hands into his pockets. Then sat. Put his feet up on the coffee table.

"My wife was honest," Billy said as his weight settled into the couch.

"Shit. Fuck. I wish we had some goddamn milk. I

hate black coffee," Nichols screamed from the kitchen. "Fuck . . . What'd you say, Billy? I didn't hear you."

"Nothing. It wasn't important."

"No. No. Something about your wife. What was the deal on you two, anyway?"

"We were just good friends. Something you'd probably call a *marriage of convenience.* She did her thing, I did mine. We had fun. Partied together, that's all. She was an honest person. I'm going to miss her."

"Yeah? So why didn't you stick around for the funeral?"

"You didn't see what they did to her . . . I'm not afraid to say I was scared. I still am."

"And you don't think Arthur Junior was sent here to find you? It's a little too goddman coincidental if you ask me."

"Maybe he was. But he doesn't know anything and he wouldn't hurt a soul. I'm sure he believes the *I've got a bonus coming* story."

"Well, the old man's definitely after you. That much is for sure. He's got Junior looking for you—and God knows who else. It won't be long before he pinpoints Paris. Who do you think the old man sent after your wife?"

"It could have been anyone. Arthur's a self-made-man. He loved to hang out with the lowlifes as well as the stuffed shirts. There were always shifty characters perched in his office. Even his driver was an oily bastard. Nestor maintains he's a Cuban, but he could've fooled me."

"You gave all this information to the Director when you were in Washington, right?"

"Yes. They said they would look into it." Billy rolled his eyes to the ceiling.

"They will," Nichols said. "If they said they'd look into it, they will. I'll try to get a photo of this Nestor character sent over here. Sounds like someone we should be keeping an eye open for."

"I'd rather whoever killed my wife, didn't get away with it, that's all. A little justice. It'd be nice."

The door opened and Austin and Petrie entered with two shopping bags each.

"I hope you've got some milk in there?" Nichols said.

Austin looked at Petrie.

"Was milk on the list?"

"Yes," Billy answered.

"Where?"

Petrie handed the list to Billy, and Billy pointed to the word "lait."

"That's milk? Well, Christ, write it in English next time." Austin then pulled a bottle out of his bag. "Rhine wine was on sale . . ." He looked at the label. "Hope it's as good as that Polish stuff."

Seventeen

The last thing Arthur Junior wanted to do was get involved in his old man's goddamn business. The farther, and the longer he kept away from the United Martyrs the happier he was. After going to high school in France and majoring in French at Stanford he'd become the ultimate Francophile. He loved the country. He loved its proximity to the Spanish golf courses. He loved its women. But most of all he loved it for its safety. He couldn't be touched. Arthur Preston Senior was afraid to fly.

For the hundredth time he looked down at the scrap of paper in his hand; 6 Rue Racine, Apartment 24, Nichols. He shook his head. Shit, he thought. Why does the old bastard have to dig his greedy claws into Paris. Paris is my city. He has New York—and all of America for that matter. Why can't I have France and be left alone?

But Arthur was the dutiful son. He'd do what he'd been asked to do. He would look for Billy Barton. If he found him, he'd tell him to contact Sam Zuckerman. What the hell? If Billy had a bonus coming, it was the least he could do. However, Arthur vowed to only give it this one afternoon of his life. That was it. If things got more involved than he liked, if this mission started to take up too much time, he'd simply head south for a little golf.

He jumped onto the number four Métro train at Chateau d'Eau and headed in the direction of Port d'Orléans. Arthur loved the Paris Métro. It was efficient. You could get just about anywhere, and in no time at all. And it was filled with a youthful vitality. Smiling faces. Tourists and Parisians, all enjoying life. Why take a cab?

Every Métro car had its own freelance musician. On board to entertain the masses and pass the hat. Today it was two squabbling guitar-toting Armenian brothers. So close in age, they could pass for twins. They had their act polished to a comic brilliance. Each with a different idea on the proper tempo for some obscure B.B. King masterpiece. They both carried small battery-powered amplifiers and were nearly as good as the great Mr. King himself. It was an outstanding show. The entire carload of men, women, and children was beaming with smiles when the hat was passed. And the dueling guitarists served to take Arthur's mind off his father as the subway rolled under the Seine toward the Left Bank.

But nothing lasts forever, and Arthur soon found himself skipping up the steps of the Odéon Métro stop and on his way to 6 Rue Racine.

When he reached the building he scanned the buzzers for Nichols and leaned on the button for a good five seconds. He waited. No reply. He pressed it a second time. Nothing. Arthur then pulled one of Sam Zuckerman's crumpled business cards from his wallet and began to write a note for Billy Barton. This was turning out to be easier than he originally thought.

Joe Bradlee didn't recognize Arthur when he came up behind him. He only said, "Pardon," and waited for him to step aside. He then opened the locked door with his key and moved inside.

"Monsieur, s'il vous plaît, avez vous connaissance de—" Arthur started to say, but was quickly interrupted by Joe.

"Whoa, hold on there, pal. My French isn't that good. It's okay, but you've got to slow down. Who are you looking for?"

". . . Billy?"

". . . Yeah?"

"I'm Arthur Preston. You used to work for my father."

"Oh, yeah, Jesus, Arthur. How the hell are you? I didn't recognize you at first. What brings you to Paris?"

"Just a little business. Are you okay?"

"Yeah . . . Sure . . . What do you mean?"

"I don't know. You look different. You seem a little rougher around the edges. But sturdier for some reason. That was supposed to be a compliment." He looked at his shoes. "I don't think it sounded like one."

"Thanks. No. I follow you. I had one of those damn red-eye flights a few days ago. You know, the kind you can't sleep for shit on, no matter how hard you try? Seats don't go back far enough, so your head keeps falling forward? Seems to screw me up for weeks. I probably need a shave, too." Joe rubbed his chin in an exaggerated fashion.

"Well, anyway, I ran into Sam Zuckerman just before I left. He said you had some kind of bonus coming. He wants to talk to you. I was just supposed to tell him where you were, but I figured you might as well call him yourself, right?"

"How the hell did you find me?"

Joe hoped the hell he wasn't laying this bullshit on too thick.

"It's a long story. Coincidence. Some guy on the plane—I forget his name—said he'd worked with you a long time ago. Said you used to visit this Nichols guy . . . ?"

Joe looked to the name above the buzzer. "Yeah. I've stayed here for years. It's convenient. Zuckerman didn't go into any details, huh? It'd be nice to know what the hell this bonus thing is all about. Or more importantly, how much."

"No . . . no details, sorry. Look, I can call him if you want. It doesn't make any difference to me. It'd probably keep my old man from having a cow. He's not keen on any improvisation by the peons."

"Yeah, now that I think about it, that's probably the best plan. I hate talking to Zuckerman, anyway. He depresses the shit out of me. He's such a fucking weasel."

"I know what you mean. What is it with him, anyway? If I didn't know better, I'd say he had a little habit for the white rabbit."

"Beats me." Joe shrugged. "Maybe you could just give him this address. He can mail me whatever it is. That way I don't have to listen to his voice."

"Sure, if that's the way you want it."

"I'll give you the phone number, too." Joe scratched

it out on the scrap of paper Arthur had written the address on. "Maybe Sam'll need to talk to me for some reason."

"You're sure you're okay? I mean . . . you know . . . you seem less . . ." Arthur rolled his hands and fingers around looking for the right word.

"Less . . . ? Less what, Arthur?"

"Well, you know, less . . . you know. I mean, weren't you and that Lazlo character an item?"

"Me and Lazlo? Nah . . . Lazlo was a good guy. We just did a lot of blow together. Hung out. Had a few laughs. He might have been gay, if that's what you mean, but we never got into it."

"Nestor told me you were off the coke."

"Nestor?"

"My old man's driver?"

"Oh, yeah, shit, Nestor. Yeah, he's right. I've cleaned myself up, but it's amazing how that crap can affect your memory in the long run . . ." Joe rubbed his chin again, trying to visualize what Nestor looked like. "Nestor, huh? How the hell is he?"

"As oily as he's always been."

"Doesn't surprise me. I don't think Nestor'll ever change."

Arthur seemed to study Joe for a long time and then almost shouted, "I know . . . I know . . . Jack Harper."

"What? You know Jack Harper?"

"No, no, I don't know him. I just remembered, that's all. It was Jack Harper. That's the name of the guy on the plane who said he knew you. Said you used to work together. Know him?"

"Jack Harper was on the plane with you? You're sure that's who he said he was?"

"Yeah. Why? Who is he?"

"Uhh . . . Just some guy from the old days . . . And he's in Paris? Now? You're sure?"

"We got off the plane together at Orly. Why? What's up?"

"When'd you get in?"

"Yesterday morning. What's up?"

"Nothing," Joe said. "I just figured if Harper knew I was here he would have looked me up."

"We'll maybe he's found someone else."

"Thanks, Arthur."

Eighteen

"Well, alleluia, Sam," Arthur Preston Senior said with a coarse smile as he perused Zuckerman's yellow legal pad, "the little golf hustler got us better information than your *informed* FBI man. Good God Almighty, I'm impressed."

"*Junior* got the phone number. They both came up with number six Rue Racine, apartment twenty-four. I don't see what use the phone number will be," Sam said, lifting his eyebrows and putting a condescending twang on the word Junior, unwilling to concede whose man was the superior fact gatherer. "You can get a phone number out of a phone book, for gosh sake."

Preston glared at him. "My son's information is better, it's more complete. Yes or no? A one-word answer will do."

". . . Yes."

"Good . . . I just wanted to be sure we understood each other."

A departing La Guardia jetliner rattled the Rikers Island windows. Zuckerman placed his yellow legal pad back into his attaché case and pressed the brass snaps down until he heard their familiar click-click.

He then stood and walked over to the still vibrating window glass. He peered through the bars. Out across the churning water. Onto the houses and boats adorning the coast of the Hunts Point section of the Bronx. "What's next?" he said.

"We send Nestor to Paris."

"Do you think that's wise, Arthur?" He turned back to the old man. "My FBI contact says to bear with him. Hold off for a few weeks. I have confidence in him. It might be a better idea to work on his timetable. Harper's very methodical. Very sure. Precise, would be a good word."

"I'm beginning to have very little use for you and your good words. I don't want to wait. I don't want to take chances on someone I haven't dealt with. I don't trust those jackals. Don't forget they're the ones who put me in this cesspool in the first place. Besides, the next thing you know, this *contact* of yours gets cold feet and I'm sitting in Federal court staring at Billy Boy in the witness box. You go ahead. Play along with your FBI pal. This *Harper*, or whatever his name is. Set it all up. It'll be a backup. Plus, it's nice to have the goods on one of these Feds. It might come in handy down the road. But I trust Nestor. He's come through for me in the past. I want this cockroach Billy gone. And the sooner the better."

"Okay. I'll try to get Nestor out on a flight tomorrow."

"Don't try, Sam; just do it. Lord, I'm so sick of lawyers, I can barely keep my food down."

As Zuckerman passed through the last pedestrian security gate and walked toward Nestor and the waiting limousine, he found himself thinking of his days at Columbia Law School. He wondered how it had all come down to this. For twenty years he had stacked one brilliant victory on top of another. He'd become the winningest trial lawyer in the history of the Jacobs-Ashton firm. And he had done it all without paying off judges, falsifying one iota of evidence; or killing a single witness. But here he was, preparing to send Nestor, Arthur Preston's switchblade-toting psychopath, over to Paris to eliminate a somewhat innocent person, having already contacted a mercenary FBI agent weeks earlier and paid him a small fortune to do the same blessed thing.

But Zuckerman had become addicted to winning. The thought of losing a case was just too much for him to handle. And he was definitely going to lose the Preston case if Billy Barton made it back to New York to testify. Sam sighed deeply as he walked the last few paces to the waiting car. It's too bad, really, he thought, Billy Barton wasn't such a bad guy. We had some good times.

"Hey, Sam-u-el, my man, cheer up," Nestor said with a beaming smile. "You look like you lost your best fucking friend, dude."

"It's this place. It's depressing as hell. You got any blow with you?"

"Sure, man. But I don't think this parking lot is a good place to be doing lines, if you get my drift," Nestor said as he made exaggerated head movements toward a guard tower.

"So let's roll."

Zuckerman slid into the front seat with Nestor and the Cuban eased the big car onto the highway. In no time they were speeding off toward the Triboro Bridge and Manhattan. After they hit the FDR Drive, Sam cut a line of cocaine on the opened glove compartment and drew the powder deeply up into his nose.

"Aw, Christ." He coughed. "Jesus. God . . . Don't you want to die like a baby? Thanks, Nestor. I needed that."

"No problem, my man, that's what I'm here for."

"Mr. Preston wants you to go to Paris, France, for him. He's got something that needs to be taken care of." Zuckerman coughed twice more.

"Billy?"

"Yeah. We found him."

"I like Billy. He's a good man. But I guess it had to come down to this shit. He shouldn't have fucked up like this. Look at the trouble he's got his ass into, the dumb maricone. You talk to cops and no fucking good will come to you in the end. That's what my mother used to say."

"My mother used to say shit like 'Foul language is an indication of a poor vocabulary and inferior education.' "

"Is that supposed to be some kind of a fucking joke, man?"

"I don't think so. She's a very serious woman. It was not easy growing up with her. She even went with me to the bar exams."

"Yeah, Moms can be tough. Mine used to take me to Plaza Vieja when I was a kid, then point out who was an informer for Castro. Who to keep away from. And she wasn't subtle about it, either, man. Moms ain't subtle about nothin'."

"Tell me about it. You'll have to leave for Paris tomorrow. I'll get your plane tickets. Find you a place to stay." Sam bent down and sucked up another line of cocaine. "Whoa, yeah. Jesus . . . this is decent stuff." He coughed again, then dabbed the remaining powder with his pinky finger and spread it on his tongue and lower gums.

"Go easy, man."

"Whoosh . . . Jiminy Cricket." He pushed his skull back into the headrest. "You don't speak French, do you?"

"Hey, man, I didn't get my inferior motherfucking education in the fucking Bronx, you know. I went to school in Havana. I was speaking Spanish, French, English, Russian, and Latin before I was ten motherfucking years old. Tell that to your fucking serious Mamma."

Nineteen

Joe pulled a small piece of paper from his wallet and eyed the phone number he'd scribbled on it. 50.24.61.13. Only then did he realize it was just a few digits off from the 6 Rue Racine phone number. Son of a bitch, he thought, she's got to live in the goddamn neighborhood.

He tossed the paper beside the phone and walked into the kitchen, where he pulled a bottle of Smirnoff Blue Label vodka from the freezer and poured a heavy shot into a glass. He threw the frosty liquid down his throat and poured a second shot before returning the bottle to the freezer. The afternoon sun had heated the apartment to an almost unbearable 95 degrees and the damn vodka had absolutely no effect in cooling him off. Joe brought the glass to his lips, but then stopped to observe a slight trembling in his left hand. "Shit," he said out loud, "where the hell did that come from?"

In the Secret Service, Joe hadn't been much of a drinker. Sure, he'd throw a few beers down every now and then, or one or two stiff vodkas after a particularly exhausting day with the politicos. But never more than two. And never in the morning. Never in the afternoon like now. And when he'd stepped out, took his leave, for the year he'd been married, he never went near the stuff. But all of that changed one day in April. April first, to be exact. April Fools' Day. Joe shook his head and finished his second vodka. Pulled the bottle back out and poured a third. Wondered if the drinking would stop. Wondered if the memories would stop.

His wife, Nina, and his stepson, Eubie, had been riding the A train, on their way to meet Joe at Central Park South for a late lunch. At 1:31 P.M. a small man dressed in a Brooks Brothers three-piece suit and navy blue camel hair overcoat entered the train at West 14th Street. The doors closed behind him. Before they opened again at Pennsylvania Station on 34th Street, the man had run three clips of ammunition through his AK-47, killing all seventeen of his fellow passengers, Nina and Eubie included. He then calmly dropped the weapon, exited the train, and disappeared into the bustling train station's lunchtime throng. Leaving behind him a pile of tangled bloody bodies, and a dozen emotionally wrenched families with nothing but a handful of brutal memories to haunt their remaining days.

Joe poured himself another vodka and thought of something his old man, Buster, used to say: "Chocolate's the best love substitute in the world." Joe walked to the window, downed the vodka, laughed, and said, "Shows what the fuck he knew, the dumb bastard."

He then returned to the living room, picked up the phone, and dialed 50.24.61.13. It was answered after four or five rings.

"Oui?"

"Danielle?"

"Oui . . . ?"

"Do you speak English, by any chance?"

"Who is this?"

Joe detected little or no accent when Danielle switched to English.

"My name is Joe Bradlee. I'm a friend of Jack Harper's. Is he there?"

"Pourquoi . . . ? Why would he be here?"

"Well, he's in Paris. Where does he usually stay?"

"Not here, *certainment."*

"D'accord. Fine. Listen, I need to get a hold of him. Do you know how I can do that?"

"It doesn't sound to me like you're such a good friend of Jack Harper's, if you don't have a telephone number for him."

"I had a feeling you were going to say something like that."

"Then you shouldn't have called . . . I'm sorry, I can't help you, Monsieur Bradlee."

"Well, listen, he did give me your number. He said you were a good person. Said I should give you a call if I needed help."

Danielle let out an audible sigh, and considered hanging up the phone. She knew she should have. She knew what was coming, but she didn't do it.

"What kind of help do you need?" she said, and then silently cursed herself for taking the bait.

"I wish I knew . . . Maybe we can meet somewhere? I hate these goddamn telephones."

"I work . . . I work in my home. I'm very regimented. And ... I'm in the middle of something important."

"How about when you're finished?"

"That may not be until later this evening. I don't know."

"That's fine with me; later is okay."

"Do I know you from somewhere, Monsieur Bradlee? Have we met before? There's something familiar in your voice."

"No. I don't think so."

"You're in the same business as Jack Harper though, aren't you?"

"Sort of . . . but not really."

After another sigh she said, "Do you know Café de Flore?"

"Yes."

"I can meet you there at nine tonight."

"Thank you. How will I know you?"

"I'll wear a vest."

By nine Joe'd cleaned up his act. After hanging up the telephone he'd returned to the kitchen for another drink but somehow ended up dumping the remainder of the bottle down the drain. It was an almost Pavlovian reaction to something in Danielle's voice—or something she'd said. Or didn't say. He almost thought he knew her also. And he'd spent the past five hours trying to figure out what the hell she'd done to make him dump the vodka out. He never came up with an answer.

When Joe approached Café de Flore every sidewalk table was occupied. Couples held hands, tourists took photos of one another, and waiters in long white aprons and black neckties scurried about. He strolled inside and stood by the bar. Then turned and glanced around the room, looking for a woman in a vest.

"Bon soir, monsieur," the bartender said as he cleared a dirty beer glass and swiped at the wet ring with a cloth.

"Bon soir. Nothing right now, I'm waiting for someone. *Merci bien."*

The bartender smiled. Said, *"Oui, monsieur."*

Joe looked out over the patrons, through the opened windows, and on into the advancing twilight. All the street and shop lights had come on. L'heure Bleue, the Parisian blue hour, was gone and the city was going through her final transformation, on her way to becoming the City of Lights. After about five minutes his eye was caught by a woman on the far street corner waiting for the stoplight to change green. She was tall, almost his height, with shoulder-length brownish-blond hair, and seemed to stand out among the small crowd patiently waiting at the light with her. Maybe it was how she carried herself—a self-assured look in her eye, that gave her an almost exotic appearance. It made her seem far better looking than she probably was. She wore a vest.

The light changed and she skipped across the street and into Café de Flore.

Joe approached her. His voice cracked as he said, "Danielle?"

"Monsieur Bradlee . . ." She extended her right hand and Joe took it. It seemed unusually warm, even for a hot August night in Paris.

"You can call me Joe."

"Okay, Joe." Her smile was equally as warm. "Why the sad eyes?"

"Can we get a table?"

"Sure."

"What sad eyes?"

"I don't know. You looked overly sad for some reason . . . and now you don't anymore. They're gone."

"Instant personality analysis?"

"I don't know . . . maybe."

"Why don't we grab that table." Joe pointed to the corner and they moved over to it. After they sat Joe said, "Did Jack tell you I'd be coming over to Paris?"

"I haven't seen Jack in almost a year."

"You're kidding?"

"No . . . Why?"

The waiter arrived and Joe said, "Have you had dinner?"

"Not yet."

"Deux menu, s'il vous plaît."

"Oui, monsieur."

"Can I buy you dinner?" he said after the waiter left. "We can go to a nicer place if you like . . . Jesus, what's that stuff on you hands?"

She started to laugh. "It's a plaster resin. I was working on a piece and lost track of time. I'm lucky I remembered to throw this vest on. It'll wash off."

"Piece?"

"Sculpture. This place is fine. The food's good here. I'll be right back."

The waiter returned with the menus and Danielle strolled off to the ladies' room. Joe watched her cross the cafe floor, pass the bar, and disappear up the stairs. Her movements were incredibly graceful. Almost like a lioness. Joe tried to remember what

Harper had said about her. "She works for no one—not us, not the French. She's just good people." He found himself wondering just what the hell Harper had been getting at. But more importantly he wondered why Harper had come to Paris and not contacted him.

Although he was unaware of it, Joe had kept his eyes glued to the stairway for nearly five minutes, until Danielle reappeared. He watched her cross back over to the table. She seemed to float into her chair.

"You move like a dancer," he said.

"I used to be one. I'm from Bayeux originally. Dance is what brought me into Paris."

"Dance?"

"Dance."

"When was that?"

"Sometimes your eyes get very sad. Has anyone ever told you that? Other than me, that is? It's a little . . . unnerving."

"Sorry. You remind me of someone. Would you like a drink?"

"Espresso's fine."

Joe motioned to the waiter.

"Oui, monsieur?"

"Deux espresso, s'il vous plaît. And some water . . ." Then, "Sorry, my French isn't perfect," more to Danielle.

"Pas de problème, monsieur," the waiter said and moved off.

"I hate to keep coming back to this Jack Harper business," Joe went on, "but would he call you if he was here in Paris? How good of friends are you?"

"Maybe we should start with you. Why do you need to talk to him?"

"It's a mess, really. You know who he works for, right?"

"Yes."

"Well, I'm sort of working with him . . . on more or less a freelance basis. At any rate, he was supposed to meet me in two or three weeks. Here. In Paris. But I got word he's already here. I'd like to get in touch with him."

"He's in New York."

"How can you be so sure of that?"

"I called him there less than two hours ago."

"I thought you said you hadn't talked to him in a year?"

"I said I hadn't *seen* him in a year. Look, I just don't want to be involved in this business anymore. I want to be left alone."

"But you called him in New York?"

"*Merde* . . ." Danielle drew the word out. She looked Joe over and then glanced to the ceiling. Then out the window. "Mr. Jack Harper literally saved my life a few years ago. I won't go into it, but I'd do almost anything for him. I just don't want to be involved with your type or your business. Not anymore." She continued to stare out the window for a long while and Joe knew better than to say anything. ". . . On the telephone . . . there was something in your voice I recognized. I don't know what. Jesus, this is stupid. I thought maybe I knew you. I called Jack in New York to find out what you were up to. He was very evasive. He only said I should meet with you. He said you weren't like the others . . ." She turned back to the table. "So here I am. He's in New York . . . believe me."

"Can you give me the number?"

"No. He said he'd be here in two weeks. On the thirteenth. He asked me to tell you that. Listen, I think I should go . . . Thanks for the coffee, but this has been a mistake."

"No. Don't. Stay." Joe put his hand on her arm. Again it felt unusually warm. He looked far into her eyes and considered what he could tell her. Harper said to trust her, which meant she must know just about anything Harper knew—even if she wouldn't admit it.

Joe released her arm and pulled the lemon twist from his espresso cup and bit down on it. "I'm not one of those guys," he said. "That type. Jack's right. I used to be. I'm not. I'm just some dope they grabbed because I look like some other dope. I'd like you to have dinner with me. I won't say another thing about Jack Harper. You have my word on that."

Twenty

After dinner Joe walked Danielle back to her studio. It was a short distance but their pace was slow. It took them almost fifteen minutes. She asked him to come up for a coffee, but he passed. He lied and said he had work to do, thinking he wanted to keep her as a good friend. Not following his heart. Not this time. He gave her the phone number to 6 Rue Racine, said good night, and headed home.

When he unlocked his apartment door the phone was ringing. He looked at his watch. It was half-past midnight.

"Jesus . . ." He picked the phone up. *"Oui?"*

"So, who the hell was she?"

It was Andie.

"Who?"

"Miss Key Largo . . . the Lauren Bacall-looking bimbo you were eating dinner with all night, that's who. Little miss tall and skinny?"

Almost instantly, Joe found himself wishing he hadn't dumped the goddamn vodka down the drain. "She was just a friend from the old days."

"That sounds like so much bullshit to me. Was it . . . *Danielle*?"

"No. It wasn't Danielle."

"Are you sure? She looked like a goddamn *Danielle.* Only someone named *Danielle* would wear a vest . . . in August. It's so French it makes me sick."

"I think I'm starting to see a mean side to you. Where were you? And how did you know where the hell I was?"

"Mean? You think this is mean? You haven't seen anything yet. You don't know *mean.* And don't change the subject, Billy. Was it Danielle?"

"Okay, it was Danielle . . . Christ, what difference does it make?"

"I thought you flushed her number down the toilet?"

"She was the one who called me."

"Oh, Jesus, that's really lame."

"No. Honest to God. She was trying to get a hold of the guy who owns this apartment. Nichols."

"And you felt compelled to take her out to dinner? Because your good old buddy, *Nichols,* wasn't there? Come on. Give me a break."

"Where were you? I didn't see you."

"Of course you didn't see me. You were too busy mooning over *Mademoiselle Danielle.* I was next door at Les Deux Magots . . . trying to enjoy myself."

"Why didn't you come in? Say hello? There's nothing going on there." Of course it was the last thing in the world Joe wanted—to get these two women together. Danielle seemed to have a way about her that would definitely ignite sparks in Andie. He couldn't put his finger on what exactly it was, he just knew he was better off keeping her far away from the redheaded temptress.

"I'm coming over," Andie announced.

"What? It's after midnight, for Christ's sake. Listen, why don't we have lunch tomorrow?"

"*Why don't we have lunch tomorrow?* What the hell is that? Why don't you want me to come over? That's the question."

"It's late, that's all."

"Bullshit. She's there, isn't she?"

"Who?"

"Who? The bitch Danielle, that's who. Put her on. Let me talk to her."

"You're crazy. You know that?" Joe started to laugh. "There's no one here."

"Then I'm coming over."

Joe began to protest once more but Andie had hung up the phone. He entertained the thought of calling her back. There seemed to be little point. She'd still insist on seeing the apartment for herself. Joe knew the type. Nonetheless he was surprised at how quickly she showed up at his front door.

"Come on in. Look around."

"Well, of course she's gone by now. Jesus, Billy, what do you take me for, an idiot?"

"Does this seem like I'm in a no-win situation here? Or is it my feeble imagination working overtime?"

She came over and wrapped herself around him like a boa constrictor. "I think we should just fuck, and forget this whole thing ever happened. Now that I'm here, it's impossible not to forgive you."

He pried himself loose and said, "Nothing happened. There's nothing to forgive. Jesus . . . Do you feel like taking a walk? It's hot in here."

"No. I told you what I feel like doing; I want to eat you up."

"I feel like some air."

"I just got some, thanks. It's just as hot outside."

Joe walked to the couch and flopped down. He was fighting an uphill battle. Andie followed and stretched out prone, placing her head in his lap. She then unbuttoned her blouse and allowed it to fall open.

"They're very nice," he said, barely glancing at her exposed chest. "Is that all you ever think about?"

"Mostly. You seem to bring it out in me."

Joe stood and walked to the window while Andie remained seductively spread out on the couch.

"This is no good, Andie, you've got to give me a little room here." He turned and studied her. She said nothing. Only gazed back with a sexual leer that more than emphasized her earlier statements.

It was no use. It would have taken a man of iron to resist her. And Joe wasn't particularly feeling like a man of iron. He was feeling more like a child. A child lost in a maze of who to trust and who not to trust. His mind flashed once again to Harper. Arthur Junior wouldn't have lied about meeting the agent on the plane. Arthur seemed as oblivious to deceitful behavior as anyone Joe had ever met. But Joe also had a strong feeling about Danielle. He believed her when she'd told him she'd spoken to Harper in New York earlier that evening.

Joe had always trusted his gut feelings in the past, his sixth sense. And his sixth sense was telling him that both Arthur and Danielle had been telling the truth. However, his rational mind was telling him it was impossible; someone had to be lying. In the end, he opted to believe Arthur. He was too much of a clod to be a good liar. Agent Harper was obviously in Paris and was avoiding him. Joe would find him. And he would find out why Danielle was covering for him. It's too bad, he thought. I liked Danielle. Damn.

Andie stood and walked toward him, letting her blouse fall to the floor along the way. Again she latched on to him like a goddamn snake. They kissed a long kiss and walked together into the bedroom where she turned out the light. They both fell sound asleep at around one forty-five.

At nine a.m., on the dot, the telephone rang. Andie sat straight up in bed. Joe groaned. He began to fumble for the receiver, but she positioned herself over him and pulled the whole works across to her side of the bed. Joe rubbed his eyes and tried to sit up, but she pushed him back down and sunk her hips into his groin. She mumbled something into the mouthpiece, returned the receiver to its cradle, and placed the telephone back on his side.

"Who the hell was that?" he said.

"Wrong number . . ."

"Well, who'd they want to talk to?"

"Some bimbo wanted to talk to a guy named Joe."

Twenty-one

Nestor stepped out of the Orly-Sud terminal almost at the exact moment Danielle had made her misguided phone call to Joe. He was very close to drooling. Nestor hadn't seen this many good-looking women since he was a bouncer at the Pink Pelican Club in North Miami, and it took a good deal of self-control to keep from pouncing on some poor unsuspecting college student and dragging her into the luggage room and showing her a good time. But he resisted the temptation. He told himself the ladies would wait, then moved off to the taxi stand.

After four minutes he was sliding into the backseat of an orange Peugeot station wagon.

"Oui, monsieur?" the driver said, barely acknowledging Nestor's existence. Considering the swarthy Cuban to be no more than an annoying housefly.

"Trente et un Avenue George Cinq, s'il vous plaît."

The man raised his eyebrows. *"L'Hôtel George Cinq?* Are you certain, monsieur? This is a very expensive hotel. *Premiere classe.* Perhaps you've made a mistake?"

Nestor sized the man up as the racist he was. He placed his left hand on the driver's shoulder, brought his mouth to within an inch of his ear, and whispered, in flawless French, just enough to straighten him out. A loose translation of what Nestor had said would be: "Just drive the goddamn car, you little piece of shit. If I need your advice on what class of hotel I should stay in, I'll piss on that bald fucking head of yours. Until then keep your fucking mouth shut and drive. Dig?"

The driver glared at Nestor through the mirror and considered his options: Become indignant? Throw this chocolate-colored man out of his car? Refuse to move? Call a policeman? But Nestor's reversed expression was quickly analyzed by the driver. The man realized he was lucky to have gotten off as lightly as he had. He counted his blessings, pushed his cab out into the traffic flow, and kept his mouth shut for the entire drive into the Eighth Arrondissement—as he was told. Nestor settled back for the ride and looked over Zuckerman's map book and a folded slip of paper with 6 Rue Racine, Apartment 24, scratched in the lawyer's shaky scroll. Zuckerman, Nestor thought. What a fucking weasel.

The Hôtel George V was a good thirty blocks from Billy Barton's apartment, and Nestor wondered why Zuckerman had chosen a place so impractical. But these reservations were quickly forgotten the moment Nestor entered the hotel. He understood, at once, the lawyer's rationale; no self-respecting weasel would stay anywhere else.

Unlike the surly taxi driver, the hotel staff greeted Nestor as though he had been a time-honored guest returning from too many years in the Orient. His hand luggage was swiftly lifted from his shoulders while a shapely young blonde in an overly short skirt, and dramatically large breasts, escorted him directly to the front desk. Within seconds he had been checked in and directed, by the young blonde, to his room, where he found his baggage neatly laid out on mahogany luggage stands.

Nestor had, once again, an exceedingly strong urge to throw the blonde onto the bed and give her the fucking of a lifetime, but he let it drop, handed her twenty francs, and again whispered in French, "I hope I'll be able to see more of you? I've got something with me you might be interested in, mademoiselle."

"I somehow doubt that, you goat of a Neanderthal," was what the blonde was tempted to say, but she came up with, *"Merci bien, monsieur,"* and closed the door on her way out.

Like everyone else arriving on an overnight flight, Nestor was feeling the effects of a lousy night's sleep. He called down to room service and ordered up some breakfast, "sans café." Then jumped into the shower. Breakfast arrived and Nestor worked on his plan of attack for the next few days.

Zuckerman had arranged for an open-ended plane ticket, so Nestor wasn't on a particularly tight schedule, but, as with Billy's wife, he liked to get these things over and done with, than get the fuck out. The longer he waited to move, or the longer he hung around, the better the chances someone would associate his face with a bloody carcass somewhere.

But this was Paris, not Westport, Connecticut, the site of the last butchering, and it would be nice to loiter for a while. Sample some of the local ladies. Dip the old Cohiba a few times. And all of this presented Nestor with a bit of a dilemma: Should he hang out for a couple of days, nail a few broads, and then whack Billy-Boy, or waste the little maricone first and get laid second? Nestor bounced his options around in his head as he finished his eggs Florentine and toast. There was no question: the little blonde piece of ass who had shown him to his room had worked Nestor up. He was more than ready to tear into something warm and wet.

He stood and walked to the window. The Parisian traffic was loud and heated. Car horns battled with one another. The streets had become jammed with an early lunch crowd. The air was steamy. Hot. Smoggy. Dirty. Nestor stepped over to his suitcase and rummaged through the clothing until he found an ivory inlaid ebony-handled Italian stiletto. He lifted it to arm's length and slowly pressed a small silver button. An eleven-inch steel pigsticker shot from the handle with such force it snapped Nestor's wrist in a short jerk. He smiled and pressed the cold metal to his nose.

He then crossed to the bed, removed his George V robe, and sat with his head propped against the padded silk headboard. Methodically Nestor tapped the tip of his switchblade onto his bare thighs, alternating from right to left. With each tap the blade pierced the skin like a razor, leaving a small prick where a droplet of blood would eventually form. After six or seven taps on each leg, he placed the knife on the nightstand, sighed lethargically, and solidified his plan.

Nap for five hours. Get a late lunch. Visit number 6 Rue Racine. Carve up the maricone scumbag, Billy

Barton. Then go claw up a good woman. It was a plan Nestor could get into. A plan he could live with.

"Ciudad de la Habana," Nestor muttered aloud and laughed. He then slid down in the bed and closed his eyes and drifted off.

Twenty-two

After Danielle's phone call had awakened Andie and Joe, there had been a very long and very uncomfortable period of silence for Joe. He'd tried to make believe he wasn't fully awake, which wasn't too far from the truth, in an effort to figure out who the hell had been on the other end of the line. He'd guessed it had been Danielle, but he wanted a confirmation.

"You're sure this woman asked for Joe?" he finally said after yawning and rubbing his eyes for effect.

"Yes. Do you know someone named Joe?"

"I'm trying to think . . ."

"Well, forget about it. It was probably a wrong number." She moved her hips against him and pressed her exposed chest into his.

"What did she sound like?"

"What do you mean? She sounded stupid. That's what she sounded like."

"What I mean is, was she French? Was she English? American? Albanian? Italian? Greek? Russian? What the hell was she?"

"Albanian."

"Thanks . . . I'm serious."

"Jesus, Billy, what difference does it make?"

"Well, in case the people who own this apartment happen to ask me if anyone called, I can say: Yes, some stupid Greek girl called, but I didn't get any message or name."

"You mean the U.S. government?"

"What?"

"The U.S. government. The people who own this apartment."

"Yes. The U.S. government."

"She wasn't Greek."

"Well, what the fuck was she?"

"American."

"Thank you. That wasn't so hard, was it?"

"Maybe not, though. Her French was perfect. She might have been Canadian the more I think on it. She could of said 'aiye' at some point. You know, like the hockey players do?"

"Christ . . . American, French, or Canadian? Which one was it?"

"French. Wow, take it easy."

"Fine. French. We can drop it. That's good enough for the U.S. government."

"Is it Joe Nichols?"

"What?"

"Is that Nichols's first name? Joe?"

"Actually, I've never met this Nichols guy. Only talked to him over the phone. And come to think of it, he never mentioned his first name. It probably *is* Joe."

"Sorry. I guess I should have taken a message. Next time I will." Andie pressed herself flat on top of Joe and began to nibble at his neck.

"I have a better idea," Joe said as he gazed at the

ceiling. "How about you don't answer the phone anymore?"

She sat up and glared at him, "What's that supposed to mean?"

"Relax. Jesus. All I'm thinking is . . . is . . . well . . ." He stretched his neck to buy a little thinking time, and to focus. ". . . What if someone really is out to get to me? That's all I was wondering. It's possible, you know. I just don't want you to be getting involved in anything. The less people know you're spending time here with me, the better. I sure as hell don't want to put you into any danger."

Andie seemed to think about this for a minute.

"Maybe you're right," she finally said. "I won't answer the phone anymore. Damn, you're beginning to make *me* paranoid. Don't you think the government should be giving you some extra protection of some kind?"

"Nah. They're more concerned about something happening when I arrive in the States. And apparently they've got damn near the entire FBI ready to protect me when I do get back. Besides, I have a gun, remember?"

"Don't get me started on the gun again." She grabbed Joe's wrists and spread him out crucifixion-style. Then kissed him heavily and moved her hips from side to side until he had entered her. After only a second or two, she began moving her mouth and tongue down his left arm. When she reached his wrist she glanced at his watch.

"Oh, Jesus, I've got to get the hell out of here. Look at the time. You're going to get me into so much damn trouble."

She rolled off, ducked into the bathroom, and shouted through the door, "You shouldn't have wasted so much time trying to find out who was on the damn phone. You missed out on a great follow-up lay."

Andie showered and dressed in less than fifteen minutes and was gone.

Joe's head was spinning. Anything that vaguely resembled "control over the situation" had completely evaporated the moment he had boarded the plane at Kennedy Airport. He walked into the kitchen and opened the freezer searching for the vodka. Then glanced over to the wastebasket and the empty bottle.

"Fuck . . . You dumb bastard . . ."

He meandered into the bathroom, started a shower running, and stepped in. As soon as he was able to get a good lather worked up, the phone rang.

"Fuck a goddamn duck . . ."

He grabbed a towel and sloshed back into the living room and jerked the phone to his ear.

"Yeah?"

"Joe?"

"Yeah?"

"It's Nichols."

"Fuck a goddamn duck."

"You okay?"

"Yeah . . . Jesus . . . Okay, listen, before you say anything, I need a goddamn telephone number. This shit is getting out of hand. There's no control here. I want a number where I can reach you . . . And I want a number where I can reach that son of a bitch Harper. Some shit's going on that I don't like."

"Like what?"

"Give me a fucking number or I have nothing to say to you."

"Got a pen?"

Joe fumbled through the desk drawer.

"Okay, I got a pen."

Nichols said, "07-13-28-30."

"Fuck . . . Hold on. I've got soap all over my goddamn hands. Shit." Joe picked the pen up from the floor and it slipped from his grasp once more. "Fuck. Hold the fuck on." He bent down one more time. "Okay, give it to me again."

"07-13-28-30."

"07-13-28-30 . . . okay. Is that for you or Harper?"

"Me."

"And what's Harper's?"

"That's all I can give you."

"Jesus, fuck. What am I, negotiating for a new car, here? We're talking about my life. You bastards have hung me out to dry."

"Look, we can't have you calling the States. There's been leaks. You understand me? Harper and I have reason to believe information is seeping from headquarters like a sieve. That's the only number you get."

Joe growled like a trapped bear into the phone.

"Sorry, that's the way it's got to be," was Nichols's response.

"You fucking people . . . And there's another goddamn thing: Where the hell *is* Harper? The son of a bitch tells me he won't be here for three weeks, and I find out through the grapevine he's already here. I want to talk to that bastard. Is he there with you?"

"What are you talking about? Harper's in New York. I just spoke with him last night."

"Bullshit."

"Someone told you he was here? In Paris? It doesn't make any sense."

"He's here. I trust my source."

"Who? What source?"

"Arthur Junior, that's who. And don't tell me he's lying. He's too much of a goofball to be a good liar."

"Arthur told you Harper was here? In Paris? Why would he do that?"

"Don't ask me. Put Harper on. Let me talk to him."

"He's not here. Jesus."

Joe slammed the receiver down and walked back into the bathroom and rinsed off. The phone rang two more times while he was in the shower and a third time as he dried off. He wrapped a towel around his waist and answered it on Nichols's fourth attempt to get reconnected.

"What do you want?"

"I'm trying to figure this Harper shit out. I'm sure there's some logical explanation. Don't hang up. Look, I swear I spoke to Harper, in New York, last night. That's why I was calling. He's on his way over—as we speak. Things have heated up. Customs has informed us that Nestor left the States yesterday. He's here. In Paris."

"Who the hell is Nestor? Sounds like a fourth-place finisher in an Argentinean tango contest."

"That's not far off. He's Arthur Preston's driver and right-hand sleazeball."

"Right, right, Arthur Junior mentioned something about good old Nestor, now that I think on it."

"Billy's certain Nestor's the one who sliced up his wife. He could only be here for one reason."

"Me?"

"You . . . Well, Billy."

"Would you like to tell me what this charmer looks like, or should I just wait for someone with a Spanish accent to put a knife in my kidneys?"

"Harper's bringing photos."

"Back to Harper. I want to talk to that bastard. You guys play all the fucking games you want. But I want to talk to him."

A lightbulb seemed to exploded in Nichols's head and he began to laugh hysterically, "Oh . . . Fuck . . . Jesus . . . Hold on, you're not going to believe this. This is great."

"Try me," was Joe's dead-pan response.

"I know why Arthur Junior told you Harper was here. Jesus. I never put two and two together." He continued to laugh.

"Try to get a hold of yourself, there, Nichols," Joe said, "this could be more fascinating than you think," lacing it with a dose of sarcasm.

"No. It's actually funny, when you think about it. I came over on the plane with Arthur. I told him my name was Jack Harper. Jesus . . . I completely forgot I did that. See, I told you there was a logical goddamn explanation."

"That's fucking logical?"

"Yeah."

"What's logical about you telling someone your name's Jack Harper? Indulge me on this, will you, Nichols?"

"We don't like to use our real names in casual conversation. It can come back to haunt you. I guess I should say, I don't, instead of we."

"Doesn't seem like a great way to create lasting friendships. Jesus, you guys never cease to amaze me."

"Look, it's the truth. That's why Arthur thought Harper was here in Paris."

"No, no. That's okay. I believe you. I've had too many run-ins with you clowns not to appreciate the miraculous governmental logic in it all."

The agent continued to laugh. "Okay, now that we've got that little problem ironed out . . ."

But Joe recalled something Harper had mentioned earlier. "No. Hold on, Nichols . . . Harper told me someone had pulled confidential paperwork on Billy and used his name to do it. Was that you again—using Harper's name?"

"No. We never tracked that down. We don't know who it was."

"But it had to be an FBI agent, right?"

"Had to be someone right in our own goddamn building." Nichols had switched back to a deadly serious tone almost as quickly as he'd lost it. "My feeling is, it could only mean Preston's got a man on the inside. One of our own."

"Fuck."

"Yep . . . Now you see why we're playing it tight. All right, next order of business; the D.A. failed to get the trial moved back to the twenty-seventh. The best he could come up with was a week extension. That places opening statements on the sixth. We're going to have to change our travel plans. Move things forward."

"To when?"

"I'll keep you posted. It's going to take some work."

"Beautiful . . . So, let's get back to Nestor. Where is this greaseball now?"

"He's at the Hôtel George Cinq. Nestor's a party boy. Our feeling is, he'll want to fool around Paris for a few days before he tries to make a move. Harper'll be in tonight. We'll get you a photo first thing tomorrow morning."

"So I just sit tight? What if the Nemesis Nestor comes by before then?"

"He won't. Besides, you've got a gun. Blow his fucking head off, for all I care."

"Spoken like a true American." Joe dropped the receiver into its cradle and proceeded to dress. When he was done he went back to the phone and dialed Danielle's number.

"Oui?"

"Danielle?"

"Oui."

"It's Joe."

"I know."

"Jesus, you know?"

"Well, I mean, you've got a fairly recognizable voice, especially for Paris."

"I guess so. Umm, listen"—he took a long breath—"you didn't happen to call me this morning, did you? Around nine?"

"Oui, Oui?"

"Yeah, well, there's a problem. I don't think the maid understands English too well."

"I asked for you in French. I think the *maid* understands both languages *très bien.*"

"Yeah . . . This is going to be tougher to explain than I thought."

"You don't have to explain anything to me."

Joe found himself somewhat disappointed Danielle

wasn't more upset Andie had been in his apartment. Had answered his telephone.

"But, I'd like to explain it to you," he said. "I'd like to see you again."

"I'm working right now."

"I didn't mean right now. How about later?"

"I don't think I should."

After a dead space, Joe said, "Okay . . . Sorry . . . You're probably right."

"Okay? Sorry? You give up that easy?"

"I don't want to push. I just thought we could yak over some coffee or something."

"This is a mistake . . ." She sighed through the phone. "I should have seen this coming. Jack Harper is craftier than he lets on." She sighed once more. "I'll tell you what we can do . . . I'm going to Musée Rodin this afternoon. I have some work to do there. Why don't you stop by around four?"

"I'll be there. How will I find you?"

"It's a small museum. Just look around . . . you'll like what you see."

"I will?"

"If you don't, I've misjudged you."

Joe spent the day strolling the Latin Quarter and the Left Bank, slowly working his way west along the Boulevard St. Germain until he eventually reached the gardens of the Rodin Museum.

Andie, on the other hand, had spent her day on the Right Bank, and by five-thirty had grown weary of the Parisian streets and crowds. She decided to swing by 6 Rue Racine before heading back to her hotel. When she arrived at Joe's building she opened the heavy door and pressed the buzzer marked *Nichols*—

24. She waited and pressed the button a second time. After a minute Mrs. Meighan opened the inner door and stepped out.

"Bon soir, mademoiselle," she said upon seeing Andie, appearing not to recognize her.

Andie grabbed the door before it had a chance to close and said, *"Bon soir, madame. Merci beaucoup."*

And as the old woman stepped out into the August evening, she paid little attention to the tall Cuban who slipped in behind her.

Nestor's moves were hawklike once inside the vestibule. He seized Andie from behind and cupped his hand over her opened mouth. Then pinned her against the still cracked inner door. She struggled for freedom but he pressed his entire weight into her, forcing her into the hallway. As the door swung shut he pressed her up to the wall and moved his mouth alongside her ear.

"Your timing couldn't be better, sweet stuff. What's that they say about . . . knocking off two birds with one stone?"

Twenty-three

Joe had wandered around Rodin's *The Burghers of Calais* for what seemed like an eternity. Time was completely lost on him. The six larger-than-life figures comprised one of the most powerful pieces of art he'd ever seen, and he found it impossible to tear himself away from these tormented creatures that had been so masterfully solidified in this now green and weather-beaten bronze. He had entered the museum gardens, approached the sculpture, and circled it counterclockwise with every intention of moving on to the next work, but the Burghers grabbed him and refused to let go. He reversed his direction and viewed them in a clockwise perspective, then leaned for a long while on a peeling poplar tree watching tourists rub at the bronze, touching a finger, or nose, or dangling rope, or the mammoth key. He then moved around and squatted by a large glass panel that had been placed in the stone wall to allow passersby to view the work from the street. He stayed there for another twenty minutes, until his knees ached, embracing the new-found angle. He then stood and paced some more, mesmerized by their colossal hands and feet. He peered under their palms and studied their agonized faces and hollowed-eye sockets, and he felt a strong temptation to stand up alongside of them, position his feet in the pools of collected rain water, as if this would somehow place him directly within their thoughts. Eventually he tore himself away and moved farther down the path, but he continued to look back every now and then, half expecting the Burghers to be following, as though he were walking point, and they'd become his platoon of war-weary reinforcements.

About thirty yards down the gravel path Joe came upon two huge bronze doors. Each probably twenty feet high and six feet wide. They led nowhere. Nothing existed behind them. They were simply on display. The two panels were littered with masses of anguished figures in varying stages of torture and despair.

"Christ," Joe muttered to himself.

"La Porte de l'enfer," Danielle said as she moved up beside him.

"Which means?"

"The Gates of Hell. I thought you were going to get here at four?"

"I've been here since three. What time is it?"

"They're closing. We've got to leave. I wanted to show you something inside, but it's too late. They're locking up. You would've liked it."

"Sorry, I got hung up on those six characters over there. I don't know how long I stared at them. I just couldn't seem to move away. Déjà vu . . . This door's also unbelievable."

"It's inspired by Dante's *Inferno.* That's Dante seated at the top. And of course the masses below are the damned."

"I think I recognize a few of them." Joe pointed to the bulk of a man who appeared to be tumbling into the depths. "That guy up there is a former senator from Nevada, I'm sure of it. It's reassuring to know he got what he deserved."

Danielle smiled. "Come on, we have to go or we'll be locked in for the night."

"Too bad. I'd like to go in. Whenever I thought of Rodin in the past all that came to mind was that damn *Thinker*, and so many brain-dead time-servers at the U.S. State Department have *Thinker* paperweights on their desks, it's enough to keep you off old Auguste until hell freezes over."

They started walking toward the exit gate, but remained quiet. As they passed by the Burghers, Danielle said, "You're with the United States State Department?"

"Jesus, God, no. Perish the thought. I've just had some dealings with them in the past. A pretty inefficient bunch, but there's no point going into it."

"Why not?"

"It's boring."

"Why don't you try me."

"I used to be with the Secret Service. We dealt with the State Department more times than I want to remember. That's all . . . Like I said, a pretty inefficient bunch."

They passed through the main gate and stood for a minute on the sidewalk. Neither sure of which way to turn. Finally Joe said, "You want to get a cup of coffee or something?"

"What about your *maid*? Won't she be worried about you?"

"Oh, yeah, the *maid*. I forgot about her. I don't even want to go back there. Jesus." He looked up to the terraced apartments across the street. "I can explain all this."

"Why do you think you have to explain anything to me? So, you have a *maid*. Lots of men do."

"It's not that I have to explain it to you; it's more that I want to explain . . . for some reason. And then, that in itself is something I'm trying to explain to myself. Does that make any sense?"

"No."

"It's just that you remind me of someone."

"Who?"

"My wife."

"Your wife? You've got a wife and a *maid*? *Mon Dieu.*"

"She wasn't really the *maid*."

"You're kidding? Not the maid? My God, she sure could've fooled me." Danielle's sarcasm was thicker than heavy cream. It made Joe laugh, and she in turn, laughed at him.

"She's just someone I met. Honest. It's not what you'd call a relationship."

"I think that's something you'd better worry about explaining to your wife, not me."

Joe glanced back to the Burghers and bit into the inside of his lower lip. Then, after a minute or two he said, "Feel like walking?"

"Sure. Which way?"

"This way?" Joe pointed east.

"D'accord . . ."

"I've got an idea. Why don't you show me your work."

"I don't know . . . There's an old sculptor's saying, 'Never be the Auguste Rodin follow-up act.' I don't think you'd be very impressed."

"Try me."

She smiled again. Said, *"Bon. Allons-y."*

They worked their way down the rue de Bellechasse until they reached the river and turned right. Most offices had now closed down, and the sidewalks had become more crowded than they'd been in the early afternoon. But there was no jostling or pushing and shoving; the throngs had been released into a balmy Parisian August evening, and the city had passed to an atmosphere that bordered on blissful laziness. *L'heure Bleue*, the blue hour as some would have it, was moving in on Paris. It was a time to stop, have a café or wine, a cigarette or cigar, a little conversation, talk politics, read a newspaper.

Danielle and Joe walked slowly along the quay. They would stop every hundred yards or so and comment on the barges. Some were hauling cargo, while others had been refitted into houseboats and had transformed their decks into patios and gardens, with laundry on drying lines flapping in humid city air.

"So, now that I know you so well," Danielle said, and again with a fair amount of sarcasm, "tell me a little more about your *maid*. Or would you like to start out with your wife?"

Joe stopped. He leaned his weight on the stone wall designed to keep Parisian drivers from veering into the Seine and looked out across the river, onto the Tuileries garden where he and Andie had had lunch a week ago. Danielle positioned herself on his left. Almost close enough to touch, but not.

"I'm sorry," she said, "it's none of my business . . . I really do love this city." She took in a large breath of air and slowly let it escape.

"My wife was killed a little over a year ago."

"*Mon dieu.* I'm sorry, Joe." She looked at him for a long time, then wrapped her arm in his and moved into him. "I should learn to think more before I . . . I'm sorry."

"No. It's okay. How could you have known that? She was killed with my stepson by a lunatic gunman on the New York City subway."

"*Oui . . . C'est vrai.* I remember reading something about that. There were many people killed. It's the type of American news the French newspapers are fond of printing. I'm sorry, Joe."

"Just one of eight million stories. Life goes on."

"We don't have to talk about this . . . I'm sorry."

"I've never talked to anyone about . . . I've never met anyone I wanted to. That's what I was trying to get at earlier. I feel like I want to explain things to you. I don't know . . . it's something I have to figure out on my own, I guess."

". . . And thus the *maid.*"

"Pardon me?"

"The *maid.* It makes sense to me. It has a very familiar ring. You go through an experience like that, and you're left completely alone, you have no one, so what do you do? You walk around in a fog of bewilderment and you fuck everything that moves."

Joe stiffened. Hearing the word *fuck* coming from Danielle seemed out of place.

She went on not noticing his reaction. "You're looking to get something back. But you're not getting anything that resembles what you lost. You're just getting odd snatches." Danielle thought for a second. "Maybe I didn't phrase that quite right. I think snatches might have been the wrong word. I don't know, Joe. I'm not a psychiatrist."

"It sounded good. It's very rational."

"I think you're the first person to have ever used the word *rational* when describing anything I've said. I'm not sure I like it. I wouldn't want people to start thinking of me as a rational person."

"I'll never do it again."

They watched as a woman changed her son's diaper on the park bench below them.

"Do you drink a lot, too?" Danielle asked.

Joe looked at her and laughed. "I don't know . . . What do you mean by 'a lot'?"

"That's good enough. You answered the question."

"I did?"

"You did."

"Jesus."

"You're not that hard to see through. No matter what you might think."

"Well, I was hoping for something a little thicker than cellophane, for Christ's sake."

"*Non . . .*"

"Damn . . . I work so hard at it, too."

The woman below had finished with her child's changing and moved off to the left. Danielle again placed her arm around Joe's and moved close to him. He was immediately aware of how warm she was.

"I'm not so sure I'm happy I met you," she said.

"I can get lost."

"More than you are?"

Joe laughed.

She didn't. She said. "So, what are you going to do about this *maid* of yours?"

"What do you mean?"

"Like it or not, if we're going to start seeing each other, I mean on a somewhat serious basis, the *maid* has got to go. Clean your own house."

Twenty-four

The heat Andie felt from Nestor's hard body as he pressed his weight into her backside, was an extreme contrast to the cool stone hallway wall he'd sandwiched her up against. She struggled once more, but he was too big. Too strong for her.

Nestor laughed at her feeble attempts to liberate herself from his grip and placed his tongue along her exposed neck.

"Go ahead, bitch," he whispered. "I like it when they put up a little fight. Makes my dick real hard. Can you feel it, sweet stuff? Can you feel it back here?" He jammed his hips into her. "Well, can you, baby?"

Again she tried to wrestle herself free. It was a useless effort. He outweighed her by well over a hundred pounds.

Nestor kept his left hand pressed to her mouth and his right arm tightened around her waist. He pulled her back behind the stairway. He'd seen enough walk-up apartment buildings in his lifetime to know where the basement was, and under the steps he found what he was looking for. He pulled his hand from Andie's mouth and groped for the doorknob. She twisted left, and then right, but it only served to excite Nestor all the more. He began to laugh again and pump his groin into her backside.

"You're a fucking creep," she spat at him hoarsely. "I know all about you, you scumbag. Let me go, you fuck. You're biting more than you can fucking chew."

"Yeah, talk that shit, baby. I got something for that nasty goddamn mouth of yours." He pried his thumb between her lips and forced it down her throat as far as he could get it. "Suck on that for a while, bitch. I'll give you something bigger and better when I get this sweet little ass of yours downstairs."

Andie began to gag and choke as Nestor once more wrenched her tightly around the waist.

"Venga," he snapped. He dragged her through the doorway and then wrestled her down the stairs to the darkened basement. He started to fumble with her brassiere and then in frustration shoved his hand under the elastic and pinched at her breasts and nipples. Again she contorted herself in an effort to wriggle free. A dangling wire from an overhead light fixture brushed Nestor's ear. He removed his hand from her mouth and yanked on it, sending a red-yellow light to the damp corners of the basement. The room was loaded with old and broken furniture and appeared to have not been visited by a soul for fifty years. Three mattresses had been stacked on the far wall. Nestor wrenched Andie over to the thick moldy pads. He kicked one down to the floor and threw Andie onto it, facedown.

"It's your lucky day, baby. You won't be scratching those knees and little titties of yours on the stones."

He then reached under her skirt and tore her panties off.

"Let's have a look at that tight ass of yours."

She began to scramble away, but he grabbed her skirt at the waist and pulled her back into his distended trousers.

"You fucking bastard. I know all about you." Again she said it in only a loud gritty whisper. "I know why you're here, you fuck."

"Yeah, well, I should fucking hope so, sweet stuff. And you're about to get to know me a whole hell of a lot better before this night's out—once you feel this big dick up inside you."

"You fucking lowlife scumbag."

Nestor then stood and worked the buckle on his belt with his left hand as the right fumbled with his zipper. Andie used the quickly evaporating seconds to grope for her handbag. Once she reached it, she found the clasp, slid her right hand into the bag, and again made an attempt to scramble away from him. But he was too fast. He caught her left ankle and brutally dragged her back onto the mattress.

"Oh, baby, that's a sweet ass you have. I may have to give that a good fucking, before I'm through with you. Um-um, you got my dick hard like a motherfucker."

Andie deftly flung herself over and onto her back. She kicked Nestor hard in the chest and then, in an almost overly calm voice, said, "You're not going to fuck anything, ever again, you Cuban faggot."

In her right hand—and firmly supported with the left—she held a nine-millimeter semiautomatic pistol. The weapon had a four-inch silencer fitted to the barrel. It was pointed directly at Nestor's quickly shrinking member.

"Goddamn, baby, that's a big gun . . . You're sure you know how to use that thing?" Nestor grunted and then laughed a somewhat tenuous laugh.

Andie lowered the pistol, aimed the muzzle at his right kneecap, and pulled the trigger. The bullet nearly vaporized the joint and Nestor dropped to the floor like a sack of potatoes.

"Does that answer your question . . . Nestor?"

Nestor wasn't certain what had bewildered him the most: the quick turn of events, the unbearable pain emanating from his right leg, or the fact that this broad knew his name. "Who the fuck are you?" was all he could think to say.

"So you came to whack Billy . . . Zuckerman could not leave it alone, could he?"

"Who are you . . . ? What the fuck's going on? How do you know Zuckerman? Where'd you get my name?"

"That's not important. Although, you could always ask the little weasel lawyer who I am, but then the odds of you seeing the sleazy bastard again are slim, to say the least." She squeezed off another round and sent a bullet through Nestor's now limp private parts. He howled, clutched at his bloody groin, and dropped facedown between Andie's spread legs.

"You fucking bitch," he muttered and rolled off to one side.

"You couldn't leave it alone, could you? We told Zuckerman we'd deliver Billy. We told him everything was under control. But he's got to go into a goddamn sweat. He couldn't wait. He's got to send you over to fuck things up." Andie stood. "You ruined my panties, Nestor. I don't like men who ruin my things. Especially my panties."

"Punta . . . loca."

"Well, it's been fun, Nestor . . ." She pointed the pistol to Nestor's forehead.

"Wait . . . Goddamn, baby . . . Hold on . . . Hold on . . ." He was almost crying. The pain shot up from his lower body and tore at his brain. A white froth began to form at the corners of his mouth. "Zuckerman didn't tell me shit," he spat out. "What the fuck's going on here? Yeah . . . Yeah . . . Okay . . . He sent me to whack Billy. That's all I know. God, look at me . . . Nothing's left."

"Well, I'm not Billy, am I? So why'd you bring me down here? Unless Zuckerman told you to take me out, too?"

"No, baby. I wasn't going to hurt you. Damn . . . I just wanted to knock off a little pussy." Tears drained from his eyes and he pressed his lids down and contorted his face in an effort to ease the spreading agony. "That's all . . . I don't know you . . . It wasn't anything personal. I was just after the pussy, baby. That's it. I wasn't going to hurt you, I swear to Christ."

"Well, I'm a sensitive girl, Nestor. I'm sorry, but I took it sort of personal." She moved the pistol to Nestor's other kneecap and dropped a bullet into it. Again he howled with pain as his bones splintered into the stone floor.

"Listen . . . Jesus Christo . . . I didn't come here to hit you. I swear. I don't know who the fuck you are. You've got to believe me. Zuckerman didn't tell me shit."

"I think I do believe you, Nestor—if it means anything to you. But that doesn't imply I'm about to let you get up and walk out of here." She smiled at his collapsed body. "Although, I think you'd have a little trouble doing that anyway—with those bad knees of yours. You've got to be one of the biggest fucking slimeballs I've ever seen." She brought the pistol back up to his head. *"Adios, amigo."*

"You goddamn bitch," were Nestor's final words.

Andie put the nine millimeter back into her handbag and retrieved her torn panties and four expended brass shell casings. She then dragged Nestor's body back behind the stairwell. She placed one mattress over him and arranged the other two neatly on the floor to soak up, and hide, where Nestor's sticky blood had stained the ancient stones. She then removed two condoms from her bag, opened the foil, rolled them out, spat into each, and tossed them, along with their wrappers, onto the mattresses. She straightened out her skirt and blouse and walked back up to the lobby. When she stepped out of the building, Mrs. Meighan was returning with two net shopping sacks filled with groceries.

"I could have told you Billy wasn't here, dear," the old woman said, without looking up.

"Oh, that's okay, Mrs. Meighan . . . Everything worked out for the best."

Twenty-five

When Andie returned to the Hôtel Salomé the Algerian desk clerk smiled and handed her a two-hour-old message:

"Call your brother at work," it read.

She thanked him and headed up to her room. She first took a long shower, then opened her address book and dialed the switchboard at the FBI building at 26 Federal Plaza in lower Manhattan. She asked for Agent Drew Stevenson. After a minute, her brother came on the line.

"Stevenson, here."

"Drew, it's Andie."

"Are you at your hotel?"

"Yes."

"I'll call you back in ten minutes. I'm in a meeting."

Andie walked over to the dresser. She removed her nine-millimeter pistol, broke it down, cleaned it, and replaced the four expended rounds in the magazine. Her phone rang, almost to the second, ten minutes after she had hung it up.

"Oui?"

"How's France?" Drew asked.

"Fine. What's up?"

"I needed to get to a phone booth. The office isn't secure anymore."

"That sucks."

"It probably never was."

"That sucks even more."

"I assume you were able to hook up with Billy on the plane?"

"Yes . . . That all worked out very smoothly."

"Then why haven't I read anything startling in the newspapers yet?"

"I'm taking my time. I'm having a little fun. It's Paris, for Christ's sake."

"Well, knock off the *little fun.* It's time to get to work. We've got a couple of big problems. First, I don't know if Zuckerman is trying to cross us or not, but something's up. He's sent that sleazeball, Nestor, over to Paris. And I have to assume the spic's there to eighty-six Billy."

"I'm ahead of you on that one. Nestor's been taken care of."

"Permanently?"

"Permanently."

"Good. Couldn't happen to a nicer guy."

"What's the next *big* problem?"

"The D.A. couldn't get the postponement he wanted. Opening statements are set for September sixth. That means the Bureau's going to have to move Billy back to the States within a week. You're going to have to find him and finish the job. No more *little fun.*"

"You FBI guys can be such sticks-in-the-mud sometimes." She laughed.

"Just do it, Andie. Get serious. This is the biggest payday you're ever going to see . . . I'm ever going to see."

"I'm trying to come up with something that looks good. Original. Something that'll keep the Feds and the gendarmes from investigating things too closely."

"Just do it. They're going to investigate. Billy could walk into their office and blow his own goddamn brains out, and they're going to investigate closely. Just do it and get the hell out. I'll cover your tracks."

"That's no good. Your buddy Nichols has already contacted me. He knows I've been with Billy. He's even got me reporting to him on Billy's activities."

"You're fucking kidding me?"

"Nope . . ."

"How the hell did that happen?"

"It just did. There was nothing I could do but play along with him. That's why I had to move a little slower. Anyway, I'm not worried about an alibi . . . I just want to make this look good. How much time do I have?"

"Less than a week. Christ, they could move him home tomorrow for all I know. Don't waste any more time."

"I'll come through. Have I ever let you down?" she cooed.

"No. And this isn't a good time to start."

After Agent Stevenson hung up the phone he rummaged through his wallet until he found Sam Zuckerman's business card. He dialed the number.

The switchboard answered, "Jacobs-Ashton."

"Sam Zuckerman, please."

After a few seconds he heard, "Mr. Zuckerman's office."

"Is he in?"

"Yes, sir, who should I say is calling?"

"Jack Harper."

Twenty-six

When Danielle and Joe finally climbed the last of the five flights of stairs and entered her studio the sun had fallen below the Parisian rooftops. It had illuminated the sky to an orange-red in the West, while leaving the eastern horizon to darken into an almost black cobalt blue. The studio/apartment consisted of two rooms. The first had a bank of floor-to-ceiling windows cut at a twenty-degree angle to the floor. They looked out over Rue Guisarde and were flooded with a diminishing northern light.

"I'll show you my work in a minute," she said. "Let me make some coffee first." She moved into the other room and Joe followed.

The second room mimicked the dimensions of the first, however the small dormer windows faced to the south over St. Sulpice. Looking past the church, and down the narrow Rue Ferou, a glimpse of the emerald-green Luxemborg Gardens could be seen. The furnishings were typically artistic. A long, dark oak table, with six nonmatching chairs had been littered with sculpture magazines, half-written letters, sketch pads, and an unusual collection of stainless-steel utensils, undoubtedly intended for molding nothing into something.

A small kitchen was wedged into one corner, and an unmade double bed, with wrought-iron head and foot posts, rested on the far wall. On the opposite side of the room sat an overstuffed couch with an empty crate that served as a coffee table.

"This is a nice place," Joe said.

"*Chez moi* . . . I'm not very good about making the bed. Sorry." She made a pot of espresso and lit the gas stove with a kitchen match. "This shouldn't take long."

"No rush." Joe sat at the table and picked up a copy of *Sculpteur.* It was entirely in French. "There's a magazine for everything, isn't there?"

"I guess so."

"How'd you get into this? I thought you said you came to Paris to dance?"

She moved to the table and sat next to him. "I did. I studied dance for over five years. And while I practiced during the day, I worked in a club at night. It's the tourists' chance to see bare-breasted young women and make believe they are being terribly French. It made sense to me back then . . . I was younger. But then I met a sculptor . . . I fell in love with him almost instantly. I fell in love with his art. He was a genius. I think I pictured myself as the next Camille Claudel." Danielle laughed and shook her head. "This is boring. Suffice it to say, 'Never fall in love with a genius.' "

"No. No. Go ahead. I'm not bored. I just wanted to know why you stopped dancing."

"I moved on. People move on."

"Do you do that a lot?"

"What? Move on?"

"No. Shut down a conversation when it moves in on you, so that people can't get close?"

"You're one to talk 'Mr. ex-Secret Service, Mr. ex-Marine."

"Did I tell you I was in the Marine Corps? I don't think so."

"You didn't have to. I also dated one of your embassy guards. He was the only man I ever went out with who opened and held doors for me. Now you."

"Leave it to a Marine to screw it up for everyone else."

Danielle laughed, said, "The coffee's ready," and went back to the stove.

". . . And don't think I'm going to let you get away with 'I moved on.' Why did you stop dancing?"

"Persistent, aren't you?"

"When I want to be."

"Okay . . . I fell in love with this sculptor. His name was Fred—"

"Fred? His name was Fred? You fell in love with someone named Fred? I hate that goddamn name. I always have. I assume he turned out to be an asshole."

"Thank you . . . You didn't let me finish. His name was Frederick."

"Frederick, Federico, it's all Fred."

"Anyway, we lived together for a little over four years. He taught as well. And after a while I picked things up. Sculpture. I like working with my hands. I moved on from dancing. Happy?"

"Yes, I am. So where's old Fred now?"

"Still teaching."

Joe waited, but Danielle didn't add anything.

"I'm going to have to pry this out of you, aren't I?"

"Okay ... *Merde* ... I came home one day and found him in bed with two of his students. One boy, and one girl ..."

"Jesus ..."

"He said, 'Jump in. Or close the door on your way out.' So I left."

"What an asshole. I could have saved you a lot of time and aggravation. Everyone named Fred is an asshole."

"It's amazing how quickly you can fall out of love with someone. You don't want any sugar, do you?"

"No, thanks."

"Anyway, by then I was done dancing. You use different muscles ... and it's nice to be able to see your work."

"And what about Jack Harper?"

She put a coffee in front of Joe and sat back down. "What is this? The third degree?"

"I told you everything there was to know about me."

"That's such a bunch of dirty wash water," Danielle said with almost a guffaw. "You've told me nothing."

"I told you about my wife."

"Okay, but that's it. And it wasn't overly detailed. We haven't even touched on your *maid*."

"I'll answer any question you want. But, first, how do you know Harper? He told me to look you up if I was in trouble. I mean, Jesus, if I get into trouble, what are you going to do for me, make a paperweight?"

Danielle picked her coffee up and moved over to the couch. Joe turned his chair around so he'd be facing her. She slouched down and let out a long sigh that more resembled a groan and said, "After I left *Frederick,* I did, what I will refer to as 'Doing the Joe Bradlee.' In other words, I began fucking everything that moved . . . And drinking. It wasn't a pretty picture. I started getting in with a sort of tough, druggy crowd. Anyway, it turned out that this one guy wanted to smuggle a few kilos of cocaine into the States. He wanted me to put it into a sculpture, or build a piece around it, or something. I turned him down. I didn't want to get involved with dopers . . ."

She trailed off and sipped her coffee. Joe waited for more.

"Well, this guy became pretty abusive. I'm sure you know how some of these coke people can get when they're not tooting up."

"I've seen a few."

". . . I was lost. It was a bad time for me. So, I molded a piece for him. I built it hollow and told him I didn't want to know anything. Three days later Jack Harper was at my door."

"Sometimes the efficiency of these guys can be mind-boggling, can't it?"

"I never thought men like Jack were supposed to give you a break. In France the detectives are known to be very tough."

Danielle looked as though she were about to cry. It prompted Joe to take his coffee and move beside her on the couch.

"It's unusual for an American to be as *sensitive* as Jack," he said, "most of the time they're real fucking hard asses . . . like me."

"*Oui* . . . Anyway, Jack believed my side of the

story. They picked the guy up, and he never asked me to testify. Either here, or in the States."

"Good old Jack Harper. What a guy. I think I see what's coming."

"*Oui* . . . Well, for the next three years, I would get telephone calls from Jack. 'So-and-so needs to be put up for a few days,' or 'We need your studio for a weekend.' Things like that."

"Who were they?"

"I don't know. There wasn't any sex involved or anything like that. They were just people who wanted to keep a low profile for some reason. I didn't think I was in a position to turn him down. But they all seemed to attract some—let's say—unsavory characters."

"And this is your concept of someone 'literally saving your life?' "

"It may sound stupid, but he did. I think I was this close"—Danielle held up her thumb and forefinger with a quarter-inch gap between them—"to losing it. He just woke me up. I got back to my work . . . my life took shape again. Anyway, the visiting strangers all stopped a little over a year ago. I thought it was done. Now you see why I didn't want to meet you. I'm just afraid it's going to start all over again . . . I have a chicken in the refrigerator. Do you want to stay for dinner?"

"I'd like that."

"What about the *maid*?"

"She doesn't have to know."

"Oh, you're such a funny guy," Danielle said facetiously. "But I think you're missing my point . . . ever so slightly. Who is she?"

"Her name is Andie—"

"Andie? I hate that name. Everyone named Andie is a slut, didn't you know that?"

"Somehow I think if I had told you her name was Mother Teresa I would have got that same reaction. That's not to say I didn't deserve it."

"You did. Why don't you tell me about . . . Andie . . . the slut."

"I met her on the plane coming over here. She's very good looking, and she's very aggressive. I don't think many men would be able to resist a come-on from her. I didn't."

"Has she moved in with you?"

"No."

"Then she shouldn't be too hard to get rid of, should she? It would just take a little shove on your part."

"Shove?"

Danielle chuckled. "You're right . . . you have to do what you think's best. I wouldn't want you to hurt her feelings."

Joe looked at her sideways, wondering if she was serious about that.

"It's over," he said. "It's been over. It was just one of those, as you so aptly put it, 'fuck anything that moves,' situations. I feel like I'm over that faze of my life for some reason. It's amazing how quickly that can happen."

"So, no more 'fucking anything that moves,' right?"

"Right."

"Does this mean I'm going to have to stand perfectly still for the rest of the evening?"

Twenty-seven

Joe walked into apartment 24, 6 Rue Racine at ten the next morning to a ringing phone. Danielle had thrown him out. She had work to do. She needed to be alone to do it. She told him he could come back at six-thirty. Not before. Joe wouldn't have bothered to answer the damn phone, but he somehow thought it might have been her. He would have liked to have heard her voice again even though it'd only been twelve minutes.

"Where the fuck were you all goddamn night?" It was Jack Harper—the real Jack Harper. "We figured you'd managed to get yourself killed."

"I was out."

"Brilliant . . . Why didn't I think of that. You were out. In case you didn't know it, we're trying to keep you alive, you dumb bastard."

"I can handle myself."

"I'm not so sure of that. We've got an operation to run here. If you want to get yourself killed, do it on your own time. Do it after I'm done with you."

"Yes, Dad."

"I need to talk to you. I'm coming over. I'll be there in a half hour. Don't go anywhere. I've got pictures of Nestor."

"Autographed? They must be worth a goddamn fortune."

"Just don't go anywhere, you fucking dick-head." Harper hung up the phone.

Joe walked over and put his thumb and two fingers into the three bullet holes in the bedroom door, as if he were grabbing a bowling ball. His evening with Danielle had forced him to forget why he'd been sent to Paris in the first place. He'd forgotten he was scheduled to return to New York; that he was being set up to flush out some nameless assassin who would appear from nowhere; a man no one would know, or recognize. He had forgotten about the Cuban, Nestor—who might possibly only be a backup. He had forgotten about Andie. And, he hadn't taken the time to consider that he was dragging all these people into Danielle's life.

He removed his fingers from the door and strolled into the bathroom. He gazed into the mirror and spoke to the reflection. "You're such a fucking asshole." Joe then removed his shirt and lathered his face. He had only shaved his upper lip, when the phone started ringing.

"Fuck me."

He stomped back to the living room and pressed the receiver to his soapy face.

"Oui."

"Where the fuck were you all goddamn night?"

"Jesus, Andie. I'm shaving. I'll call you back in five minutes."

"I won't be here. I won't answer the phone. I won't even hear the damn thing ringing. Where were you? I tried to call you all night."

"I was out."

"No kidding . . . ?"

"Listen, Andie." He took a long breath. "We've got to call this thing off . . . They've moved the trial up . . . I'll be leaving soon . . ." Joe stammered. "Look, we're no good for each other . . . I've got to concentrate on the job ahead . . . You have your work . . . It's just not going to work out." He took another breath. "Jesus . . . Well, aren't you going to say something?"

"Where were you last night? I sincerely hope you weren't with that bitch, *Danielle.*"

"Christ, no, are you nuts? She's not my type. I went out and tied one on. I got in around three a.m. and passed out. I didn't even hear the damn phone ring. Jesus, I have to get off the line. My head is pounding."

"I don't know. That sounds fishy to me . . . I'm coming over."

"No. Don't. Don't do that." The words flew from Joe's mouth. "I mean, you can't . . . You can't come over here."

"She's there, isn't she?"

"No." Joe fumbled for a lie. "I haven't seen her, honest." And then, as the situation began to clear in his mind, he realized the truth would work just fine. "Listen, it could get dangerous around here. I want you to stay away. Some FBI men are coming over. Apparently Arthur Preston has sent some sort of hit man over here to kill me. I know it sounds strange, him being a charities broker and all, but you've got to believe me. It's the truth."

Joe waited. There was a long silence.

"My brother's in the FBI."

"What? Your brother's in the FBI?"

"My brother is in the FBI. I could call him up right now and find out if you're telling the truth or not."

"That's great. Do that. Call him up. I think you should do that. Call him up. He probably knows all about this. Is he with the New York Bureau?"

"I don't want to lose you, Billy." She had turned her voice into something softer than goose down.

"The FBI will take care of me. Don't worry."

"I mean, I don't want to lose our relationship. I have to see you again."

"It's no good, Andie. I'll be sequestered for months with this trial. I've got to concentrate my efforts. We can't see each other anymore. We just can't." Joe could hear her crying on the other end of the line. "Listen, you don't love me. It was just a fun roll in the hay. Come on. Don't make it any tougher than it already is."

"I want to see you . . . even if it's just one more time," she managed through her sobs.

"Jesus . . ."

"Please . . . ?"

"Okay, okay . . . Let me talk to these FBI people and find out what their schedule is. They may not want to let me out of their sight until they find this hired killer Preston's sent over. I'll call you later. Okay? How's that?"

"I want to see you alone, Billy."

"We'll work it out. I promise."

"Maybe I can come over and make you dinner . . . I'm a good cook. We could have some fun for dessert."

"We'll work it out, okay?"

"Okay."

Joe hung up the phone, looked to the ceiling, and

screamed for all the world to hear, "Jesus. God. Somebody help me." Then finished shaving.

Harper arrived with a predicted punctuality. He walked directly to the bedroom door and eyed the three holes. "Nichols told me about this. You never found out who she was, huh?"

"I thought that was your job? Nichols figured she was a junkie. I reluctantly went along with him. Was I wrong in doing that? Going along with Nichols?"

"Nah, that was probably it. We've had a lot of shit stolen out of here. The place stays empty for too long. We should put some of the lights on timers." Harper handed Joe a five-by-seven photograph. "Here's our friend Nestor. Seen him?"

"Christ, he's a dead ringer for Roberto Clemente."

"Who?"

"Roberto Clemente. He played for the Pirates back in—"

"I know who the fuck Roberto Clemente was. Let me see that." Harper grabbed the photo back. "Jesus. You're right. I never noticed that. Roberto. Man, you had to love him . . . Talk about a class act. Here. Keep it. We've got plenty."

"Thanks."

"You haven't seen him then?"

"Nope. Have you got someone tailing him?"

"I'm sorry to report," Harper said with a mock sadness, "he's given us the slip. He checked into the George Cinq and left before Nichols had a chance to send someone over. He never returned last night. He could be anywhere."

"Fuck me."

"He's a blade man. I don't think you'd have any

trouble handling him. He could take Billy out easily, but you'll be okay. Just sleep lightly. Don't turn your back on anyone."

"You're so reassuring, Jack."

Harper went to the kitchen and began to look through the cabinets. Joe felt a distinct invasion of privacy as he watched the agent, but remembered it was as much Harper's apartment as it was his. Harper picked the empty vodka bottle out of the trash and appeared to read the label. He gave Joe a sour look, then dropped it back into the basket.

"Where were you last night?" he called.

"Out," Joe called back.

"With Danielle?"

"Jesus, my life's an open fucking book here. Everybody knows more about Joe Bradlee than I do."

"She phoned me in New York. I told her to help you out if she could. What was so important that you had to look her up?"

Joe joined Harper in the kitchen.

"Because you bastards left me fucking hanging out to dry. I wanted a phone number. Hers was the only one I had."

"I don't want her around if Nestor shows up. Make her keep her distance."

"I've arrived at that decision on my own. But thank you so much for your sagely advice."

"Stay away from the booze."

"I have."

Harper again glanced at the trash can and the empty bottle.

"That's ancient, for Christ's sake. No one picks the

trash up around here. Things sit for days. I dumped most of it down the drain."

"And don't disappear anymore. If you go somewhere, keep in touch."

"Yes, sir . . . What's the new schedule? When do we move? Nichols said the trial's been pushed up."

"To the sixth. Monday. A week from tomorrow. But we're keeping you and Billy here for as long as we can. Nestor's our big break. As soon as that fuck makes his move . . . Bam. We take him, we squeeze him, and old Arthur's ass is locked up for good."

"I like that word *we.* It has a nice ring to it. Do I have some backup here? Do you put a tail on me? Since you seem incapable of tailing Nestor."

"Either Petrie or Austin will be outside this building at all times. If you go anywhere, they'll be close at hand. There's no way Nestor's going to get past them."

"I'd like to meet these two boys. I want to know what they look like."

"Petrie's out front already. But trust me, Joe. You'll know who they are when you see them. They're whiter than white, and both bear a striking resemblance to Ephram fucking Zimbalist. They blend in about as well as a turd in a toilet bowl. I don't want to bring them up here. I don't want Nestor to spot them. They reek FBI."

"Gotcha."

"One more thing . . . This wasn't something I particularly went along with . . . it was Nichols's idea . . . But . . . we've had Andie reporting back to us. You know, just so we'd be able to sort of . . . keep an eye on you."

Joe began to chuckle. He shook his head, walked back to the living room and over to the couch where he flopped down lengthwise. Before he could bring his laughter under control, Harper had worked his way to the door.

"You guys are fucking amazing," Joe was finally able to vocalize.

"It wasn't my idea."

"So, what you're trying to tell me is, Andie's one of the good guys. She's on our side?"

"She's on our side. You can trust her."

Twenty-eight

"This better be good," Arthur Preston growled at Sam Zuckerman, "I'm missing the Yankees' game."

"Well . . ." Zuckerman began. But a Delta jetliner had very little trouble drowning him out. He'd lost his enthusiasm for any vocal jousting with multimillion-dollar aircraft.

"Will you speak up, you weasel? I can't hear a blessed thing. These planes are driving me crazy. What am I paying you for, anyway? Give me that little girl's ashtray you're always toting around. It's the only thing you're useful for."

The lawyer pulled his portable ashtray from his attaché case and set it on the table. He then sucked in a large breath of air as if trying to grasp a final bit of fresh oxygen before the old man lit up. Arthur struck a match and torched the tip of his cigarette.

Zuckerman squinted and said, "I'm afraid I have some bad news, Arthur . . ."

"What is it?"

Zuckerman stood. He shuffled over to the small window. Looked out and said, "Nestor's been killed."

"What . . . ?" Arthur hurled Zuckerman's attaché case from the table. It sailed across the room and cut into the lawyer at the back of his knees, knocking his feet out from under him. He clutched at the window bars as he fell and was left hanging like a slave at a whipping post.

"Jesus, Arthur," he squealed.

"What do you mean 'Nestor's been killed,' you pitiful little worm?"

"My FBI contact, Harper, he told me Nestor tried to kill his man in Paris—and paid the price. Harper's very unhappy. He doesn't trust us anymore. He's raised his price . . . I knew it was a mistake to send Nestor to France." Zuckerman was close to tears.

"You call Paris. Try to find Nestor. If he *is* dead, there's got to be a body. Will you get a hold of yourself, you sniveling idiot. How do you know this Harper can be trusted? How do you know he's not a government plant? How do you know it's even his real name?"

"We can't try to contact Nestor. We can't. God, Arthur. We have to avoid being connected with him in any way."

"He's my chauffeur, you cretin. I'd say I'm connected with the greaseball already. I've got to think . . . Good God."

"Arthur?"

The old man didn't seem to hear his lawyer. His mind was spinning. "Maybe it's okay. If Nestor's dead, he can't be pinned to us. Are you following me? Dead men don't talk."

"Umm . . ."

"If we're asked, Nestor was on vacation. That's it. We don't know any more than that. We don't know where he went. You got it? Sam . . . ?"

"You know"— he rubbed the back of his knees as he regained his footing—"it might work."

"It'll work . . . if you don't foul it up. Now"—Arthur took a long drag from his cigarette—"What's going on with this Harper?"

"He wants another two hundred and fifty thousand." Zuckerman prepared for the ashtray to be thrown, but was surprised by Arthur's calm.

"Good," the old man said. His thin lips formed a crooked and pale smile.

"Good . . . ?"

"Yes. There's no way he's a government plant. If he was setting us up, he'd be afraid of losing us. He wouldn't push the price up. Not by that much. No, he's no plant, he's just a greedy man." He took another drag. "You see, Sam, you can always trust greedy men . . . as long as you can afford to feed them. But you're a lawyer, I shouldn't have to tell you that."

Zuckerman bent down. He began to pick his papers up from the floor and stuff them back into his attaché case. Arthur crushed his cigarette out and tossed the ashtray into the case without closing the lid or waiting for the embers to cool. The lawyer flipped them out with an old subpoena, then stamped at them with his foot.

The old man watched him with a sadistic smile glued to his face. "When can this Harper deliver Billy-boy's head?" he said.

"He told me forty-eight hours if we're willing to pay. He says his man in Paris is the best, but we can't wait forever. The FBI will be moving him back to New York soon."

"Arrange for the cash. But I want a guarantee. You

tell this Harper, if he doesn't come through, he's going to be alongside Nestor before he knows it. I'm getting back to the ball game." Arthur stood, walked to the steel door and pounded on it. "Get me out of this place, will you? The company around here is enough to make me puke."

"I'm trying, Arthur, I'm trying." Zuckerman sighed.

"I'm not talking to you, you putz, I'm talking to the guard."

Twenty-nine

Joe found waiting for six-thirty, the hour at which Danielle said she would allow him to return, to be one of the most agonizing waits of his life. He'd considered calling her, but knew it would only disturb her work; plus he felt things should be explained to her in person.

He found it strange, that here he was, attempting to call off two embryonic relationships, with two different women, for two entirely different reasons, on the very same day. Andie, because he'd become infatuated with Danielle. And Danielle, because he didn't want her walking into Harper's nest of vipers.

He'd remained in the apartment at 6 Rue Racine the length of the day, for fear the phone would ring again—Harper with information on Nestor's whereabouts, or Danielle asking him to come over early. It never rang.

He'd spent the first half of the afternoon working on his French. Then pulled a volume of Shakespeare from the bookshelf and began reading *The Taming of the Shrew*. It was slow going. He kept looking at his watch and thinking of Andie for some reason; and then alternately thinking of Nestor, half expecting the slimy bastard to slither through the open bedroom window any minute. Eventually he switched to *A Lover's Complaint,* but it didn't help speed up the hours or calm his paranoia with regards to Nestor.

At five-thirty Joe decided he'd waited long enough. He threw the Shakespeare onto the couch and stood. He went to the kitchen for some water, but was stopped by a soft tapping on the front door. Three short knocks. He turned his head slightly and smiled. It was show time.

"Fucking Nestor . . . you son of a bitch," he said under his breath. "Knocking right at the front door . . . You've got balls, I'll give you that." Joe continued on into the kitchen and pulled the .32 automatic from the oven. He quietly chambered a round and slipped back out to the door. He listened for a minute. The hallway was completely silent. He waited. After a moment there was a second tapping. Only slightly louder. More forceful. Joe reached for the handle. When he had a firm grasp on it, he twisted it sharply counterclockwise and threw the door open. Joe kept the pistol tight to his chest. He remained tucked behind the door jamb, and called out, "Come and get me, you slimy bastard."

Silence was the only response. He waited.

"Nestor, you scumbag. Give it the fuck up before I turn your ass into Swiss fucking cheese."

"Billy . . . is that you?"

Joe stepped out from his hiding place and moved into the doorway.

"Oh, Jesus . . . Sorry, Mrs. Meighan. I was expecting someone else." Joe let the automatic drop to his side. The old woman seemed close to tears. "Don't get upset. I was watching a police movie on TV. I don't know what I was thinking of . . . Is there something I can help you with, Mrs. Meighan?"

"You don't have a TV," she managed to choke out.

"Right . . . It was a book. I have a vivid imagination," Joe said in a too caustic tone. "What can I do for you?"

"One of my cats wandered off." She was trembling. A tear had worked its way down her left cheek.

Joe looked at his watch. "Look, I'm sorry about your cat, but I'm just off to a meeting. I really don't have the time to look for him right now."

"Her."

"Okay. Her. But I'm busy." He glanced over her shoulder and looked down the hall. "Isn't there someone else in the building who can help you?"

"But you have a gun."

Joe cleared his throat, "I don't think I'm following you here, Mrs. Meighan . . . And, I know this is going to sound rude, but I'm now running late, and . . . I don't like cats. I've never liked cats. They give me the creeps and make me sneeze."

The woman burst into a wail of tears.

"Okay, okay. Jesus. Calm down, will you? Where did you last see him . . . ? Her?"

"I've found him already."

"Jesus, God . . ." Any ability to camouflage his impatience had left him. "What the hell do you need me for?"

"He was in the basement," she sobbed.

"So, what's the problem?"

"There's a man in the basement."

Joe reacted swiftly. He grabbed Mrs. Meighan and

dragged her into his apartment and slammed the door. He sat her on the couch. "Stay here. Do not move." He eased his way back over to the door and said, "What does this guy look like?"

"Roberto Clemente."

"Who?"

"Roberto Clemente. He used to play for the Pittsburgh Pirates . . . ?"

"Yes. Yes. I know Roberto Clemente . . . Listen, this guy's very dangerous. I want you to—"

"He was killed in a plane crash, so I know it's not really Mr. Clemente. Delivering food to storm victims."

"Right. Look. I want you to stay here. I'm going to go down to the basement. If anything happens to me, there's a man across the street. He looks a little like Ephram Zimbalist . . ."

"More like Robert Stack, I would say."

"Whatever. He's an FBI agent. He can help you. If Roberto Clemente shows up, scream bloody murder. One of us will get to you."

"I'm not worried about Roberto Clemente. He's dead."

"I know he's dead, Mrs. Meighan. I'm talking about the guy in the basement."

"Oh, he's dead, too," she said through a fresh flood of tears. "Somebody shot his Willy-Whacker off."

Thirty

Andie wasn't stupid. She knew Billy was avoiding her. He had somehow managed to get himself stuck on Danielle. She wasn't happy about it, but he was going to pay the big price in the end. She was pissed. He'd get his. It was the bitch Danielle, Andie was thinking about. Her professional side told her to let it all slide. Take care of business; do away with Billy, and cover her tracks. But Andie had another side to her. A side consumed with a heavy dose of jealousy. No woman was going to get the best of her. The bitch Danielle was going to pay as well. Andie was pissed.

She picked up a small black notebook and thumbed through the pages until she came to the spot where Danielle's phone number had been written. The spot where she'd copied it from the cocktail napkin that had fallen from Billy's shirt pocket at thirty thousand feet. At the time she had assumed it was a number for a police connection, or possibly the FBI. She'd been surprised to find out there actually was a Danielle.

Andie remembered Billy saying Danielle was a friend of the people who owned the apartment on Rue Racine. It might have been a lie, but the people who owned the apartment were the United States government, and if Danielle was a friend, it meant she was most likely an operative of one government agency or another.

Andie picked up the phone and dialed.

"Oui," Danielle answered.

Then, in Andie's best South Carolina drawl she inquired, "Is this American Airlines?"

"I think you have the wrong number."

"Oh, I'm awfully sorry."

Andie hung the phone up and said, "Good . . . the bitch is home."

She then went to the dresser and opened the top drawer. She lifted her nine-millimeter pistol out and placed it under her arm. She pushed aside two or three pairs of panties and some stockings until she found the silencer. She fitted it into place, slid a clip of ammunition into the gun's handle, and chambered a round. Then put the weapon gently into her handbag.

She next pulled out her map book of Paris. She remembered the location of Danielle's building from when she'd followed Billy and the bimbo back to the place a few nights ago. She'd know it again when she saw it. She'd recognize Danielle's studio at the top. But Andie wanted an address to give a cab driver. It was a close enough walk, but not much fun in high heels. And she didn't dare take a chance on running into Billy. Number 6 Rue Racine fell directly between her hotel and Danielle's apartment. She scanned the map. She'd ask for the Palais du Luxembourg. Front entrance. It'd be close enough.

Andie could sense her emotions were taking over as she watched her hands tremble with the pages of the map book. She would continually force herself to stop and take a deep breath. Slow herself down. And it would calm her for a few minutes. But it didn't take long for her to become hopping mad again. She had no idea what she was going to do to Danielle, but she was going to make it hurt.

She grabbed her bag, ducked down the two flights to the lobby, and out onto the street. The Rue de Hôtel Salomé was overly narrow. No taxis would venture down unless an arriving passenger had requested it. And that could take forever. Andie trotted down to the quay. The lights were just beginning to warm up across the river on the Île de la Cité and Notre Dame. Andie paid no attention. She'd seen it already.

Every cab was occupied. She glanced at her watch. Five-thirty. "Shit," Andie said aloud. Again she pulled her map book out and surmised how long of a walk it would be. It didn't look long, but she knew better. The map's distances were deceiving. She stuffed it back into her bag and scanned the traffic. After a few minutes, a taxi slowed down to a crawl and eventually came to a stop on the opposite side of the street.

Andie jumped. She worked her way through the moving cars and was at curbside before the passenger could open the door. She helped an old woman out, then slid in and slammed the door.

"Palais du Luxembourg, entrée principal. I'm in a rush . . . *S'il vous plaît."*

"Mais mademoiselle, the old woman has not yet paid me."

"How much?"

"Vingt-deux francs."

Andie fished through her bag and handed the driver two twenty franc notes. "Keep it. *Allons-y."*

"But, mademoiselle, I am on call. I cannot take a fare from the street."

Andie leaned forward. Her breasts nearly fell from her blouse and her voice again turned softer than soft, "It's very important for me to see my father. He's very ill. Won't you please bend the rules, just this once?"

By the time she'd finished, the man probably would have taken her to Berlin if she'd asked. But he only smiled and said, *"Certainment, ma cherie."*

The ride took less than ten minutes. She paid, jumped out, darted across the wide Rue de Vaugirard, and down the block to St. Sulpice. The church bells were ringing, but they were lost on her. Andie crossed the plaza. She walked up to the entrance to Danielle's building and tried the door. It opened easily. The lock appeared to have been broken long ago.

Andie slowly began the climb to the top floor. With each flight of stairs she would stop. She would take a deep breath. Try to relax. Get her wits about her. Organize her thoughts. Formulate what she would say. What she would do.

When she reached the last landing she glanced up to the skylight, then to the lone door. It was decorated with a brass knocker, and the number 13, also in brass. Andie took her last deep breath, stepped to the door, and tapped the knocker four times.

Danielle was at the sink washing her hands when she heard the knock. She called out through the door. "Hold on, Joe. My hands are a mess with plaster. You're early . . . It's fine. I'm all finished. Let me get this stuff off? You don't mind waiting out there for a minute, do you?" She washed the last bit of plaster from her hands and grabbed a towel. "All done. I'm on my way."

When Danielle reached the door she tossed the towel over her left shoulder, slid the two bolts, put a huge smile on her face, and flung it open.

Andie had a glare on her face that would've stopped a freight train. "I want to talk to you," she spat.

"Oh, oh. Don't tell me. You must be the *maid*."

Thirty-one

FBI agent Jack Harper was led to the basement of number 6 Rue Racine by agent Nichols. He took one look at Nestor's body and brought his eyes across the room to meet Joe Bradlee's. Bradlee was leaning against a dusty bookcase with his arms folded across his chest.

"Why'd you have to kill the bastard?" Harper said. "Now there's no fucking way we can prove Arthur Preston sent the scumbag over here."

"I didn't kill the greaseball," Joe groaned. "He was like that when I came down here."

"They look like thirty-two markings to me."

"Terrific. What are you? A forensic specialist all of a sudden?" Joe walked over to Nestor and stood at Harper's side. "Look close. Look at the spread on the powder burns. Ten'll get you twenty our boy used a silencer. I've checked the building. No one heard or saw a damn thing—and the thirty-two you left for me isn't grooved for a silencer. You know that."

But Harper pushed it. "Just level with me. If you whacked him, it's no big deal. We move on."

"Jesus, does this look like something a normal person would do? Paste him in the kneecaps, blow his fucking balls off, and then pop him in the head?"

"Who said you were normal?"

"I saw a fag killing like this once," Nichols offered in an official tone. "Sometimes these guys can get into some pretty gruesome shit."

Harper smiled, glanced back down at Nestor, and said, "You're not a *fag*, are you, Joe?"

"Oh, you guys are a bundle of laughs today."

Nichols continued, "It stinks of a homosexual hit. Look at the poor bastard. It shouldn't happen to anyone. Only fags do this kind of stuff."

"You're too much, Nichols." Harper was now chuckling at the agent. "You're about as homophobic as Daffy Duck on a Key West weekend. What makes you think a broad didn't do this? Remember old John Wayne—whatever the hell his name was? Wife removed his joint with a filet knife? It makes sense. John Wayne drags some bimbo down here for a little fun and games and gets more than he bargained for. There's a couple of rubbers over there." Harper pointed. "See if they're wet, Nichols."

"Are you crazy? You see if they're wet. I'm not touching those fucking things."

"Christ," Joe muttered. Then crossed over to the mattress. Bent down to get a closer look at the condoms. Harper followed.

"They're still wet," Joe declared. "You guys happy? But that just confuses the issue more. Nestor drags a woman down here, has his way with her, and uses a rubber—not once, but twice? It doesn't wash. I think someone's trying to make this look like something it wasn't."

"Like what?" Nichols asked.

"I don't know. It's confusing as hell." Joe said. He

straightened and checked his watch. "Look, I've got to make a phone call. I told someone I'd meet them. I'll be back in a few minutes."

"Who?"

"None of your fucking business, who. It's social."

"I don't want Danielle mixed up in this," Harper declared, as though he'd become her long lost father.

"Jesus, what do you think I'm trying to do? I don't, either . . . I'm trying to lose her. Push her away. I'll be back."

Joe trotted up the stairs and Harper walked back over to Nestor's corpse.

Nichols moved up next to him and said, "What do you think? Think Bradlee smoked him?"

"I don't know . . . I guess he could have, if he caught Nestor down here with someone . . . then flown off the handle. But, if he did, I've read him all wrong. I always figured he was the type of guy who'd take a fair amount of pride in bringing a schmuck like Nestor in alive. He knew how important he was to us. If we had Nestor alive, Bradlee'd be done here. He could go home. We'd be done." Harper rubbed his mouth and chin. "Nah, Bradlee didn't shoot this bastard."

Nichols bent down and rolled Nestor's head to one side, careful not to get blood on his fingers. "Well, if it wasn't a thirty-two it was a nine millimeter. I'll put money on that. What do you want to do? Call the gendarmes? Or Removals?"

"I don't think the French are going to give a shit about Nestor. We'll get Removals in here after dark. Tell Mrs. Meighan we're sorry. It won't happen again. I guess we're going to have to increase her allowance by a few francs." Harper moved to the other side of the basement and ran his hand along a dusty paint can. "Feel her out. See how upset she is. But if she plays hardball, wants too much, remind her we can easily farm her apartment out to someone else and send her back to Pittsburgh."

"Right . . ."

"And find out if she's seen any strangers coming and going. We know Andie and Danielle have probably been frequenting the apartment, but maybe someone else's been hanging around. Something stinks about this."

When Joe reached the apartment he poured himself a glass of water, chugged it down, and dialed Danielle. He could feel the tension in her voice even though she only said, *"Oui?"*

"Danielle, it's Joe."

"Oh . . . Hi . . . Jeeze, *Billy*, I thought you'd be over here by now."

"Billy?" Joe held the receiver out and stared at it for a second. Then brought it back to his face. "Where did you get that name? I never gave it to you."

"I wish you'd at least been open enough to give me your real name . . . but I've been set straight."

Joe's mind was racing to keep up. Danielle knew his name. Harper had even backed it up. But she was now playing a game with him. "Listen, Danielle, my name is Joe. You have to believe me. I've been honest with you. I swear."

"Oh, I know that."

"Then what the hell's going on?"

"I've got some company here, Billy."

"Ahh, shit . . . Can you talk at all?"

Danielle's voice took on a staccato tone, "Almost . . .

Your friend Andie is here. She wants you to come over. And Billy?"

"Yes?"

"I want you to know, I do care for you . . . Never forget who you are, okay?"

Joe could hear a muffled sound from the other end as Andie tugged the phone away from Danielle.

"Hello, Billy. How's it hanging?" Andie cooed into the receiver.

"Andie, what the hell's going on? What are you doing there? What the hell are you up to?"

"Easy there . . . I don't like to be cheated on, my dear." Her voice was low and sexual. "I'm the jealous type, in case you hadn't guessed, and I'm pissed off. It's time you both got what you deserve . . . a good fucking."

"Listen, Andie . . ."

"No, no. You listen, Billy. I want you over here. Pronto. I won't touch her until you get here, but don't take too long. I want you to watch her suffer. But I won't wait all night."

"Andie, this is pointless. Just leave her be. She doesn't mean anything to me. If you want, I'll never see her again. We can go out and have some dinner tonight. How's that?"

"Be here in fifteen minutes. And come alone."

Andie hung up.

"Shit," Joe growled.

He trotted out of the apartment and took the stairs two at a time. When he got to street level, Harper and Nichols were just emerging from the basement. Harper called to him, "Hey . . . hey . . . where're you going?"

"Out."

"Well, hold on. I'll get Petri to go with you."

"Jesus, Jack. I don't need these guys. It's over. Preston's man is dead, for Christ's sake. I'm going out for a drink. I want to be alone."

"I'm hoping he'll send someone else."

Joe stopped and walked back to Harper. "Okay, look. I'm sure he will send someone else, but I just need a few hours to myself. You don't think Preston has the wherewithal to scramble a new hit this fast, do you? He probably doesn't even know that oily bastard's dead. And if he does, my guess is he's going to try to set it up for New York . . . if he wants to go again. I mean come on, he's running out of options."

"I think he's right, Jack," Nichols said. "I think we should start working on the move. The sooner we leak the details, the more time Preston has to dig up another hit man. My guess is, Bradlee's safe here in Paris."

"All right," Harper groaned. "Just keep in touch . . . And don't hit the booze too heavy. Things may shape up faster than you think."

Joe shrugged, "I've been very well behaved for the last few days—thanks to our friend Danielle, I might add." He patted Harper on the cheek. "I won't let you down, Dad. I promise." He then turned and strolled out of the building.

Once on the street, Joe looked first left and then right until he spotted a man in a gray suit. A man bearing a striking resemblance to Robert Stack. Gotta be Petrie, Joe thought. He pointed to the door to let the agent know he was wanted inside. Petri waved back. Joe then put his hands in his pockets and strolled off to the west. He tried to casually whistle a tune, but no sound came out. He stopped for a second and glanced at the sole of his shoe as if he'd stepped in some dog shit. He then walked to the curb and scraped the leather against the stone. He looked back to Petri, who shook his head and laughed. He then crossed the street and entered 6 Rue Racine. Joe continued to saunter indifferently.

The moment he rounded the corner, Joe took off in a full sprint. The sidewalks were narrow and filled with evening strollers. He found it impossible to maneuver around them without knocking people over, so he took to the street, jagging in and out between the moving cars. Horns blared at him constantly. Drivers leaned out of windows and cursed him as they jumped on their brakes.

Within five minutes he was at the entrance to Danielle's building. He tore the door open and raced up the five flights. Once on the top floor he jogged the short distance to studio 13 and lowered his right shoulder to meet the numbers, breaking the lock and leaving a splintered door jamb in his wake.

Danielle was sitting on the couch with her arms folded across her chest. Andie had perched herself on the empty crate that served as the coffee table. She sat cross-legged facing Danielle. Her elbows propped on her knees.

"Where the hell did you get that?" Joe said, referring to the nine-millimeter pistol, *avec* silencer, Andie had trained on Danielle's left breast.

"Kind of phallic, isn't it?"

Thirty-two

"You made good time," Andie said without moving her face in Joe's direction. "It took *me* forever to find a cab."

"What the hell is going on?" Joe began walking toward the two women as he talked. "Go ahead, get jealous. Okay. That's fine. But, Christ, Andie, there's no reason for this. It's juvenile in the extreme."

"Stay away from me."

"I'm not coming near you." Joe held his hands out in a gesture of peace. But kept moving closer.

"I'm warning you. I know how to use this."

Joe continued to inch closer, not believing her, until he was within six feet. Then said, "Listen, I'm going to sit on the couch with Danielle, okay? That way you've got us both out in front of you. How's that sound?" He didn't wait for an answer. He slid in and dropped down next to Danielle. She felt very warm, almost feverish as she pressed her body against his. But still had a surprising air of calm about her.

"See . . . *Pas de problème,*" he said to Andie. He looked at Danielle. "You okay?"

She trembled slightly but put on a good tough-broad

act, considering the situation. "Why didn't you tell me your real name, you creep?"

"You know, that's the one thing that's saved your little *Danielle* here in all of this, Billy; you lying to her about your name. My assumption is, you think more of *me* than her. Or you don't want her to know who you really are. Either way, I'm almost happy about that." Andie waved her pistol back and forth between Danielle's chest and Joe's. "The phony name lets me forgive you for knocking something off on the side . . . To a certain point, that is . . . I'm still going to take a good deal of pleasure in watching you both suffer, though."

Joe's voice took on a conversational tone as he crossed his legs. "What do you want, Andie? She doesn't mean anything to me. You've got to know that. Like you said, I was knocking off a little something on the side . . . She's a lousy lay. Is that what you want me to say? Is that what you want to hear? Well, she is. She's a lousy lay. There. I said it. Crummy blow jobs on top of it. So, let's just go get some dinner and leave her be. What do you say? We'll have a good time. Make a night of it."

Danielle jabbed Joe in the ribs with her elbow and said, "You're a lousy lay, too, you . . . you . . ."

"Shithead?"

"Yes, shithead."

Andie began laughing and Joe studied her. He eyed the pistol moving between them. He analyzed the gun and considered his options. The pistol was cocked and the safety was off. It would take little or nothing for Andie to squeeze off a round. His initial thought was that she didn't have it in her to pull the trigger. But the damn thing could go off too easily by accident. And, Jesus, who knows what a jealous woman is capable of?

As Joe analyzed the situation, and the pistol, he seemed to notice the silencer for the first time. He looked up to the ceiling and muttered, "Christ." This was no normal gun. It was the same gun that had nailed Nestor.

"What's the matter, Billy-boy?" Andie was still giggling over Danielle's comment.

Joe rolled his eyes up and pushed his head down into his shoulders. "Oh . . . fuck," he groaned. Joe moved both hands to his chest as a pained expression swept across his face. He clutched at his shirt tearing the pocket. He attempted to stand but only rose halfway and flopped back to the sofa, then tried again to climb out of the seat.

"Oh my God, he's having a heart attack," Danielle cried. "Let me call for a doctor."

"Don't move," Andie shouted as Joe collapsed on top of Danielle. Andie then jumped up and began to move off to one side.

But Joe was too quick for her. As he covered Danielle with his body, he brought his legs around to his right and entwined them with Andie's, sending her spinning to the floor. He'd hoped the shock would've jarred the pistol from her grasp, but she'd held on like a vise. Joe then scrambled off of Danielle and on top of Andie. He grabbed her wrist and knocked it three times against the hardwood floor. No good, her grip was like steel. She brought her knee up to meet Joe's groin. He growled as an acute pain shot through his entire midsection, then rolled off to her left. Joe managed somehow to retain his grip on her wrist, but Andie was able to line Danielle up in her sights and squeeze off a round.

The bullet narrowly missed Danielle's left ear and soared across the room, where it ripped into a life-mask of her former lover, Frederick, tearing his nose off.

"Jesus Christ, Andie," Joe bellowed, "this isn't a game. The fucking thing's loaded." He rolled back onto her and wedged his thumb into the gap between the firing pin and hammer. Andie pulled the trigger once more and the hammer slammed down on Joe's thumb. "Ayeee, shit."

"You bastard," Andie said, "give me that pistol." Again she kneed him in the groin, and again he rolled off to one side. This time he lost his grip on her gun hand, and when the hammer met the firing pin, another round was sent flying. Took off in the direction of the kitchen.

Andie rolled on top of Joe and brought the silencer up to meet his nose. She snickered. "Sorry, Billy. If it makes you feel any better . . . I thought you were a great lay."

As Andie brought her right index finger to meet the trigger, what was left of Frederick's life-mask crashed into her flame-red hair just above her right ear. She arched her back, lifted her chin, and rolled her eyes up into their lids. Andie stayed like that for almost five seconds, then she toppled off to Joe's left. Her head bounced twice on the floor and she settled in an unconscious heap.

"Oh, God, you don't think I killed her, do you?" Danielle said. She brought her hands to her face.

Joe struggled to erase the pained expression from

his face as he rearranged his testicles. "I don't know whether to say I hope so, or I hope not."

"Look at her."

"I'm looking."

"She can't be dead, do you think?"

Joe removed the nine millimeter from Andie's limp right hand and took her pulse. "She's alive." He examined her head. "She'll be fine. Here, take this." He handed the pistol to Danielle.

"I don't want that thing." She took a few steps backward as though it had been contaminated with smallpox.

Joe stood, removed the bullet from the chamber and the ammunition clip, and placed it all in the refrigerator.

"Will that be okay in there? It won't explode or anything, will it?"

"It'll be fine." He walked over to Andie. He picked her up and spread her out on the sofa. "Would you bring me a damp towel or something? For her head. She's got a hell of a lump here."

"Sure."

Danielle's eyes began to narrow into slits as she studied Andie. "Why don't you pull her skirt down to a respectable level? At least cover her underwear." She then stepped into the bathroom and returned with the towel. Joe had adjusted Andie's skirt. "That's better. Thank you."

"So, what the hell went on here?" he said.

"She came over. I let her in. And she pulled the gun out . . . She kept calling you Billy. It confused me at first, but then I remembered you telling me you were here because you looked like somebody else. I played along. I covered. I don't think I blew it for you. I'm sorry you thought I was such a lousy lay."

Joe smiled at her. He picked up the plaster from the floor and said, "Too bad about old Fred. I was really fond of this piece."

"Here," Danielle handed the damp towel to Joe, "you do the first aid. I'm not the Florence Nightingale type."

He walked to the couch. He sat alongside Andie's head and rested the cloth on her expanding lump. "This is confusing me. I never pegged her to get violent like this. And that gun? Do you have any idea where it came from?"

"You're asking me?"

It was just about then Andie began to regain consciousness, but she remained still. Kept her eyes closed. Wanting to listen more than anything.

"I wasn't really asking you. I was more thinking out loud. It's the type of gun a professional killer would use. How'd she get it?"

"You don't think she was sent to kill you, do you?"

"I don't know what to say. We found a Cuban guy dead in my basement. That's why I was running late. I'd bet money he was killed with that same gun."

"That would seem to narrow down your list of suspects, wouldn't you say?"

"I guess so." He looked down at Andie. "But she has a brother in the FBI."

"What's that supposed to be . . . ? A clean bill of health?"

"Well, no, but . . ."

"Why don't you just leave her on the couch and

come over here with me. You look too comfortable with her head buried in your lap like that."

Joe left the towel on Andie's head and joined Danielle at the table.

"What are you going to do?" she said.

"Wait until she comes to. I've got a few questions for her."

"How about we call the police? Or is that something that would upset your sensibilities?"

"No . . . It's an option. Let's just hear what she has to say."

Andie only caught every other word as she struggled to regain full consciousness. She remained absolutely still. Trying to dissect what little information she was receiving. Filtering it through her groggy brain and throbbing head.

"I still think she's just insanely jealous," Joe continued. "Did she say anything to you that would make you think otherwise? Make you think she's some sort of killer?"

Danielle thought for a minute. "Well, it wasn't anything she said, it was more something in her eyes—"

"I'm going to kill you, you son of a bitch," Andie shrieked. She flew off the couch and charged toward Joe. He stood and turned to face her. There was a crazed look on her face. When she reached him, he grabbed her forearms and forced them down to her sides. He then wrapped his arms around her and carried her back to the couch. Andie clung to him as best she could and began to sob uncontrollably, "He tried to rape me . . . He dragged me to the basement . . ."

Joe found it impossible to understand her through the flood of tears. "Slow down. Relax. I'm not going anywhere. Take a breath. Danielle, bring me a dry towel, would you? What's the problem, Andie?"

"He tried to rape me . . . He threw me down the basement steps . . . On the mattress . . . He tore my clothes . . ."

Danielle arrived with the dry towel. There was something about this story she wasn't buying, but she couldn't put her finger on it.

"I was so scared, Billy . . . I hate you . . . You weren't there. Where were you? You let me walk right into him. God, it was so horrible." She continued to sob hysterically.

"Okay. Okay. Try to settle down. Danielle, could you make her some tea or something?"

Danielle rolled her eyes to the ceiling, and moved off to the kitchen area.

"Just take it easy. Get your breath and relax," Joe said. He then placed Andie's head on his lap. "It's going to be okay." He stroked her hair.

"I'm sorry, Billy. I just lost it."

"It's okay . . . Who tried to rape you?"

"That Cuban guy, Nestor. It was horrible . . . He had a gun . . . Oh, God . . ."

"Tell me what happened. You don't have to worry about him. He's dead."

Andie almost gagged on her tears. "I know . . ." She coughed. "I killed him."

"What . . . ?"

"I'm confused, Billy . . . He had a gun. He put it down on the mattress . . . and then he pulled out his . . . his . . . his, you know, *thing*. It was so horrible. I grabbed the gun and . . . and I shot him. I was crazed. I don't know what got into me . . . I think I . . . I . . . mutilated him."

Joe coughed. "Mutilated. Yeah, that's a good word."

"Oh, God."

Danielle arrived with a tea bag in a cup of cold water and Andie rolled onto her side, leaving her face buried in Joe's crotch. She looked up and said, "Thank you, dear."

Danielle set the tea down on the crate. She moved back to the table, sighed, and began thumbing through a magazine.

"It's his gun. It was the Cuban's," Andie choked through her continued flood of tears. "I was mad at you . . . I thought it was all your fault . . . You off with *her* . . . It just seemed like my life was falling apart. God, what's going to happen to me? I'm scared, Billy. Honest to God."

"Don't worry. The FBI is taking care of the Cuban. Even if anything comes up, it was a clear case of self-defense. But nothing will come of it . . . I think we should get you back to your hotel. Maybe have a doctor go over you. Get you something to relax you a little bit."

"I hate to stick my nose in here, where it may not belong . . . *Billy,*" Danielle interjected, "but don't you think we should be addressing the fact that your little redhead here came into my house and held a gun to my chest for fifteen minutes, and then tried to blow both our heads off? I think she may need a little more than *something to relax her a bit.*"

"Billy, you're right," Andie sniffled. "Maybe you could take me back to my hotel." She pressed her cheek into Joe's groin. "I'm sorry I kicked you here. I'll make it up to you. I'll make it feel better."

"That's not what I'm talking about," Danielle hissed. "What makes you think she won't try this stunt again?"

"You know I was thinking, Andie," Joe said, in an almost monotone, "there were two condoms on the mattress . . ."

Andie stopped crying as quickly as she had started. She sat up on the couch and glared at Joe. "What are you two saying? All of a sudden I'm being given the third degree? All of a sudden the victim is now the guilty one?"

"I don't know. They appeared to have been used. It's just a little confusing, that's all."

"Well, they were there when he dragged me down to the basement. It was disgusting . . . I was almost raped. Can't you understand that? I want to go back to my hotel. I'm not feeling well. I've been through a terrible ordeal." Andie grabbed her purse and headed for the door. She then stopped short, turned, and said, in an overly professional voice, "I guess I should see that the Cuban's gun gets to the FBI. They'll probably want to check it out. Where'd it get to?"

"I can handle that," Joe said. He stepped over to her. "Let me take you home." Joe looked to Danielle, who had taken the untouched teacup to the kitchen sink and dumped it. "I'll call you later to find out when's a good time for me to come back for that gun."

"Yes, do that . . . *Billy*. And try to stay out of trouble in the meantime. Will you do that? For me?"

"I'll call you . . ."

"I'll be sure to hold my breath."

Thirty-three

"I guess we'll have to walk," Joe said after ten minutes of searching for a cab.

Andie clutched his arm and pressed her lips to his ear. "Will you spend the night with me, Billy? I don't want to be alone."

Joe started walking toward the Boulevard St. Michel. Andie held on. They walked in silence for five or six blocks.

"Well . . . ?" she finally said.

"Well what?"

"Are you going to spend the night with me?"

"I can't help but think, if Danielle hadn't cracked you over the head with that piece of shit plaster casting, you would've blown my brains out. Am I right or wrong about that?"

They walked for another block.

"You may be right. I can't believe I would be capable of it, but I guess it's a good thing she stopped me. I would've been in a ton of trouble. I can now see how people feel justified in pleading a temporary insanity defense. I went off the deep end. I'm sorry. It won't happen again."

"I'm greatly relieved. Are you hungry?"

"A little."

"We'll pick something up for you to take up to your room. Should I find a doctor for you?"

"Billy . . . ? You sound so . . . removed."

"Jesus Christ. You tried to blow my fucking head off." Joe's vocal level had the effect of making everyone within twenty feet stop and gawk.

"I said I was sorry."

"Sorry isn't going to cut it, Andie. I'm leaving for New York in a few days. I want you to stay away from me. I want you to stay away from Danielle. Okay? I want you to promise me that. If you can't do that, I'm going to report all of this to the French police . . . And I'm not kidding."

"Just one more night . . . ? Please, Billy? I don't know why, but this whole situation has made me incredibly horny."

She reached into Joe's torn shirt and began playing with his chest hair.

He removed her hand. "Will you knock it off? I'm pissed about this. I'll leave you right here on the street if I have to."

"You just want to get back to that bitch. You're probably hornier than hell, too. It's always that way after a good fight. I could just eat you up right now."

"Fight? You call that a fight? I call it attempted murder, for Christ's sake."

"But it's over." She squeezed herself into him.

"Look . . . I'm going back over there and I'm going to pick up that gun. That's it. I'll never see her again after that . . . I feel like shit for messing her life up."

"What about my life? Look at me. I'm the one who got raped."

"Almost raped."

"It's the same thing."

"What . . . ? What do you mean *the same thing*? How do you figure that?"

"I wouldn't expect a man to understand. I can't believe you're turning out to be this insensitive. Let's just drop it." She crossed her arms pushing her breasts nearly out of her blouse, and walked ahead.

"Jesus . . ."

Joe had an overwhelming desire to hang a quick left and disappear into a Greek restaurant. But unfortunately he'd bought Andie's story. He felt obligated to at least return to her hotel. He followed behind her for a few more blocks, then grabbed her arm as they came abreast of a sandwich shop.

"Hold on. Let me get you something to eat."

"You want me to sit in my room, by myself, alone, and eat a sandwich for dinner?"

Joe was on the verge of screaming. Pulling all his hair out. His jaw was clinched tight. So were his fists. Andie read the tension.

"All right," she said, "maybe we should spend a night alone. We can get together tomorrow. What's on your schedule?"

Joe dropped his hands into his pockets and shook his head. He looked up and over to the Cathedral of Notre Dame, then let out a long, aggravated breath. "Come in here and pick something out to eat."

It took ten minutes for Andie to find something she liked and another ten to get her back to the hotel.

"You can get upstairs okay?" Joe asked when they'd reached the lobby.

"You won't come up?"

He only shook his head.

"You won't go to see that bitch tonight, will you?"

"I don't want to leave that gun there."

"But you can get it tomorrow?"

"Sure." Joe sighed.

"What would you like to do tomorrow?"

"I think I'm done with my free time in Paris, Andie. I'm in the hands of the FBI from now on. This dead Cuban has them very uneasy. I do what they tell me to do."

"Well . . . I guess it's good night then, isn't it?"

"Yes. Maybe we'll see each other again sometime . . . Look, it was fun, Addie. Except for tonight . . . We had a good time. We move on. That's the way it is."

"Will the FBI ever allow us to be alone?"

"I doubt it. Not after the Cuban."

"We'll never make love again? I can't live with that."

"We'll both have to."

"I'm going to work something out."

"Just let it drop."

"I'll figure something out."

"Jesus . . . Good night."

"Good night, Billy. I'll call you."

"Don't. Don't call me. Let it be."

"How else will I know you're not running off to see *Danielle*?"

Joe placed his hand on the nape of his neck and rubbed hard. "Good night, Andie." He turned and left without looking back.

The streets had become crowded with Parisians and tourists out to enjoy a summer's evening in the Latin Quarter. Music drifted from jazz clubs, and headwaiters waved to passersby, beckoning them to step in for the meal of a lifetime. Joe found an empty table in front of Les Trois Mailletz, a small jazz club he'd frequented years ago. He ordered a small carafe of wine and listened as the music drifted out from the club's opened front door.

When the wine arrived Joe was thinking of Danielle. How he'd mucked up her life. What he was going to do about it. The pistol could stay in her refrigerator till the cows came home. The FBI didn't need it. They were happy to have Nestor disappear quietly. There was no need for Joe to go back for it. There was no need for him to see Danielle again. So he'd let her be. It wasn't the decision he wanted to come up with but he'd go through with it. It seemed the only fair thing.

The flip side: Did he dare leave Danielle alone with Andie still on the prowl? Was the flash of jealousy a onetime thing, or would she be back?

Joe ended up staying at the outdoor table for dinner but his concern for Danielle gnawed at his stomach for the entire meal. He finished up with two espressos, which only served to make him more uneasy. He wandered into the apartment at 6 Rue Racine a little after ten. The phone was ringing and he wasn't in the least bit surprised.

"Oui?"

"Billy?"

"Yes, Andie, what is it?"

"Where have you been?"

"I stopped for dinner."

"I don't believe you."

"Then don't."

Joe hung up the phone and walked to the bathroom

and turned the shower on. The phone rang again. He stripped out of his clothes as it continued to ring. It stopped the moment he drifted under the water but rang three more times before he stepped out. He toweled off. Went to the kitchen and poured himself a tall glass of water. The phone rang once more. He picked it up. The acid from his espressos was still grating his gut.

"Listen, if you call this number one more fucking time, I *will* go over to see Danielle . . . And when I get there, I'm going straight to her refrigerator. I'm going to take the nine-millimeter pistol, silencer and all, and I'm going to come over to the Hôtel Salomé, and I'm going to unload the entire magazine into that thick head of yours. Are you with me on this, Andie? I'm not kidding. I'm that pissed off."

There was no answer from the other end.

Joe waited.

She laughed.

"Well . . . ?" he said.

"*C'est moi* . . . Danielle."

"*Mon Dieu* . . . *Je suis désolé* . . . She's driving me nuts. She's a friggin' basket case. She's out of control and I don't think she has the slightest idea what the hell's going on, or what she's doing."

"I wouldn't count on that, Joe."

Thirty-four

"Can you come over? I'd feel better if you were here." There seemed to be a cracking in Danielle's voice Joe had never heard before.

"Listen . . . Danielle . . . Jesus, I don't know . . . I'll be gone in a few days. I feel like a bum for bringing this mess into your life. I don't want you involved in any more of it. It's such a bunch of B.S . . ."

"I am involved."

"You don't have to be. Maybe I can come back to Paris. Maybe after this mess blows over. When I'm done. Without this crazy woman crawling around every corner."

"That's what I'm saying, Joe. You're not hearing me. She's not crazy. Not in a million years."

"You're trying to tell me her performance this evening was normal?"

"Not normal, no. But I'd say definitely a *performance.*"

"I don't think I'm following you . . ."

"All I know is, I sat there for fifteen minutes while she pointed a gun at me and I wasn't frightened for a moment. I can't explain it . . . Now, she's nowhere in sight and she scares the life out of me. She wasn't going to hurt *me*. She wanted you. She was waiting for *you*."

"She was jealous."

"It goes beyond that. Trust me, Joe, I've got a bad feeling about all this . . . I want to talk about it. With you. Not on the phone. Come over. It'll only take you a few minutes."

"Do you know how to work the gun?"

"Pardon?"

"Just in case."

"I'm not touching that gun."

"Well, hide it better. Put some lettuce on top of it. Make it look like a salad. I'll be there in ten minutes, max . . . Is the lock working or did I break it?"

"One of them still works."

"Good. Lock it. I'll see you in a bit. Don't let anyone in but me, okay?"

"Thanks, Joe."

He dropped the receiver in the cradle and started to count slowly to ten. When he hit eight, the phone rang one more time. He picked it up and said, "Yes, Andie, what is it?"

"How did you know it was me?"

"Just a lucky guess."

"Who were you talking to?"

"The FBI."

"I don't believe you."

"Listen, I'm going to go to bed. Please don't call me anymore. I need some sleep. I'm not going to answer the phone. If you call me, I'll take it off the hook."

"How about I come over? I'd love to fuck your brains out right now."

"I've got to get some sleep, Andie. I won't answer the door if you come, so stay put. Besides, I have a strange feeling my brains have already been fucked out."

"You can't get away from me that easy, Billy. Here . . ."

Joe heard a scratching noise coming from the other end.

"Do you know what that was?" Andie said.

"No."

"That was me rubbing the phone between my legs . . . How about a nice BJ?"

"Good night, Andie."

The evening was still warm. Joe took his time getting to Danielle's studio. The streets were thinning out. The remaining people were mostly lovers, strolling, having finished a late meal. He climbed the five flights and she opened her door wearing only a terry cloth robe. She put her arms around his waist and pressed into him. Again Joe was surprised at how hot her body felt.

"You just opened the door like that? You don't ask who it is?"

"I recognize your footsteps. Your knock, too."

Joe closed the door and said, "Which one of these locks still works?"

"This one." She pointed.

"Sorry about this thing. I'll have Harper find someone to fix it for you. He's somehow under the misguided impression that he's become your long lost father. Did you know that?"

"I love Jack." She smiled broadly.

"Yeah, I love Jack, too. He has a way of growing on people."

Joe locked the door and took Danielle's hand. He walked her to the couch. They sat together.

"Do you have a constant fever, or something?" Joe said. "You feel like you're roasting all the time."

"My body temp's higher than average. Like a dog. It's always been like that."

"Curious . . . I think there was some Tennessee Williams's character who had that same problem. I like it, though." He leaned into her slightly. "Tell me what you're thinking is about Andie."

"You don't think these events are strange?"

"Sort of . . . But I don't see what you're getting at."

"Does this happen to you a lot? Women trying to shoot you? Because if it does, I don't think I want to know you anymore."

"And . . . I don't want you to get involved. Wasn't I saying that earlier?"

Danielle let out a long groan. "You don't get this, do you? That woman pointed that gun at my face and pulled the trigger. How far do you think the bullet came from blowing my head off? A few centimeters? Less? She then stuck the thing up your nose, and if it wasn't for Frederick's life-mask, you'd be more dead than Saint Denis. You'd have no head. It's not jealousy, Joe. I hate to bruise your ego like this, but she came here to kill *you*. She still thinks you're that Billy guy. Don't you see it?"

"I don't know . . . I hung out with her for a week. She's had plenty of opportunities."

"You've just got some macho-macho hangup that

says no woman you've gone to bed with would ever want to have your head on a plate."

"Would you kill me?"

"I'm seriously thinking about it, you . . . you . . ."

"Would you like a quality American obscenity to finish your thought? I've got a million of them."

Joe pulled the drawstring to her robe and it fell open to the waist. She stood, retied it, and walked to the table.

"Don't you touch me, you bastard, I'm not finished with Mademoiselle Andie. And I won't be finished with her until you see my point."

Joe smiled.

"Take that stupid grin off your face. Seriously, Joe, listen to what I'm saying . . . I've seen jealous women before. I've seen women I truly believed were capable of killing their husbands. God knows most of them have deserved it, but Andie didn't have that look in her eyes when she got here. I sat on that couch, right where you are, for fifteen minutes, and we said nothing. Not a word. It was as if she was waiting for a bus to arrive. Can't you see it? She's cold. She's cold as ice."

"You know, now that you mention it, old Nestor's wounds were pretty clean. Not the type of thing a hysterical rape victim could pull off."

"And there's another thing. How did she know his name was Nestor?"

"She never called him Nestor. She only said he was Cuban."

"*Non.* No. No. She sat right there, on that same couch, crying her head off, and said, 'That Cuban guy,

Nestor, blah, blah, blah, he tried to rape me.' I heard her say it, I swear to God, I did. I know. I've never heard that name before in my life."

"So? Nestor told her his name?"

"*Non. Non. Non.* It sounded strange to me when it came out of her mouth. Think about it. Some guy drags you down to the basement and says, 'Hi, my name's Nestor . . . Now bend over baby doll, I'm going to drive your ass to Brooklyn.' I don't think so."

"That was catchy. The Brooklyn thing. Who taught that one to you? Fred? Who would have guessed he was so cosmopolitan?"

"I'm just telling you it stinks. I wish I had something to throw at you, you're such a . . . a . . . a . . ."

"Jerk?"

"Jerk."

"Okay. Okay. I'm beginning to buy this. Come back over here. I feel like you're in Oregon, for Christ's sake."

Danielle came back over and dropped onto the couch. "Keep your hands to yourself."

"I will. I've got to think," Joe said with a new seriousness. "It's just not fitting together for some reason. What have we got here? There's no question Nestor was sent to Paris to pop Billy, or me, or whatever . . . But where does Andie fit in? Preston wouldn't send two people. And why would one kill the other? It doesn't make sense. And Andie's brother is in the FBI, for Christ's sake."

"Would you stop with *her brother's in the FBI.* That doesn't mean anything. Look, Joe, it doesn't matter if

I'm right or wrong about Andie's motives. The fact is, she tried to kill you. You *know* she was going to pull that trigger. You're an idiot if you think otherwise. All I'm saying is, stay away from her. She's up to no good."

Joe put his arm around Danielle and said, "Can I touch you now?"

"Yes."

"I can't believe I didn't see this."

"I can."

"It's not a *macho-macho thing*, if that's what you're thinking."

"Right . . ."

"We still haven't figured out why she waited all this time."

Danielle crossed her arms over her chest. "Maybe it's because you're such a great lay?"

"I hope I didn't detect any sarcasm in that statement?"

"I hope you didn't, either."

"Well, what about you?"

"What about me?"

"Do you think you're safe? Do you think if I stay away from you, she'll leave you alone? This is the situation I was trying to avoid." Joe stood and moved over to her dormer window and gazed out onto the street lamps of the Luxembourg Gardens. "Shit," he said. "I was trying to let you live a simple life."

"Who want's a simple life? There'd be no art. War and turmoil create art, not simple lives."

"It just seems like I'm digging a pit you'll never be able to crawl out of."

"I'm a big girl."

"Crawl out . . . That's it . . . *Orpheus Descending.*"

"What?"

"*Orpheus Descending.* That's the Tennessee Williams's play where the guy has the hot blood."

"Can you come back over here? I feel like you're in Oregon."

Thirty-five

"Try it again," Harper shouted to Agent Petrie from the kitchen. He seemed mesmerized by the glaring street lamps and the empty Rue de Rivoli as he stared out the window. "The bastard has to be home by now."

Petrie dialed and waited.

"Nope. Nothing."

"Shit. Where the fuck is he?" Harper turned and walked back into the living room.

"He was pretty lovey-dovey with Stevenson's sister all last week. Maybe he's shacked up with her," Nichols said.

"Call her up, Petrie."

"It's two o'clock in the morning, Jack," Petrie groaned. "Why don't we get some sleep and pick it back up tomorrow? You're the only one on New York time. The rest of us are beat."

"Just call her, okay? I don't want to lose this bastard. We're too close."

Petrie picked up the receiver but Nichols stepped in. "Here, give it to me. I'll call. She knows my voice." He then looked to Harper. "Do you think we should fill her in on what's going on? She may be able to help us down the road if she knows a little more."

Harper seemed to think this over for a minute. Then said, "Help us? In what way? No, I want to phase her out of this. We owe that much to Stevenson. I don't want any more innocents involved. Whoever whacked Nestor is still out there. And until we come up with a decent explanation for who greased him, and why, nothing we have leaves this room."

"Right."

Nichols phoned Andie and was off in less than a minute.

"She said she'd talked to 'Billy' earlier. He was going to bed and wouldn't be answering the phone."

"That's a big fucking help," Harper said. He paced the length of the living room twice. "Call Danielle."

"Jesus, Jack, give it up. You want to wake up the entire goddamn city, just because you think it's eight in the fucking morning?"

Harper looked at his watch and said, "Eight at night. It's not even dark yet in New York. Just call her and stop bitching."

Nichols crossed back to the phone with mock exhaustion plastered over his face. It rang an instant before he could pick it up.

"Yeah. . . ?" He held the receiver at arm's length in Harper's direction. "It's for you."

"Who is it?"

"Two guesses."

"Bradlee?"

"Verrrry gooood."

Harper snatched the phone from Nichols.

Joe said, "I figured you wouldn't give a shit me

calling you this late because you're probably still on New York time."

"Okay, first off, you've got to answer the fucking phone from now on. We can't have bullshit communications. If we've got to move—I've got to know where you are. Clear?"

"Yes, Dad."

"Second, I still can't get a line on this Nestor thing. Whoever killed him is—"

"Andie killed Nestor."

This stopped Harper cold. He stammered. Then eventually said, "Run that by me again."

"Andie killed Nestor."

". . . You're sure?"

"She told me so herself. She claims he tried to rape her. She wrestled the gun away from him, and she shot him."

"What . . . ? What . . . ? Well, why didn't she stick around? Why didn't she call the cops? Why didn't she look for help? It came off more like a professional hit, if you ask me . . . And where's the gun? He's twice her size, for Christ's sake, she wrestled the gun away from him? From Nestor?"

"That's what I like about you, Jack . . . You ask a lot of questions. You don't just take things for granted."

"You don't find it a tough scenario to swallow?"

"Now that you mention it, it's getting tougher by the minute. I can't believe I didn't see all this."

"Why would you see it? You were too busy getting your machinery overhauled."

"She also tried to kill Danielle and me."

"What . . . ?"

"I knew you weren't going to like that part. She

claimed she was in a jealous rage. Came to Danielle's waving Nestor's pistol. It was very convincing. Anyway, the point is, there's really nothing to pin on her. And her story could be the truth, for all we know."

"Something tells me you have a plan. And something tells me I'm not going to like your plan."

"I just think she should be watched until we get the hell out of Dodge, that's all. I'm going to stay here with Danielle until—"

"Wait. Hold on. You're with Danielle? Now?"

"Yes. If Andie's jealousy thing is real, Danielle could be in a shitload of trouble."

"You're a fuck, you know that?" Harper was now roaring. "I told you to keep Danielle the fuck out of this."

"Take it easy, will you? Jesus. I tried. I had no choice. Believe me, I care for her as much as you do . . . Look, all we have to do is report this Nestor thing to the gendarmes. They'll hold Andie for a few days while they investigate; and most likely let her go. She's got a good self-defense case. But at least we'll know where the hell she is."

"Won't work."

"Why not?"

"Nestor's at the cannery."

"What?"

"At the cannery. He's being sautéed into Beagle food as we speak. We've got no body—we've got no crime."

"Shit . . . Well, put one of your guys on her. Tell her it's for her own protection. She's got to be watched, Jack."

"I don't have the personnel. Hold on. I've got to think this over." Harper let the phone drop to his side. He looked around the room, hoping that somehow the number of agents had multiplied. It hadn't. He brought the receiver back to his face. "Okay, I'm going to move you in here."

"What about Danielle? I'm not leaving her alone."

"All right, all right, let's back up here, okay? What do we know about Andie? She's a hit man? Preston hired her? Do you have any theory on this? Because it's not making sense. I don't buy any of it. Her brother's with the Bureau, for Christ's sake."

"Danielle thinks having a brother in the FBI doesn't constitute a foolproof alibi. But if you think about it, maybe they were both attracted to guns for some reason when they were growing up. Never outgrew them? Maybe it runs in the family?"

"Thank you so much, Dr. Freud."

"Well, Christ, I don't know. I'm just trying to get a handle on it."

"Okay. Why'd she wait a week if she's here to hit you?"

"I don't know."

"Why'd Preston send Nestor over if he'd already hired Andie?"

"I don't know."

"You know what I say?"

"No. What do you say?"

"I say we give her another chance."

"What . . . ?"

"We give her another chance. That's what this is all about, right? Connecting a hired gun to Preston? If that's what she really is, there's only one way to find out. Joe," Harper cackled, "I'm afraid you're going to have to dip your weenie into her one more time . . . for God and Country."

"I don't like this."

"I don't blame you." Harper chuckled again. "Look what she did to poor Nestor's joint."

"Can you hold on for a second?"

"Sure."

"I'm going to wake Danielle up. I'd like you to explain this to her . . . I think this is going to sound somewhat better coming from the father figure."

Thirty-six

Andie watched the sun inch its way up and over Paris's smoggy summer skyline. It was scarcely nine a.m. and she guessed the temperature had already soared to eighty-five degrees. It was going to be a hot one.

Time was running out. Billy was due in court in less than a week and it was safe to say the FBI would be moving him to New York within a day or two. She had to get close, and she had zero time to waste. And, she had other problems: She no longer possessed her nine millimeter, Billy wasn't talking to her, he'd refused to see her, and if she was going to pull this off, she'd need an ironclad alibi. The only other option would be to make his death look like an accident.

She picked up the phone and dialed the States. A groggy Agent Stevenson answered after the fifth ring.

"Yeah . . . ?"

"Drew, it's Andie. I'm sorry to wake you. I'm having a little difficulty with my French."

"Let me get the light . . . Okay, what's up?"

"I'm . . . not sure . . . how to . . . phrase this . . ." Her staccato speech was a code. She waited for the all clear.

"This phone's safe," he said. "Go ahead. What's up?"

"Have you got a backup? In case I blow this? I think they're going to move him sooner than I hoped for and things have gotten too damn sticky. I may not be able to get close anymore."

"Damn."

"Sorry."

"I managed to squeeze Preston for another quarter mil because of Nestor. We can't lose Billy now . . . Let me find a cigarette. Hold on."

Andie carried the phone to the window and opened it, as if somehow Drew's smoke would be capable of passing through the satellite hookup. The hot air blew both the curtains and her robe open.

"Sorry. I'm back," he said as he pulled the tobacco into his lungs. "I've got a backup plan. It'll be messy though. It needs work. It involves a lot of timing, and I'm going to have to disappear if we go that route. The money makes it worth it, but I'd rather Billy never gets to the airport."

"I'm sorry, Drew, I can't guarantee it. But I'll give it a try."

"I don't want you caught. That's no good. It's not what we're after. If you miss him, you miss him . . . But if Billy is coming back, it's imperative I have that flight number as soon as possible. They'll be a lot of wheels to set into motion and very little time. And Preston isn't about to release final payment without a confirmation."

"I'll work on it."

"Get it done if you can . . . I want this payday."

Andie hung up the phone and stood at the open window with her robe dangling from her shoulders.

She watched as two pigeons screwed on the opposite window ledge. After a few minutes the phone's bell pulled her away from the sideshow across the street.

"Oui?"

"Andie, it's Billy."

"I never want to see you again as long as I live, you bastard."

She slammed the receiver down and went back to watching the pigeons. When the phone rang again, she had a smile as wide as the English Channel stuck on her lips.

"Yes?"

"Look," Joe said, "I'm sorry, okay? I'm through with Danielle. There was nothing there. You're smart enough to know that."

"I really don't want to see you, Billy. I want to get you out of my system."

"I'm leaving tomorrow. It's all been set. Can't we spend this last day together? It'll be fun. Go see a few of the sights we've missed. That's all. It doesn't have to be any more than that."

"I don't know . . ."

"I'll see you in an hour, okay?"

Andie let out an elongated sigh for effect and whispered, "Okay . . . I probably shouldn't, but okay."

When Joe arrived an hour later, Andie was still in her robe and nothing else. The front desk had called to say he was on his way up and when she opened her door for him the sash was dangling at her sides. She let the robe fall to the floor where it gathered in a heap around her ankles.

"I think you should get on your knees, Billy, and apologize," she said.

"I thought we were going to see some sights?"

"You said that, not me."

He walked to her and gave her a long deep kiss.

"This may sound strange," he eventually said and walked to the open window, "but I can't seem to get this vision of what you did to Nestor's genitals out of my mind. It's temporarily put sort of a damper on my sex drive for some unexplained reason."

Andie picked her robe up and considered pushing him out the window, but they were only one flight up. There was no guarantee he'd end up with anything more than a broken leg. She sidled up behind him and slid her hands deep into his trouser pockets until she found what she was looking for. He tried to turn but she tightened her grip.

Joe winced and bent slightly at the waist.

"Jesus, Andie."

"I'm just trying to figure out where this thing's been for the last few days."

She loosened her grip and Joe managed to spin away.

"See," he said, "that's the type of behavior that makes me very uneasy about removing my clothes in your presence. Unlike Nestor, I'd like to hold onto that thing for a little longer. Look, why don't you get dressed and we'll go out for a big breakfast. How does that sound?"

"Only if you say we'll come back and jump into bed."

"We've got all afternoon and all night . . . assuming I can get this Nestor stuff out of my head. I'm not leaving until noon tomorrow."

"What flight?"

"I don't know. What difference does it make?"

"I just like to know," Andie said as she moved into him and placed her head on his chest. "When people I care about are flying, I like to know the flight numbers. That way I can call the airline and make sure they've landed safely."

"The FBI didn't fill me in. They're very cagey with that kind of information."

Andie considered whether to call Nichols and try for the information herself, but decided it would be too risky. If the FBI was in the least bit suspicious of her, it would blow everything. She pressed her body into Joe's and purred, "You can get it for me, can't you?"

"Okay . . . I'll give them a call. I don't think it'll do much good, though."

Joe crossed over to the phone and dialed 07-13-28-30. Andie recognized the number from her daily calls to Nichols. He answered after two rings.

"Nichols . . ."

"Yeah, Nichols, this is J-, J-, Jesus." Joe coughed and bent at the waist a degree or two to cover his gaffe. "This is Billy. Jesus, sorry, had a little pain in my stomach. Must've been the coffee I had this morning. Listen, I need to get tomorrow's flight number from you."

"I gave you all that shit earlier. You've got the memory span of a fucking flea."

Joe pressed the receiver tightly into his ear to keep Andie from overhearing Nichols's half of the conversation.

"I know that," Joe continued, "but I'd just like to give it to a friend. She can be trusted. Yes, I'm very close to her."

Nichols began to pick up on the situation. "Oh, I think I'm with you now. Do you need me to repeat them? Or do you remember it all?"

"Just trust me for once, will you? She just wants to call the airline and make sure we got in okay. That's it."

"Well, shit," Nichols said, "I don't know what the fuck you want . . . so here it is again; American Airlines, flight Forty-five Q, leaves Orly at twelve-fifteen p.m. tomorrow, arrives Kennedy two twenty-five same day . . . Anything else?"

Joe scribbled the information on the hotel notepad and said, "Thanks . . . Yeah, it'll be kept confidential."

He hung up the phone and handed the paper to Andie.

"Thanks," she said.

"Just make sure you don't let anyone else get a hold of it. The FBI definitely thinks someone's out to get me. Of course you almost saved that person a lot of trouble last night. Don't think I've forgotten all that crap with Nestor's gun."

"I was worked up. I'm sorry. It won't happen again."

Joe stepped back to Andie, gave her a light kiss, and said, "Come on, get dressed, we'll get something to eat."

As they sat at a window table in a cafe on the Boulevard St. Germain, Andie's mind kept jumping to bizarre scenes from old Alfred Hitchcock movies. She'd look up from her omelet, gaze at Billy, and envision herself throwing him off the Eiffel Tower or the L'arc de Triomphe. Dropping poison into his coffee or stabbing him in the shower later in the evening. Running him down on the face of Mount Rushmore with an airplane. It was only when Billy was paying the check, that she became aware of the man across the street. He'd been standing in more or less the same spot for their entire meal and bore a striking resemblance to Robert Stack.

Thirty-seven

After Agent Nichols had finished his phone chat with Joe, he'd gone back to his position at the window and his binoculars. Billy was still in bed, a late sleeper. Harper had ducked over to the American Embassy to insure his call to the Director would be untapped and well scrambled. Austin was out getting breakfast and Petrie was tailing Joe and Andie. There wasn't much for Nichols to do but keep an eye on the teenyboppers sauntering through the Tuileries.

A half hour later Harper and Austin walked through the door together. Nichols hadn't moved from his perch for the entire length of their absence.

"You never get bored with that, do you?" Harper said and placed a paper bag on the coffee table. "I brought you some breakfast if you can tear yourself away from the young stuff long enough."

"Awww, Jesus. Come here, Jack. Look at this one. I'll bet she's only sixteen."

"You're a sick fuck, you know that?"

"I'd expect that comment from Billy, but not you. Come here. Jesus, those titties are just out there, man. Hard as fucking nails. God, they're nice."

"Any calls?"

"Yeah, Joe called. Wanted the flight number again." Nichols kept the binoculars pressed to his eyeballs as he spoke. "I couldn't tell if he'd forgotten what the fuck the number was or if he was trying to make it look good for Andie . . . Oh, shit, you got to come over here, Jack. This one's too fucking much. And she's real dark, too. Just your style."

Harper walked over to Nichols and took the glasses. "Where?" he said.

"About fifteen feet to the left of the fountain at eleven o'clock. Tight black skirt. She's bending over trying to feed the goddamn pigeons. Have you ever seen an ass like that in your life?"

"She's younger than my fucking niece, you sick bastard."

Harper headed to the kitchen, keeping the binoculars.

"Hey, where're you going with the glasses?"

"We've got work to do."

The two other agents followed Harper and got comfortable around the kitchen table.

"Okay," Harper said, "here's the skinny. Nichols, you and I are taking Bradlee out to Orly tomorrow at ten a.m. for the twelve-fifteen American flight. We try to show him off as much as we can without looking too damn obvious. The State Department's setting a car up for us. They've been told it's low priority, but they know who we're moving. I'm sure they'll be good for a few leaks. The word'll get out. American Airlines has been alerted to increase security. Double-check all passengers and all luggage. That should start the rumor mill there, too. The Director's dropping hints to the French papers, The *Post*, the *Daily News*, and *Newsday*. Anyone who can't pick up that Billy

Barton is coming into New York on American Airlines flight Forty-five Q from France tomorrow afternoon, is probably brain dead in Iowa. Austin, you and Petrie are scheduled to bring the real Billy in four hours later on Delta Seventy-one. The Delta flight departs Orly at four-fifteen, arrives, Newark, New Jersey, six-thirty. The Director'll be there to greet you personally. You'll head straight to lower Manhattan. I've got your tickets and paperwork here."

Harper handed Austin a manilla envelope and continued.

"It should be a piece of cake. No one's in on this except the Director and the people in this room. If we're lucky, none of it will be necessary. Andie will put a bullet through Bradlee's brain, and that will be the end of it."

"I wouldn't count on it," Nichols said. "I've known her brother for a coon's age." He looked at Harper and considered rephrasing *coon's age* but pushed on instead. "He's a good agent. Tough when he needs to be. If his sister was in the shit, up to no good, he'd be wise to it. And, he'd be the first one to haul her ass in, too. Nah . . . she could have whacked Bradlee anytime she wanted. Why wait this long?"

"You're probably right. It's too bad we didn't catch old Nestor in the act. It may have been Preston's only stab at Billy. Is he awake yet?"

"I'm right here," Billy said as he walked through the doorway and headed toward the refrigerator. "How long's this coffee been on?"

"It's fresh," Nichols said. "I made it up a little over an hour ago."

Billy squeezed his eyes together, dumped the entire

pot down the drain, said, "Obviously *fresh* is a relative term around here," and made up a new batch.

"The milk's fresh," Austin threw in triumphantly.

"Thank God for small favors."

"You know, Billy," Harper was more thinking out loud than asking a question, "We're sitting around here wondering if Old Man Preston would send someone else for you . . . someone after Nestor."

"Well, whatever he does, he does through that weasely lawyer of his, Zuckerman. If you want to know what Arthur's up to, all you have to do is put a tap on Zuckerman's phone."

"I can't think of anything I'd rather do, but he'd be as free as a bird if we got caught doing that shit. It is against the law, in case you didn't know."

"Trick is," Billy chuckled, "don't get caught. It's life's biggest lesson. And don't sit there and tell me you guys don't use illegal wiretaps. You insult my intelligence."

The three looked at one another for several minutes without speaking, just listening to the coffee drip into the glass carafe. Finally Austin said, "Jack . . . ?"

"Nah, this Director's not about to go for an unauthorized wiretap. Not with this case, anyway. He wants Arthur Preston so bad he can taste the son of a bitch. And he's got him, as long as Billy here has his day in court. This Bradlee setup is only insurance. He can't, or won't, authorize a tap. Either way, I wouldn't waste my time asking him."

"Oh, Nichols," Billy said as though he had just remembered something funny, "guess who I woke up dreaming about?"

"Umm . . . Michael Jackson?"

"Not hardly. Andie."

"Well, hell's bells, there's a step in the right direction."

"It wasn't a sexual dream. I'm sorry to disappoint you."

"Shit, if I had a dream about Andie Stevenson, the maid would be in that bedroom right now, changing the fucking sheets."

"We can always count on Nichols to add a touch of class to any conversation," Harper said. Then looked to Billy. "So, you remember her, huh?"

"Yes. Exactly. It was a few years ago. One of those big weekends. Memorial Day. Labor Day. Fourth of July. In Newport. The Rutherford estate. It was a huge party. The whole weekend was this huge orgy scene. I think everybody balled everybody if you want my opinion."

"I was about to ask for it," Nichols interjected.

Billy continued. "There was enough cocaine floating around to sink a damn battleship. Shit, I keep forgetting . . ."

"We don't care about that shit, Billy," Austin said as he made a mental note to place the Rutherfords of Newport on a DEA watch list.

"Anyway, it was the weekend Lazlo died, and it was real fuzzy, so that's probably why I didn't remember her at first. It was Labor Day, that's right. Lazlo died on Labor Day."

"Who's Lazlo?" Harper asked, mostly out of politeness.

"Just some guy I used to hang out with. He dealt in coke as a sideline, which I figure I'm safe in saying, since he's dead. You can't report him to the DEA." He raised an eyebrow to Austin as if he had been reading his mind and continued. "He supplied the whole damn weekend. We were all pretty bummed out when he killed himself."

"At the party? He killed himself?"

"He was kind of a manic-depressive type. Apparently he owed some mule a bunch of cash. He'd become real paranoid about someone was always out to kill him and that sort of thing . . . I really liked him. He had a great personality. Completely unpredictable."

"How'd he kill himself?" Nichols asked, getting into it more and more.

"I don't know. It was like three or four in the morning. Nobody was there. He was sitting out on the diving board and shot himself in the head. The gardener found him in the morning. It was a real mess . . . Anyway, that's what I was dreaming about this morning when I remembered I knew Andie. She was at the Rutherfords' that weekend. That's when I met her. The day Lazlo died."

Thirty-eight

Andie had no idea how the hell she was going to lose Robert Stack, exterminate Billy, and then miraculously make it look as if she didn't have a damn thing to do with it. The task seemed insurmountable and it consumed her thoughts. She'd have to improvise, that's all there was to it. Wait for an opening. Wait for things to fall into place, and hope to Jesus she could pull it off. She was grateful Drew had a backup strategy. She was not feeling in the least bit optimistic.

"Are you okay?" Joe asked as they strolled along the quay D'Orsay. They'd been walking for fifteen minutes, and Joe wasn't sure, but it might have been the first thing he'd said since leaving the cafe.

"Sorry," she said, "I'm just sort of preoccupied all of a sudden . . ."

She smiled weakly.

And then with a newfound enthusiasm, "Have you ever gone to the top of the Eiffel Tower?"

"No."

"Let's, okay? It's a good day for it. The haze seems to be burning off."

"Sounds good to me."

They continued to walk along the river for four or five more blocks. Then, as if by magic, arching far up into the sky, the 984-foot mass of steel and rivets that comprised the Eiffel Tower, appeared before them.

"It's really something, isn't it?" Joe said. "When you're this close."

Andie grabbed his hand and said, "Let's go. I love it up there . . . scares the shit out of me, but I love it." She pulled him across the street, into the surrounding park, and on up to the ticket booth.

"Deux, s'il vous plaît," she laughed to the ticket seller, and added, "all the way to the top."

The woman smiled back, took Joe's money, parceled out the tickets, and said, *"Merci, monsieur."*

"What do you want to do, Billy? Go all the way to the top and work your way down, or stop along the way up?"

Joe eyed the chart by the ticket window.

"Well, let's see, we've got a stop at 187 feet, one at 377 feet, and another at 899 feet. I say we take it one step at a time."

They moved into the elevator with twelve Japanese tourists and Andie said, "It's a good thing we came early. This place is going to be a zoo in about two hours. We should have it pretty much to ourselves."

"I was born on one of these," he mumbled to himself. She didn't hear it.

The tower was started in 1887 and finished in 1889. It served as the gateway to the world's fair of that same year. It was, however, the only structure remaining, the others having been torn apart for scrap and replaced with gardens. It's a good thing this was

France, Joe thought. Any other country would have put in stylish government buildings instead of grass.

He also found himself wondering if the elevators had been refurbished. Most likely, but the ride wasn't overly smooth. The machines clanged like hundreds of ball-peen hammers stuck in a falling tin drum. He glanced around to see if it was an Otis, but found no evidence.

Andie moved close and put her arm around his waist. He in turn put his arm over her shoulder. She pressed into him and brought her face to his. One of the tourists swung his camera around, snapped a flash photo of them, and cackled hysterically.

"Have you ever noticed how some people are easily amused?" Andie said with a growing scowl.

"Don't let it bother you. He's having a good time . . . It's just their way."

"What? Sneak attacks?"

The elevator doors opened before their conversation could continue any further down the Pearl Harbor route. They waited as the tourists ran for the gift shop, then headed off in the opposite direction.

The heat of the street was still with them, but there seemed to be more oxygen at this level. A slight breeze blew Andie's hair away from her face. Small strands would catch the sunlight. The effect seemed to give her a golden-red halo, much like a Renaissance painting of the Virgin Mary. She appeared absolutely angelic and Joe said so.

"This sun electrifies your hair. Makes you look rather . . . virginal, if you want my opinion."

Andie nearly choked. "I haven't heard that word

since I was fourteen . . . You know, it's curious though, now that you mention it, do you think anyone has ever got laid up here?"

"Is that all you think about?"

"I think about other things."

"Like what?"

"Lots of things . . . It's your fault. You bring it out in me."

"Right."

"And you brought it up, too."

"I did?"

"Well, sure, talking about virgins. What am I supposed to think about?"

Joe wasn't following her rationale, but he let it slide. For some reason he found his mind drifting to Danielle, and her theory that Andie was out to get him. And Harper, trying to set it all up. Joe'd given Andie ample opportunity to try something. She hadn't made a move. She was calm, having a good time, laughing, and seemed to have forgotten about Danielle altogether. Joe wasn't ready to jump back into bed with Andie—that part was over, as far as he was concerned. Andie obviously had other ideas. He'd just have to break it to her easy, that's all.

"Well . . . ?"

"Well, what?" he said.

"Do you think anyone's ever gotten laid up here?"

"Not on this level. Restaurant. Gift shop. Too much animation . . . You're talking about tourists getting laid, right? I mean, employees would have an easier time of it. Wait for the tower to close down. Duck into a linen closet or walk-in refrigerator for a quickie."

"That doesn't count," Andie protested. She skipped over to the railing. "I mean out in the open, with the entire city spread out below. Come here. Look at this view."

"They've probably got a night watchman. I'll bet he's done it a few times."

"Employees don't count. I mean a visitor, in broad daylight. Where's the excitement in sneaking someone up here when it's all closed down? Where's the challenge?"

"I met a guy in Miami back in eighty-four. He flew his plane underneath this. Caused a big stir with the French."

"What the hell's that got to do with anything?"

"I don't know . . . I was just thinking of dangerous acts and the Eiffel Tower."

"That's not dangerous."

"It's not? I don't think anyone else has tried it and lived to tell about it. I know no Frenchman's ever done it. This guy got his picture in *People* magazine."

"Jesus, Billy, if we grab one of those tourists and take him up to the top with us and fuck our brains out, and have him take a few snaps, we'll get our picture in *People* magazine, too. At least *Penthouse* or something. That means nothing. It's the dumbest thing I've ever heard. Who gives a shit about *People* magazine?"

"I take it that was a rhetorical question?"

Andie latched onto his hand and tugged him toward the elevator. "Come on, let's see if there's less people up one more level. We can leave the Japanese press corps here."

They slipped onto the elevator with an Italian family—mother, father, two sons. Joe said, *"Buongiorno."*

"Ehh, buongiorno, signore, lei è Italiano?" the father asked with a broad smile.

"No. No. *Sono Americano."*

And that was the end of that conversation.

Joe again put his arm around Andie. "I don't think this is such a good idea, the more I think on it. As tempting as it all sounds, it's the last thing I need, to get busted with my pants around my ankles, humping away, at the top of the Eiffel Tower, the day before I'm scheduled to go back to the States."

"Don't be such a stick-in-the-mud. We fucked ourselves half silly at thirty-seven thousand feet on the airplane. This is nothing."

"Thirty-five thousand."

The Italians gave no hint of understanding any of this, but the elevator operator raised his eyebrows and turned in their direction. He wasn't smiling. They kept quiet until they stepped out at 377 feet.

This level of the tower had, on all four sides, information placards covered in Plexiglas. They pointed the way to the sights of Paris, explaining what could be seen on a clear day and facts about the exposition of 1889 and Gustave Eiffel and the city in general. A dozen coin-operated telescopes were scattered around, along with a handful of tourists.

"This doesn't look good," Andie said. "We'll have to go up higher."

"Hold on, will you? I've never been here. Let's check out the view."

"Billy, if we wait forever, this place'll be crawling with people."

Joe walked over to a placard. Andie sighed and followed.

"The first principle of architectural aesthetics prescribes that the basic lines of a structure must correspond precisely to its specified use."

"Jesus," she said. "What does that mean? We're not allowed to fuck here? They could have put it in simpler language than that. Had a drawing of two people copulating like turtles and a red line scratched through it. Actually this thing *is* pretty damn phallic, if you think about it."

". . . And I'm sure you have."

"Who writes this shit, anyway?" she said, eyeing the placard more closely.

"That quote was from old Gustave Eiffel himself."

Andie pulled on Joe's arm and forced him to face her. Then placed her hand between his legs. "Let's go up higher. It's more open. You can feel the wind up there."

"Let me take one look over the edge from this level and we can go up, okay?"

Joe walked to the railing on the southeast side. Andie followed, took one quick glance and said, "I'm going to the other side and look at the river. It's too bright over here."

Joe watched as she strolled across the platform, short pleated skirt slapping her thighs the entire way. Of the six tourists, five were men and boys, and not one of them took his eyes off her backside as she crossed. She knew it, too. Played it for all it was worth.

Joe laughed, turned back, and looked out over the gardens, the Champ-de-Mars, and onto the École Militaire. Off to his left, the dome of the Hôtel des Invalides sparkled in the sunlight like a pot of polished gold. He detected from the Plexiglas placard that Napoleon attended the military school in 1784 and 1785. Got out at sixteen an officer.

Joe looked the length of the railing. He was the only one on the southeast side. The day was overly bright. The hot sun lulled him into a dreamy feeling of relaxation, but the setup was there. He'd make it easy for her. Test her. He thought he could control it. He was wrong.

He stepped up onto the ledge that supported the railing and positioned himself as Napoleon addressing his people. The railing met him at midthigh. He grasped it loosely with his left hand while he slid his right hand into his shirt between the second and third button—precisely as the little guy liked to do.

Joe had just begun to talk to the masses in a phony French accent when he felt it. Someone's palm at the small of his back. Applying pressure. Pushing him out. Out toward the abyss. She'd taken the bait.

But she'd taken it too soon. He hadn't had time to set up properly. There was no control. He'd screwed up, and he knew it instantly.

There was a feeling of time suspended. Of slow motion. As he looked down, the ground seemed to lift up to him, and then fall away again. Instinctively his left hand tightened its grip on the railing as he struggled to untangle his right from within the shirt buttons. The hand at his back began to push him out further. Out and off of the tower. Joe fought desperately to dislodge his right hand, but in his panic he had spread his fingers wide, making it impossible to slip it back out and through the space between the buttons.

His right shoulder began to dip down toward the park, 377 feet below, and again the grassy lawn seemed to rise up and slowly drop away. His eyes would pick up a pedestrian on the ground. Then a tree or shrub, and then shoot out to the city and on up to the sky. The round lightbulbs from the Jules Verne Restaurant seemed to pop within his eyes like exploding stars.

Joe pulled with a colossal effort. He heard two sharp cracks, almost like the sound of a .22 pistol. Two shirt buttons flew out into the Parisian haze and slowly started their descent, the breeze taking them off toward the Latin Quarter. After freeing itself, Joe's right hand dropped quickly to the railing, but his upper torso continued to fall forward, and his shoes started to slide and lose their grip on the platform. He heard Andie giggling behind him. Her voice took on an otherworldly quality.

Joe knew he was fighting a losing battle. He was going over. He just hoped to hell he had the strength in his hands to hold on. His feet slid further out from the platform. He yelled, "Shit," at a vocal level that even surprised him. And then thought, That's it? That's going to be my final words? Shit . . . ?

And then a strange thing developed. Andie moved her hand down to his waist and grasped onto his belt. She pulled backward. To the center of the platform. Joe came back with her. She was now laughing hysterically.

"Saved your life. Saved your life," she cried like a

five-year-old, and they both collapsed onto the metal decking.

"That was supposed to be funny . . . ? You scared the shit out of me." For some reason he was completely out of breath.

"Jesus, Billy, it was a joke. Don't look so serious."

"Serious? Serious? Do I look serious to you? You stand up there. Let me give you a little push. See how serious you look."

"You're not supposed to stand up there anyway. Can't you read the sign? You're lucky the guard didn't catch you. We wouldn't be able to do what we came up here for. It's going to be better at the top. Especially after this . . . I guarantee it. It's twice as far down." She tugged his hand. "Let's go."

"Look at my shirt, for Christ's sake," he said as they stood and brushed themselves off. Andie continued to laugh.

Joe's heart was still pounding at an accelerated rate when they stepped out at 899 feet. The wind was surprisingly strong, but still hot. It reminded Joe of a coal furnace with the door left open. But the incredible view made up for any discomfort.

There was only one other person on the top level. Andie let out a long pained sigh that could have easily passed for a sarcastic groan. She looked at the man and said, "Is he a friend of yours?"

"I think he might be . . . Hold on, I'll check."

Joe walked up to the tall men wearing wing tips, a charcoal gray three-piece suit, and Ray•Bans. He said, "Which one are you, Austin or Petrie?"

The man looked at Joe. He appeared to be in a state

of shock at being recognized. After a second he stammered, "I'm Austin. How did you know?"

"Call it a lucky guess."

"What happened to your buttons?"

Thirty-nine

By eleven forty-five that evening, Andie and Joe were finishing up their espressos at a small restaurant only four blocks from the Hôtel Salomé. They'd both had oysters and sea bass and were the last people in the dining room. The waiters were getting testy. It was time to call it a night. Andie hadn't tried anything funny since the Eiffel Tower stunt.

"I think I'm going to head back tomorrow, too," Andie said.

"Don't you still have work to do?"

"It's done . . . mostly. I've covered all the large fashion houses and shows. I've got all I need. It's time to move on."

"I don't know if my American flight's booked or not. Would you like me to scoot across the street and check with Agent Austin?"

"That's okay, I'll call from my room. We probably should have invited the poor guy in to eat with us. It would've been the civilized thing to do." Andie had resigned herself to the fact that she'd blown this one. It was over. Might as well enjoy her last night in Paris. And, there was something else nagging her.

Something she didn't like. Why had she grabbed his belt? Why had she pulled him back? What happened?

"Are you kidding? Invite Austin in? It would've ruined his day. He thinks he's the reincarnation of Wells's Invisible Man. Christ, it's almost midnight and he's still got his fucking Ray•Bans on."

Andie reached her hand across the table and placed it on Joe's. "I'm happy things worked out this way," she said. "I had a good time with you, Billy. But it wasn't cut out to be a lasting relationship. We're both a couple of sluts. What can I say?"

Joe choked on his coffee slightly, but he gave what she'd said a good deal of thought.

"I'm glad you feel like that . . . about having a good time, I mean. I'll think about the slut part."

He considered filling her in on Harper's entire scheme, but nixed the idea. It would only hurt her feelings. She obviously wasn't out to hurt him and what was the point? Whether she was out to do in Danielle or not still wasn't clear. But at least by spending the day with her he'd been able to keep an eye on her.

He watched Andie move her mouth into a broad smile that quickly turned into a yawn, and then a loud laugh.

"Come on," he said, "I'll walk you home."

He paid the check and they walked slowly back to the Hôtel Salomé, arm in arm, Austin about forty feet back the entire way. When they reached the lobby, she asked Joe up and he said, "Fine. Just for a minute, though. I don't want to leave *The Invisible Man* outside all night. We both have a busy day tomorrow."

Joe stayed in Andie's room for only about five minutes. It ended with a long hug, a light kiss, and an "I'll see you around, sometime," from both of them. Austin was waiting across the street when he came out.

"She never tried anything funny, huh?" he asked as Joe walked up.

"With you ten feet away? Not likely . . . I think she's clean, though. We've been barking up the wrong tree here."

"I don't trust anyone. That's my policy. Keeps you breathing longer. Makes you a happy man."

"Not so invisible, though. What is that, philosophy out of the FBI handbook?"

Joe shook his head and started walking toward number 6 Rue Racine. Austin tagged alongside.

"You know," Joe said, "I knew a guy in the Secret Service who never took his dark glasses off. I think he slept and showered with the fucking things."

"You get used to them. After a while you feel uncomfortable without them."

"Yeah? Well, this guy blew his brains out when he was twenty-nine years old . . ."

Austin let out an uneasy laugh.

"I'm serious about that shit. It's a true story . . ." Joe added, "Watch yourself, it'll catch up to you sooner than you think."

Austin wasn't sure what kind of a response Joe's statement called for, so he shut up. They walked the rest of the way in silence. When they reached the entryway to number 6, Joe turned and said, "Now what?"

"I'll come up. Call Harper. See what the strategy is. Okay?"

"Sure, it's your ball game."

Upstairs, Austin made his call and said, "Uh-uh," about ten or twelve times, then handed the phone to Joe. "Harper wants to talk to you."

Joe pulled the receiver to his face and said, "Yes, Dad?"

"How you holding up?"

"That's it? You want to know how I'm *holding up*?"

"You can be such an asshole sometimes. Has anybody ever told you that?"

"Now that you mention it . . . yes."

"Good, I didn't want to be the one to break it to you . . . Okay, here's the skinny. Slight change, nothing big. Austin's spending the night there with you—"

"What? I need a baby-sitter all of a sudden?"

"Look. We're too close. If it was going to happen here, it would've gone down by now. I'm concentrating everything on New York. This end's done. It didn't happen. I don't want any last-minute fuck-ups. Okay?"

Joe groaned and let out a subdued, "Right."

Harper continued with the official tone. "You and Austin will be picked up at seven a.m. Be ready. In the foyer. Don't forget the thirty-two. I want it back. We'll be outfitting you with some new equipment. Wear a loose shirt. We've got a vest for you."

"Nothing too flashy, I hope."

"You know, Bradlee, they're going to get you one of these days. And when they do, I want to be at your wake. There's going to be a lot of happy people there. I'd hate to miss it."

"Uh-uh."

Harper grumbled and shook his head. "At any rate, what was your final read on Andie? Austin still thinks she's up to no good."

"I think he feels the same way about his own mother. Do we have anyone on her?"

Harper didn't answer. Joe continued, "I'm buying Andie's jealousy story. Call me a sentimental fool."

"You're a sentimental asshole. I'll give you that."

"What about Danielle?"

"What about her?"

"Whatever Andie's story is, I'd hate to see her decide to revisit Danielle."

"Your concern touches me," Harper said with a small laugh. "Petrie's been with her most of the day, and I'm spending the night with her."

"You fuck." Joe's tone was that of absolute disbelief.

"It's a tough job. Someone's got to do it."

"If you touch her, you bastard, I'll kill you, I swear to Christ I will."

"She's a good-looking woman, Joe. I don't know, it'll be tough to keep my hands to myself. I haven't gotten laid in weeks."

"You fuck. I'm going over there myself. You and Austin spend the goddamn night together, you fuck."

"Easy, easy. Call her up if you want. The plan stays the way it is. Seriously, Joe, we're set. I don't want to lose Billy or Danielle at this point. As a matter of fact, I don't even want to lose you. Call her up. I'll see you in the morning. Get some sleep. Put Austin back on, will you?"

Joe handed the phone back to Austin. After the agent hung up, he called Danielle.

"Rumor has it you've got a man in there with you? I'm jealous as hell."

She laughed, "*Oui.* Robert Stack. Would you like me to get his autograph for you?"

"Harper's coming over."

"I know. It'll be nice to see him again."

"I don't think I like the way you said that."

"Tough."

"Jesus, I'm getting it from everybody. I'm beginning to feel like I don't have a friend in the world."

"You do."

Joe could almost feel the heat from her body coming through the phone lines.

"Take care of yourself tomorrow," she said. "I'm worried about you."

"Don't be. It'll be a cakewalk . . . Trust me, if anyone's going to come for me, he'll stick out just like Mr. Nestor. We'll be ready."

"I still don't like it."

"Listen, this'll be all over in three or four days. Billy'll be in court, and I'll be done. What would you say if I came back over here?"

"Fine."

Joe waited for Danielle to say something else, but nothing came, so he added, "I was sort of hoping for a hint of enthusiasm in your voice. *Fine* didn't quite do it for me."

"What do you want? I work in clay, I'm not an actress, for God's sake." She took a beat and tried it again. "*Fine . . . Great . . . I'd love to have you come back over to Paris. It would bring new meaning to my life, mon cherie.* How was that?"

"It sucked. Stick to clay."

Forty

Andie had paced the partially worn carpet in front of the telephone table for forty minutes. She did not want to make this phone call. She glanced once more at her watch. Two a.m. Eight p.m. in New York. Drew would surely be home by now. More than likely sitting by his desk waiting to hear from her. She lifted the receiver and dialed. It was the third time she'd done it. Once again she replaced the receiver in its cradle a second after punching in the last digit.

"Damn it," she said aloud.

She walked over to the mini-bar and cracked the last of the three miniature Remy Martin bottles, then dumped the contents into a plastic hotel cup. She moved over to the window. The night had become overly still and the reflection from the mighty lights illuminating Notre Dame cast everything in milky yellow. Andie crossed her arms over her chest and sipped slowly at the brandy. She was beginning to get a slight buzz. She'd hoped the stuff would've increased her confidence, but it only served to chip away at it.

She stepped back to the phone, set the cup down,

and sighed. "I've got to get this over with. Nothing's going to change. Not tonight."

She dialed the number a fifth time and waited.

"Yeah. Hello," Stevenson said in an anxious voice.

"It's me."

"How's everything?"

"Fucked."

"Shit . . . Goddamn it," he grumbled.

"I'm sorry . . . I couldn't get him alone. Every time I turned around there was some Federal type hiding in the bushes."

"Shit."

"There was no point in trying to shake him. It would've thrown up a flag."

He grumbled, tapped his fingers for a bit, then said, "Wait. Hold on . . . Why wasn't this guy with him?"

"Who? What do you mean?"

"If they wanted to protect him so badly, why didn't the Fed just pal around with Billy? Why'd he have to hide in the fucking bushes?" Stevenson waited for an answer. Got none and moved on. "I think they were on to you already. I know these guys. I know how they work . . . Sounds to me like they were setting you up."

"I don't know," she said, but thought about it.

"Something's fishy here. He should be under tighter wraps than this. Think about it. Anybody could've walked up and popped him, and made a dash for it."

"I think they figured no one would be that stupid. I sure wasn't. They would've grabbed him in a second."

"Yeah? So then they've got some hit man with tight lips and lost their star witness . . . Plus if it's done right, they'd have nothing. Zilch."

"Well, Billy said their big concern wasn't here in Paris, because no one knew he was here."

"Except for Arthur Preston, Senior and Junior, Sam Zuckerman, Nestor, you, me, the old broad who lives next door . . . Anybody I miss?"

"I don't know, it's late, Jesus," Andie said. "It didn't seem abnormal to me. Billy was very calm. He didn't appear to be sweating it at all. He would have been nervous as hell, if they were throwing him out as bait."

"I don't like it . . ." He thought some more, then said, "What's their plan?"

"American Airlines, flight Forty-five Q, leaves Orly at twelve-fifteen this afternoon. Gets into Kennedy at two twenty-five your time."

"When's he moving to the airport?"

"I don't know."

"Goddamn it, Andie. What the hell's going on with you? You're fucking falling apart on me." Stevenson was burning. "Shit! Never leave a woman to do a man's work."

Andie screamed back, "You fuck. You fucking bastard. You ever say something like that to me again, and I'll make you wish you never had a dick. You hear me, you fuck? What difference does it make when he goes to the fucking airport?"

"I want you there. I want you there when they move him. If they're not all over him, like flies on shit, I want to know about it. If they're not following procedure, I want to know. You get it? I'm putting my ass on the line here. It's not you anymore, it's me. If something's fucked, I want to know."

"Okay. Okay. I'll find out. Calm down . . . How're you going to handle this?"

"Never mind how I'm going to handle it. It's my show now. You just hold up your end. I want a report from you within eight hours. I want to know how he's being moved to Orly. Try not to fuck this up, okay? You fuck this up, and you're out."

Andie could feel her blood boiling. She was ready to end this relationship here and now. He'd been playing the charade for so long, he was beginning to talk to her like he really was her goddamn brother. It would end. Drew Stevenson was going to get his. When this was over he was going to get it good. And Andie'd go back to her real name—pack up, pull out, and start all over again as a virgin. The only thing that kept her from pulling the plug now, was the money. She'd blown the hit, okay, but she was still in for a large piece of the action. Drew wouldn't be stupid enough to cut her out. Not now. She had too much on the bastard.

"I'll call you at four a.m. New York time. I'll tell you what I see."

"Don't disappoint your big brother."

Andie dropped the receiver into its cradle. It bounced out, and she slammed it back in place. "You fuck," she said, then picked it back up and dialed.

"Hello?"

"Billy. . . ?"

"No, this is Agent Austin."

"Can I speak to Billy, please? It's Andie."

"Listen, lady—"

"Andie."

"Pardon me?"

"My name's Andie. Not *lady*."

"Right . . . He's asleep."

"Can you wake him? It's important."

"Look, *Andie*, we've got to be moving at seven. In a little over four hours. Let the guy get some sleep, will you? Let me get some sleep."

"Fuck you." She hung up on him.

Next she dialed the front desk. A very groggy Algerian fumbled at the switchboard and eventually said, *"Oui?"*

"Could you please ring me at six a.m.?"

"Oui, mademoiselle."

Andie walked back to the mini-bar. She cracked a Chivas Regal, said, "Goddamn it," and started to cry—for no apparent reason.

Forty-one

It started raining at about five a.m. It was a light rain. Andie was exhausted, but the soft sound of water dripping onto the cobblestones managed to wake her. It was darker than when she'd fallen asleep a little over two hours earlier and she now envisioned herself strapped onto a Chinese torture device. Her stomach was churning and her head was throbbing. Too much booze. Not enough sleep. Each drop of water seemed to echo like a set of castanets trapped within her skull. She stuffed her head deep into the down pillows and remained motionless for a long while. She then rolled to her left side. She waited for sleep to return. She squeezed her eyes tight and rolled over to her right side. Then onto her stomach. It was no use. She sat up. Looked at the clock. The phone rang.

"Shit," she said and went to the desk to answer it.

"*Oui?*"

"*Ils sont six heures, mademoiselle,*" the desk clerk said.

"*Merci.*"

Andie dragged herself to the bathroom and flipped the tub handle. She waited for the shower to draw some hot water up from the boiler, then stepped in. She sat in the tub for over fifteen minutes, barely moving. Eventually she stood, lathered up, rinsed off, and dried her hair. She pulled her crimson mane straight back and tied it into a tight ponytail at the nape of her neck. She slid into a pair of loose-fitting jeans and a pumpkin-colored hooded sweatshirt. She then grabbed her key and walked out.

The summer drizzle had ended, but the streets were still wet. They reflected gray and pink as the dawn's new light slithered through narrow openings between buildings. Andie walked the short distance to 6 Rue Racine. When she arrived, the small coffee bar across the street was bustling with early-morning workers. She kept her hood up, ordered a double espresso, and took a stool at the window. She was the only woman in the place. Her outfit kept anyone from noticing.

After ten minutes, at seven a.m. precisely, a Citroën sedan with diplomatic license plates and a bronze U.S. Embassy plaque on the bumper, pulled up to the stoop of Nichols's apartment building. Not the same agent Andie'd seen the previous day, but another Robert Stack look-alike, stepped out of the passenger's side, and entered the building. The driver stayed with the car. Within three minutes the agent stepped back out, placed a large suitcase in the Citroën's trunk, looked up and down the street, and nodded to someone inside. Agent Austin and Billy Barton then darted out of the building and into the car's rear seat. Robert Stack number two jumped back into the front seat and the Citroën sped off. It was good. It was clean. It was fast.

Andie ordered another espresso and a sweet roll. She finished them at the counter and listened to the

Frenchmen talk politics and women for twenty more minutes.

When she returned to her hotel it was still only eight o'clock. Two hours before she'd said she would call Drew back. She phoned him anyway. He'd been sound asleep.

"Huh? Yeah?"

"It's me."

"Jesus, what time is it? Fuck."

"It's eight here. Two there."

"What's up? Hold on. Let me get a cigarette."

It took a minute, but he came back.

"Yeah, I'm here."

"They picked him up at seven. Two agents and a driver. Diplomatic car. They were very protective. Very cautious. Happy?"

"Why so early?"

"My guess would be that they're going to outfit him with some underwear, bulletproof vest. I assume you've counted on that?"

"It's been taken into consideration."

"Who's making the move? Anyone I know?"

"Don't worry, it'll be handled."

"Is there a reason you're not trusting me with any of the details?" she said with a noticeable edge to her voice. "I'd like to know who's going to whack him."

"At this point you have no need to know. I don't know what's going on over there. Loose lips sink ships."

"Aren't you cute . . . ? Don't try to fuck me, Drew. It'll come back to haunt you. You can count on that. You can have no worse enemy than a lover scorned."

"I'm not going to screw you. Trust me. Timing has

become critical. It's a one-man show now. If only one man knows the details, nothing goes wrong. I'll talk to you in a few days. It's almost over."

Andie hung up the phone and ambled over to the window. The clouds were separating and a brilliant blue sky was just beginning to take over. She looked up to the heavens for a long time. The brighter the blue became, the whiter the clouds seemed to get. A thought glided into her mind and she smiled for the first time in eight hours. She walked back to the phone. When the switchboard answered she said, "Do you think you could get me through to American Airlines?"

"*Oui, mademoiselle.* I have the number here. Please hold for a minute."

Andie sat and drummed her fingernails on the glass tabletop.

"American Airlines, this is Blanche, how can I help you?"

Her accent tempted Andie to ask if her last name was DuBois, but she didn't.

"Yes, do you have any space left on flight Forty-five Q to Kennedy Airport today? I think it's at twelve-fifteen?"

"Let me just check that for you. How would that be?"

"That would be fine, Blanche," Andie said in a staccato voice, feeling strangely like Marlon Brando. She could hear Blanche working on her computer in the background.

"I'm awfully sorry that flight is completely booked. Oh, my goodness, it's actually overbooked," she said and laughed.

"Can you tell me if any other airlines have flights today?"

"Let me check for you, dear."

After a moment Blanche continued, "Well, let's see what we have here, shall we? Okay . . . I'm showing Air France has two flights this afternoon. One at twelve-forty and another at three-thirty."

"Thank you very much."

"However," Blanche added, "I'm also showing that they're booked as well."

Andie said, "Shit . . . that's it, huh?"

"I'm afraid so, dear, unless you'd be willing to fly into Newark, New Jersey?"

"Newark. . . ? Yes, that'd be fine."

"Well, then I'm showing Delta Airlines has a flight Seventy-one at four-fifteen this afternoon. And it has a number of openings."

"Thank you, Blanche, it's always nice to know one can rely on the kindness of strangers."

"Well, we like to help when we can."

Andie asked the switchboard to ring Delta Airlines for her. When they answered, she said, "Yes, I'd like to book a seat on your flight Seventy-one to Newark, New Jersey, this afternoon. Nonsmoking, please."

"All of Delta's international flights are nonsmoking, ma'am. For your convenience."

Forty-two

"Did you bring the thirty-two?" was the first thing Harper said as Joe entered the FBI's apartment on the Rue de Rivoli.

"Hi. Nice to see you again, Jack. How's Paris been treating you? Some weather we're having, huh?" Joe handed Harper the gun and walked to the window. He looked out to the gardens and the mist rising from the river beyond. "Shit. How come you guys get the Ritz while I've been stuck in the low-rent district for a month?"

Joe turned to eye Harper and Billy Barton emerged from the kitchen with a cup of coffee in his hand. They started at each other for over a minute. No one in the room spoke. Finally Billy said, "Hi. I'm Billy Barton." He approached Joe and extended his right hand.

Joe was stunned. It was like looking directly into a mirror. He stammered when he spoke. "Yeah . . . Jesus . . . Um . . . I'm Joe. Joe Bradlee. Jesus." He looked to Harper. "This is amazing. It's shocking, is what it is." Then shook Billy's hand. "Nice to meet you."

"I saw you in the park across the street a while ago,"

Billy said. "I've gotten over the shock . . . I must say, you're an awfully good-looking man."

They both laughed.

Joe said, "Thanks. You too." And they laughed again, but Joe was feeling a little uncomfortable for some reason. Billy had a strange look in his eye.

"Okay," Harper said, "you two can get acquainted later. Joe, take your shirt off. I want to make sure this stuff's comfortable for you." He held up a bulletproof vest and shoulder holster fitted out with a Smith and Wesson .357 magnum, model 19. The same weapon Joe had refused to carry when he was with the Secret Service.

Joe crossed to Harper and hefted the piece in his left hand. "I hate these fucking things," he said, "they're too damn big. You couldn't find me a cannon? Maybe a fifty-caliber machine gun?"

"Yeah, well it may save your life, so learn to like it."

"Yes, sir."

"Throw it on. The vest's cut out under the arm to accommodate the magnum. See how it works for you."

Joe slipped the vest on, fastened it, and lifted his left arm. He examined the cutout under his triceps and the bare skin of his chest that shone through. He started to laugh and Harper said, "What's the problem?"

"Nothing." Joe shook his head and continued to chuckle. He slipped his shirt back over his shoulders and buttoned it up. He then took the holster, slid his arms through the leather straps, and picked up the .357. He checked to see if it was loaded, it was, and attempted to stuff it into the quick-release grip under his left arm. He missed it twice, but secured the gun on his third try. He never stopped laughing throughout the entire song and dance.

"You haven't been drinking, have you?" Harper made no attempt to hide his agitation. "What the fuck's so funny?"

"You guys amaze me. Why the hell do you think I never carried one of these things?" Joe struggled to remove the pistol from the holster. It was a clumsy move to say the least. "The casings blow right into your face."

"What are you talking about?"

"I'm left-handed, for Christ's sake. First off, I can't even draw the thing from this side without blowing my balls off . . . And second, every time you shoot the thing from the left side the casings go up your goddamn nose." He was still laughing.

"How do you figure that?" Harper took the pistol and pointed it at arm's length. He put his finger to the ejection port, then moved it off to the right. "The casings go out that way? No way they hit your face—left- or right-handed."

"Fuck you. The gun's a piece of shit."

"Great, I've got a purist on my hands. A goddamn artist," Harper said.

Billy walked over to them and smiled at Joe. "Isn't that amazing? I'm left-handed, too. I guess the reason I never noticed it when I saw you in the park was because everything was just so perfect."

"Thanks, Billy," Harper said, then looked at Joe. "Well, shit. It's too late to change it now. See how your jacket fits. Fuck. I'm sorry about this, Joe. I should have checked it out. A goddamn southpaw. Sorry."

"Happens all the time," Joe said as he slipped into

his jacket. "Don't worry about it. But don't expect any Quick-Draw-McGraw stuff from me."

Nichols came from one of the back bedrooms and eyeballed Joe. "It looks good," he said and sat on the couch.

"You're Nichols?" Joe said.

"Yep."

"Well, now I know everybody. All you boys sleep here together . . . ? Looks cozy."

"Coffee, Joe?" Harper said almost too quickly.

"Sure."

"It's in the kitchen."

Harper moved off and made a gesture for Joe to join him. In the kitchen, as he poured the coffee, Harper said in a low voice, "I don't know if you know it, but Billy's gay."

"I gathered that much."

"Well, I just thought I'd warn you before you came out with any crude *fag* jokes."

Joe gave Harper a long hard look, then said, "Have I come out with any crude *nigger* jokes?"

Harper straightened. Tightened his jaw. Said, "No."

"Well, if I haven't come out with any crude *nigger* jokes, what makes you think I'll come out with any crude *fag* jokes?"

"You made your point."

"Good. This coffee's for the goddamn birds. Who made it?"

"You're a piece of work, you know that?"

"Yeah? Well, I'll bet you one thing . . ."

"What's that?"

"Billy didn't make this coffee."

Harper smiled, said, "Let's go over the plan," and walked back to the living room.

Joe followed. After settling into an overstuffed armchair, he glanced around the room, studied the agents, and said, "Nice coffee, Nichols."

"Thanks."

Joe then looked at Harper, smiled, and said, "I should've put money on it."

Harper cleared his throat and began. "Okay. This is pretty cut and dried, but let's run through it. Nichols and Joe and I will leave at ten. Joe, we sandwich you the entire way. Through the building and again out in the street. You sit tight, right between us, for the ride to Orly. I'm not expecting anything to snap here, in Paris, this is all for show. Any way we can attract attention helps. We got a nice photo in the *Herald* today." Harper held up the newspaper and handed it to Joe. "I don't even know which one of you guys it is."

"It's Billy," Joe said.

"Out at Orly, airport security will meet us at curbside. They'll check our bags with American, escort us through the concourse and metal detectors, and out to the departure gate. Play it up. Make it a good show for the people. Don't be shy . . . We'll board before the masses, and that should be it. Until New York. Like I said, I wouldn't expect anything here. Preston's next move will come in the States—that, *I'll* put money on. Any questions?"

Joe raised his hand.

"Yeah?" Harper said.

"How about I dump the vest until New York?"

"It's part of the show . . . Hey, it's good. You look like the Sta-Puff Marshmallow Man."

"What's the program for arrival at Kennedy?" Joe asked.

"I'll lay that out on the plane . . . I want it fresh."

Drew Stevenson knew what he had to do. Like Jack Harper, he, too, had worked out a plan for Kennedy Airport. The beauty of Stevenson's plan was in its simplicity; and the fact that not a soul was in on it, except Stevenson himself.

American Airlines flight 45Q was due into Kennedy at two twenty-five. Gate 4. Airport regulations allowed no one to meet incoming passengers until they had cleared customs and exited the terminal at street level. Security personnel carefully checked everyone for a ticket or boarding pass before they were free to pass onto the gate areas. Stevenson merely had to show his FBI identification to sidestep any airport security.

Stevenson would be waiting for Harper, Nichols, and Billy Barton when they stepped off of flight 45Q. He'd explain how the Director had sent him over as a backup. He'd be recognized. No questions would be asked.

Sixty-five feet down the corridor, heading north from gate 4, there would be an emergency exit. After the four men passed the door, Stevenson would pull a .22-caliber semiautomatic pistol. He had studied enough human anatomy charts and enough bulletproof vests to know where he needed to position the weapon to obtain a clear path to Billy's heart. He would fire three shots in rapid succession, thus the necessity for a .22. The recoil from a .22 would be minimal, enabling him to keep a steady hand and maintain a tight bullet grouping. It would also create just enough noise to alert Harper and Nichols. No one else.

Stevenson would then drop the gun and duck out of the emergency exit, setting off the alarm, and hopefully panicking a few passengers—after he'd cleared the area. The door would be jammed from the outside, but it would be highly unlikely Harper or Nichols would follow. A chest shot would create the illusion Billy could be saved, and that would be the agents primary concern. They'd stay with their witness and forget the assassin for the time being. This was why Stevenson would shoot Billy in the heart and not the head. If Harper knew Billy was dead, he'd give chase.

After jamming the emergency door, Stevenson would work his way to an employee washroom on the tarmac level. There he would shave his mustache completely off and buzz his hair down to a crew cut. He would change into casual clothes, throw on a longish sandy-brown wig, and emerge with a new name, a new passport, and looking somewhat like one of the Bee-Gees. Stevenson would then take an interairport bus to the International Terminal where he would board a Varig airliner for Brazil. By the time the FBI sealed off the airport, he'd be long gone.

Seven hundred and fifty thousand dollars were waiting for him in a Panamanian bank account, and another half million would be coming his way when the job was done. Fuck Andie. She blew it. She was out on her ass. It would be good. It would be clean. It would be fast.

Forty-three

Harper was right. It was a piece of cake. Joe felt like he'd walked into a movie—Star Witness being hustled out of a French apartment building, through the streets of Paris, into a crowded airport, people staring and pointing the entire way, and out onto a waiting jetliner. It was something. When the FBI wanted to put on a show, it was something.

Billy's trip took on a much different tone. He, too, had been outfitted with a bulletproof vest, but his hair had been whitened at the sides and back. He wore a beret cocked neatly off to the right side. At one-thirty, Austin took three suitcases down to the basement and loaded them into the trunk of a Peugeot sedan with smoked windows. He returned to the apartment, looked at Petrie and Billy, and said, "All set?"

They both nodded.

He said, "Let's roll."

They hit moderate traffic, but managed to get to Orly within an hour. Petrie pulled up curbside, they stepped out, looking very much like three businessmen, grabbed their bags, and walked up to the Delta counter. The car was left with the keys in it. Running.

Two minutes later a plainclothes French policeman stepped into the sedan and drove off.

At the Delta counter they checked their baggage like any other passengers, and headed for the departure gate. When they passed through the metal detector a bell sounded. They were asked to step to one side by the head security officer on duty. The man picked up a handheld metal sensor, and smoothly switched it to the off position before he lifted it to Petrie's side.

"I am sorry for the inconvenience, gentlemen. This should take me only a minute."

After checking all three, and hearing no sound from his sensor, the security officer allowed them to pass. They sat and read newspapers until twenty minutes before flight 71 was due to board. At that time they were approached by a Delta flight attendant. He said, "Excuse me, gentlemen, but would you be kind enough to show me your boarding passes?"

The passes were produced. The attendant looked them over.

"There seems to be a slight problem. If you could follow me . . ."

They stood and were led directly onto the aircraft. They held four seats in the left side of the busines-class section; 9A, 9B, 10A, and 10B. Billy was told to take 9A. Austin took 9B, and Petrie 10B. Ten A, the seat behind Billy was left empty.

After fifteen minutes a couple with two wailing brats, and loaded down with four diaper satchels entered the plane. They worked their way back. The wife stopped next to Austin and started juggling her bundles of pink baby crap searching for their seat numbers.

"Keep going, damn it," the husband grumbled. "we're back in the thirties somewhere."

They continued on to the coach section, kids screaming the entire way.

"Thank Christ," Austin and Billy said in almost perfect unison.

Another few minutes and the general boarding began. Austin and Petrie buried their noses in the in-flight magazines as one passenger after another smacked them in their shoulders and ears with their carry-on luggage as they moved onto the rear of the plane. One of the last people to board the aircraft was a shapely redheaded woman who could have easily passed for a fashion model.

"Aw, shit," Austin said, and nudged Billy. "You know who that is, don't you?"

Billy looked up and said, "Andie?"

"Right . . . Look out the window or something, maybe she'll miss you."

Andie began to work her way to the rear. She missed seeing Billy at first. What caught her attention was Agent Austin and the guy sitting behind him, Robert Stack number two. She then glanced at the gray-haired man sitting next to Austin. He was peering out the window, but she'd nibbled on those ears enough to recognize them from the back.

"Billy . . . ?"

He turned and stood. Then extended his right hand, "Andie, it's so nice to see you again. How have you been?"

Petrie groaned and slid down in his seat.

"I thought you were leaving on an American flight?" Andie stammered.

Austin stood between them. "We had a little change of plans . . . Now, I'm sure you can understand the sensitivity of what we're doing here. I think it's best if you just move on off to your seat."

Andie looked past Austin and said, "Billy . . . ? What's going on?"

Petrie then stood and put his hand on Andie's elbow. "Why don't I help you to your seat."

"You take your hands off me this second, you fuck, or I'll make so much goddamn noise, you'll wish you were back cleaning toilets in Alabama . . . or wherever the hell you're from."

Petrie removed his hand.

"Andie, dear, this can all be explained quite easily—"

Billy was interrupted by Austin. "That's enough. Can it, Billy." He bore into Andie. "This has now become a matter of national security. Either move on to your seat, or I'll have you removed from the aircraft. I can do it. Just try me."

Andie looked to Billy. He shrugged and gave her a small smile she hadn't seen since two years ago at the Rutherford estate in Newport.

"Fine," she said and worked her way back to seat 34B. She placed her bag in the overhead bin, sat, and fastened her seat belt. Across the aisle a woman was struggling with a two-year-old and an infant. It looked like the primate pen at the Bronx Zoo except everything was fucking pink. The parents were pink. The kids were pink. Their clothes were pink. The father even had pink socks on. Andie leaned across the aisle and tapped the mother on the shoulder.

"I hope you're going to keep those little fuckers quiet. Everyone on this plane hates your guts already."

"Well, I'm trying," the woman said, "you just don't know what it's like if you've never had children. It's a very special time for us." She looked to her husband. "Peter, I think we should switch seats. Can you talk to one of these girls?"

"Girls?"

"Stewardesses."

Peter couldn't *talk* to one of the *girls* because at that moment the captain came on to say they were pushing back. Andie slid over to the window seat and thought about her brief run-in with Billy in the business section.

First question: Why'd they switch Billy's flight at the last minute, or had he lied about it from the beginning? Second: Where was Agent Nichols? She knew his voice from their phone conversations. Neither one of the agents with Billy was Nichols, of that she was positive. Third: Billy's vocal quality seemed changed; more like the Newport Billy. Had they drugged him? And he seemed less solid. The gray hair was fake, that was obvious, but he suddenly seemed like a different man from the one she'd been sleeping with.

The plane steadily climbed to its cruising altitude of thirty-five thousand feet and Andie continued to search for answers to her questions. Eventually she resigned herself to the fact that she'd screwed it up one more time. She'd given Drew the wrong flight number. It wasn't a total disaster. If Drew was planning to have someone nail Billy at the American terminal, Billy wouldn't be there. Tough luck. Drew would have to make other arrangements.

She flipped her way through the duty-free catalog and shook her head at the prices. Who buys this shit? she wondered. Booze, cigarettes, stuffed bears, calculators, perfume, watches . . . Andie's gaze remained glued to a man's Seiko stainless-steel watch with more dials and knobs than a nuclear sub's engine room. It listed for two hundred and seventy-five dollars. She couldn't take her eyes off it. She flipped through some more pages but kept coming back to the watch. After a few minutes a flight attendant worked her way back to Andie's seat with her cart. Andie was still staring at the watch.

"Anything from our duty-free shop, miss?" the attendant asked.

Andie looked up and said, "Can I give you an American Express card?"

"Of course."

She pointed to the catalog, "I'll take one of these watches."

"A nice choice, I'm sure he'll love it."

"I think so, too."

After the attendant had completed running Andie's American Express card through her portable computer, she returned it, asked her to sign a slip of paper, handed Andie her receipt and watch, and moved down the aisle, ignoring the mother with the screaming brats.

Andie removed the watch from its packaging and snipped off the instruction tags with a pair of nail clippers. She set the watch to Paris time. She then unfastened her seat belt and worked her way up to the business section. She stopped when she reached row nine.

"Looking for this?" she said to Billy, and held out the watch. "You left it in my hotel room last night."

Austin was caught completely by surprise. He said nothing and looked at Billy.

Billy was a little sharper. He pushed his left wrist under his thigh in an effort to hide his own watch, and smiled at Andie. "Thanks," he said, "I wondered where that had gone to."

Andie said, "You men can be so stupid sometimes." She smiled and then returned to her seat.

Petrie moved up to Austin and said, "Let me look at that . . ." He took the Seiko and rolled it in his fingers. "What do you think? I thought Bradlee was wearing a watch this morning."

"Fuck. I didn't notice. Maybe he was, maybe he wasn't. Fuck."

"It's got to be Bradlee's. Where the hell else could she have gotten it?"

The three men looked at one another. Billy shrugged. Austin shrugged. Petrie returned to his seat.

And Andie flopped back into the window seat of row thirty-four and thought, Goddamn it . . . there's two of them.

Forty-four

One simple fact had answered all Andie's questions. And she was stunned. She was stunned that the FBI had been able to pull it off. That they were able to keep Drew in the dark about it for so long. She was stunned that she hadn't picked up the clues. The early-morning phone call for *Joe.* Danielle rambling on through her door to someone named *Joe* and then acting indignant because *Joe* had lied to her about his name. She was stunned at herself for being unable to push him off the Eiffel Tower when she had the opportunity. And for having waited forever to make a move. But what had stunned Andie the most, as she gazed out at the blue sky and snow white clouds below, was that she had managed to fall in love. She managed to fall in love with someone and she'd never even known his name. Joe.

Andie pushed her seat back and rolled her head toward the babies across the aisle. They were finally asleep. She looked back out the window and the endless blue and began to cry softly. Shit, she thought, this sucks the big one.

She had to stop it. She had to stop it now. She had two options, the way she saw it. One, she could walk up to the FBI agents in business class and tell them the truth. Tell them about herself. Tell them about Drew. And tell them to warn Nichols, who most likely was with Joe on the American flight. But it would mean her next stop would be a federal prison. And they'd no doubt throw away the key. Forget it, she thought, Joe wasn't worth federal prison. Worst came to worst, she'd get over him.

Her other option was to call Drew. Somehow, she had to reach Drew and call it all off. After all, he'd be fucked otherwise. She'd be fucked. Joe'd be fucked. Joe. She liked the name. It was a good name for him. Damn, she thought.

She grabbed a passing flight attendant.

"Are we close enough for me to call the States?"

"You can do that from anywhere in the world now. A Delta Airlines exclusive," he said. "The phone's on the bulkhead up there." He pointed. "Take a credit card."

"Thank you."

As Andie fished through her bag for her American Express card, Agent Austin turned to Petrie and said, "I don't trust that bitch for some reason. Something's wrong with that watch. Bradlee wouldn't wear a piece of shit like that. Take my seat."

Austin stood and Petrie moved up to 9B, the seat beside Billy. The agent then walked forward and tapped three times on the cockpit door. The navigator cracked it and said, "Yes?"

Austin flashed his FBI identification.

"I'd like to speak with the captain. Can I come in?"

"Problems?"

"Nothing we can't handle."

The man looked to the captain, got a nod, said, "Okay . . ."

The captain told Austin to hold on for a second while he made some adjustments in altitude, then turned in his seat.

"What can I do for you?"

"I'd like to have the cabin telephone shut down until we land in Newark."

"For what reason?"

"I'd rather not go into it."

"Well, then, I'd rather not shut my telephone system down. I've got a plane to fly. Unless you've got an emergency you'd like to share with me, I'll run this operation the way I see fit." He turned back to his control panel.

Austin surveyed the cockpit. The three men kept their backs to him. "Jesus . . . Okay . . . I'm bringing a witness back to the States. There's a contract out on his life. Someone's trying to kill him, you understand? I have reason to believe there may be one, *or more,* people on this plane who may try to convey his whereabouts to someone on the ground. It's imperative I keep that from happening. I'd like to avoid a shootout at Newark International Airport if I can. The FBI Director will be there when we land. He can confirm all of this for you when we get there. That's the best I can do."

"And that's all I wanted to know . . . It wasn't that hard, was it?"

He nodded to the copilot, who leaned forward and flipped a toggle switch.

In row thirty-four Andie screamed, "You fucking

cocksuckers," so loud, it woke the two babies across the aisle.

She tossed the now dead telephone onto the seat next to her and looked at her watch. "Shit," she said, in a far softer voice, "It doesn't make any difference, anyway."

American Airlines flight 45Q was due to set down in New York's John F. Kennedy Airport in seven minutes.

Forty-five

Flight 45Q's landing was possibly the smoothest Joe had ever experienced, and he'd been through a lot of them. Harper and Nichols had spent so much of the flight running over their blueprint for Kennedy Airport, and transfer into Manhattan, they were sounding like a broken record. And the truth was, it was no different from what their plan had been in Paris. Put on a good show for the people. Make it flashy. Don't be shy.

The three men remained seated while the plane emptied out.

"Give them time to clear," Harper said. "If it's going down, I don't want anyone hurt."

Joe was enjoying the hell out of this. Everyone looked at him with a, "Who is he? I know he's famous," glance. He smiled back at every one of them. Waved to a few.

When they were the last ones on board, Harper said, "It's show time. Everybody ready?"

Joe grinned and said, "Like Gary Gilmore said to the firing squad, 'Let's do it.' "

They stood together and walked off. Harper first, Joe in the middle, while Nichols followed. Once in the gangway the agents fanned out. Nichols on Joe's left, Harper on the right. They made a dogleg left, moved down a long glass passageway, and exited into a waiting area containing ten or eleven rows of fiberglass seats.

And it was gray.

The chairs were gray. The carpeting was gray. The walls, the ceiling, the building supports, the window frames; everything was gray.

And on the far side of the gray seats, just before the gray corridor that led to customs and the main terminal, stood FBI agent Drew Stevenson. In a gray suit. Harper didn't see him at first and Joe wouldn't have recognized him, but Nichols thought it was strange. "What the hell's he doing here?" he said.

"Who?" Harper said.

"Stevenson . . . He's right by the door."

"Shit. I don't know."

They approached the agent and Harper said, "What the hell are you doing here?"

"The Director thought you might need a little backup. Called me at six this morning, the fucker. I'm whipped. Stayed out late last night. Tied one on. I was supposed to be off today. What a pain in the ass." He laughed as he spoke.

"Man, why can't he let me run my own goddamn show?" Harper moaned. "I hate changes like this . . . Here's our man." He cocked his left thumb in Joe's direction. "He goes by Billy, nothing else. Don't mess it up."

Stevenson looked to Joe and said, "Agent Stevenson, Drew, nice to meet you . . . Welcome back."

Joe shook Stevenson's hand, but avoided eye contact, feeling somewhat uneasy about having balled his sister for two weeks and giving her the brush. And it was a stroke of bad luck, Joe missing Stevenson's eyes. The eyes said it all.

"Let's move out of here," Harper said, and the four headed north toward a yellow sign reading BAGGAGE—CUSTOMS—GROUND TRANSPORTATION. Stevenson positioned himself behind Nichols and Joe, on the left, as they took up an almost casual pace.

It was impossible to tell who felt it first, but Joe glanced to Harper and then to Nichols, and then the agents looked to each other. It was in the air. The air had become too thick. It was as if a warm flood of electrically charged ions had invaded the atmosphere. Harper said, "Do you feel it?"

And Nichols said, "Yep."

"It's going down right here. Be ready. Fifty bucks says we don't make it to the end of this corridor."

The walkway seemed to narrow on them. It'd become far more crowded than Harper had expected or hoped for. Nearly everyone coming their way was speaking a foreign language. A lot of it was Russian. Some Spanish. A little Greek.

They kept their pace up. Carefully scanning every passenger who came their way. Every passenger who passed them. Joe's eyes darted left and right. Out the windows. Up to the terminal's roofline. He opened and closed the fingers of his right hand, stretching them, trying to loosen them up, hoping to hell he wouldn't fumble the Smith and Wesson if he had to reach for it. "The Party's Over" began to play like a broken record on his chest.

After about sixty feet, Joe's attention was drawn out

of the window once more, and to a metal stairway that led from the emergency exit to the tarmac. It loomed about five feet ahead and on his right. A bright orange Day-Glo bar with the words EMERGENCY ONLY spanned the gray door. Outside, propped within the iron railing, rested an eight-foot length of galvanized steel electrical piping.

It was wrong. Dead wrong. It didn't belong. It was off like a son of a bitch. Joe scanned Stevenson's eyes and a thousand bits of information flew through his head in less than a millisecond. The eyes. The answer was in Stevenson's eyes. He took three more steps, and when Harper was abreast of the emergency exit, Joe looked at him and said, in a low voice, "God fucking damn it."

Harper looked at him anxiously and said, "What . . . ?" He glanced at Nichols and back. "What . . . ? What is it? Where? Who?"

"This fucking guy's the mark," were Joe's last words.

They say you never hear the one that gets you, whoever the hell *they* are, and they're right. Joe didn't hear a goddamn thing. Stevenson blew three .22-caliber bullets into Joe's left side and Joe didn't hear shit. He felt it, though. Initially he thought a bee had been caught under his bulletproof vest, and he reached up to scratch at his chest. What Joe was feeling was only the first round.

Stevenson hadn't counted on the Smith and Wesson being tucked under Joe's left arm. This first round glanced off the trigger guard of the .357. From there it passed back through the holster piercing Joe's skin about five inches below his armpit. It continued on, collapsing his left lung, passing a sixteenth of an inch in front of his heart, chipping the corner of his sternum, then exiting his body just to the left of his right pectoral muscle. And that's what Joe had felt. This tiny piece of fiery metal searing his chest hair as it became trapped underneath the bulletproof vest. The bee sting.

Stevenson's second round also ricocheted off the magnum's trigger guard, but managed to enter Joe an inch lower than the first. It glanced off his fourth rib and was sent down on a slight angle, where it met his diaphragm. It worked its way back up, unable to break through the tough muscle barrier, and crossed behind his stomach, where it passed neatly between his solar plexus and aorta, coming to rest alongside the wall of his right lung, but no longer having the momentum to enter and collapse it.

Round three: It hit the hammer of Joe's pistol and sheared in half. The lower portion remained with the .357 while the rest of the bullet traveled up through Joe's left pectoral muscle, exited through his skin and into the vest. From there it turned, headed up toward his head, and embedded itself into his neck on the left side.

Joe moved his left hand to his now bloody collar. Assuming it was another goddamn bee.

Harper and Nichols had heard the three cracks from the .22 loud and clear. But the sound traveled under Joe's arm down the corridor and echoed back onto them from the front. They had no idea where the sound had come from. Their eyes widened with each shot. Searching for the origin. Scanning the faces. Looking for flashes. Puffs of smoke. They came up empty. Three rounds, and with each one they became more confused.

Harper again shouted, "Who? Where? Who's the mark? Where, Joe, where? Shit, I don't see him. Talk to me, you bastard."

The next sound Harper heard was the blare of the emergency siren as the side door was flung open. He spun to his left as Joe dropped to one knee, clawing at his chest and bleeding neck.

"It's Stevenson, that fuck," Nichols yelled and he leapt for the closing door.

Harper moved for the exit, as well, but tripped over Joe, who was now down on all fours. "Fuck," he grumbled and he went down himself, face first into the carpeting.

Nichols reached the door and slammed into it with his right shoulder, but he was too late. Stevenson had already maneuvered the steel pipe into place, wedging it tightly across the outside. The door wasn't going anywhere.

"Goddamn son of a bitch." Nichols pulled his pistol. He hurdled over Harper and Joe and took off down the corridor. "He's down on the tarmac," he yelled back in Harper's direction and disappeared through the doorway.

And that was the second thing Stevenson hadn't considered: It wasn't Billy Barton. Harper and Nichols would give chase. They'd leave Joe Bradlee there to die, before they'd let Stevenson escape. They wanted *him*, not Joe. Drew Stevenson had become the man of the hour. They wanted him—and they wanted him alive.

Harper scrambled to his feet and took off after

Nichols while Joe rolled over and propped himself against the wall. It was the last thing he remembered. There was a quick vision of something that vaguely resembled an extremely cheesy planetarium show, then blue, and eventually it all went black.

Harper was almost to full speed when he saw her. It was like a vision. Except for her pale skin, she could have passed for his goddamn mother. It stopped him dead in his tracks. She had to be the oldest fucking flight attendant on the American Airlines payroll. He stood before her and placed his hands on her shoulders. Harper looked as far into her eyes as he could.

"You've got to help me," he said. "There's a man sitting by the emergency exit. He looks like he's drunk. He's not. He's been shot. He's probably going to die, but please . . . see if you can save him. Find a doctor for me."

She never said a word to Harper. She looked at the pistol in his right hand, turned to another attendant, and motioned to the far end of the passageway, "Get on the red phone. Dial six-eighteen. Ask for Brendon. Tell him Dorothy needs an emergency medical chopper at gate"—she turned and glanced toward the departure area—"gate three-A."

"Right."

The two women moved off in opposite directions faster than Harper thought was humanly possible, given their ages. He then stopped a porter, returning from the main terminal with an empty wheelchair.

"Give me that," he said.

"Hey, man," the porter complained, "I've got a pickup."

Harper hefted the chair over his head and threw it

through the plate-glass window on the emergency exit side of the corridor. It shattered like a piece of auto glass. Harper leaned out, looked down to the tarmac, and bellowed, "I'm going to get you, you son of a bitch. You hear me? You better be good. You better be the best there is, because I'm coming after you, you motherfucker."

Forty-six

Harper eyed the shards of glass jutting out from the window ledge. He then turned, pulled out his identification, and stopped some bozo with a ponytail wearing an LA Dodgers cap.

"FBI. This is an emergency. Give me your jacket."

"What . . . ? This cost me thirty-five hundred bucks. It's one hundred percent iguana," the bozo said.

"Give me the fucking jacket, asshole."

Reluctantly the man peeled off his lizard skin and handed it over. He wore a sleeveless Lakers T-shirt under it. Harper holstered his pistol. He folded the jacket in half, then placed it over the jagged window glass.

"Ahh, shit," the man said, turning his back to Harper, "that cost me thirty-five hundred bucks . . . Jesus God." The bozo began crying real tears.

Harper placed his hands on the jacket and maneuvered it back and forth until he had a good grip on the window ledge. He twisted his torso around and slowly lowered himself out of the window. As he hung full length by his palms, he could feel a gnawing strain working on his elbows and shoulders. He was not a light man. His feet still dangled a good nine feet above the asphalt decking and there was a good chance he'd break an ankle attempting this bullshit. But tendons were bound to tear in his joints if he didn't act soon. He thought it over for another half a second and released his grip.

Harper buckled his knees the moment he felt his feet touch the tarmac. He rolled to his left. Small flecks of glass imbedded themselves into his suit jacket and hair as he broke his fall—but no broken ankle. Son of a bitch, he thought. He stood. He looked left and right. About fifty feet down the refueling line, toward the next concourse, he saw an aluminum door working its way closed. He took off like a sprinter, losing a good deal of traction in the mound of broken glass.

When Harper reached the door he wrenched it open. Inside there was a long hallway, maybe forty feet, with four or five doors on either side. At the end of the hallway stood another door. Considering the time it'd taken him to reach the entrance, anyone could have made it down the hallway and exited out the other end; or ducked into any one of the rooms along the way. Slowly he eased his way down the hall. Trying each doorknob. Glancing left. Then right. Listening. Examining the blue signs that had been riveted to each of the doors. Wondering if Stevenson possessed the security codes that would free the locks.

109 DANGER HIGH VOLTAGE—KEEP OUT; locked. 108 FUEL VALVES—AUTHORIZED PERSONNEL ONLY; locked. 107 MAINTENANCE; locked. 106 MEN'S LAVATORY; open.

Harper eased his way in. It was small; commode, urinal, sink—and empty. He crossed the hall to 105 WOMEN'S LAVATORY; open—same setup as the men's without the urinal—empty. He moved to 104 MEN'S LOCKERS; open—nothing but lockers. 103 WOMEN'S LOCKERS; open—more lockers. 102 CUSTOMS SUPPLY; locked. 101 CUSTOMS LOUNGE; open—old leather couch, coffee machine—unplugged; cigarette machine, soda machine, candy machine, mirror—cracked. Harper had heard nothing—had seen nothing. He opened the final door at the end of the hall.

"God fucking damn it."

He was standing in the luggage pickup area. Three or four hundred people were pushing and shoving one another trying to grab their bags from the spinning carousels. Stevenson was nowhere in sight. Harper panned over the crowd. Eventually, off to the right, and standing by the passport checkpoint, he spotted Agent Nichols. He was doing the same damn thing; scanning the crowd for Stevenson. Harper holstered his weapon and worked his way through the passengers. It took him two minutes, but eventually he reached Nichols.

"Nothing, huh?"

Nichols shook his head.

"Shit . . . Are we sealed off?"

"Let's hope so. I phone it in. They know who they're looking for, but they won't close down—or check exiting airport traffic."

"Fuck. What's their reasoning?"

"Low priority. Too much of a hassle. No manpower. Lazy. He's armed. Budget cutbacks. Shift change. Jewish holiday . . . Which one do you like?"

"Fuckers . . . Christ, he could just grab a goddamn cab. Be out of here in a second."

"I don't think so, Jack. Think about it. Where the

fuck's he going to go? He's not showing up for work at 26 Fed tomorrow, that's for damn sure. It's checkout time for old Drew. Ten'll get you twenty he's got a plane ticket. And it ain't for Poughkeepsie."

Harper thought for a minute. Scanned the crowd. Turned, and watched three officials checking passports.

"You're right," he eventually said. "Where do you think he'll try to get to?"

"My guess would be Kuwait . . . maybe the Emirates. Preston had to pay him a fucking fortune to pull a stunt like this. It's the easiest place to set up a financial base. People don't ask questions. Nobody'll put the squeeze on you. They've got too much cash of their own."

"There's no point alerting passport control. He's got a new name by now. Probably shaved the mustache, too." Again Harper looked out over the crowd, "Let's get to the International Terminal. See who's going where."

The two agents pulled their IDs, held them up for the passport control officer, ran out to the ground transportation strip, and pushed their way to the front of the taxi line. Once in a cab, Harper said, "Take us to the International Terminal."

The driver was Indian and spoke with a heavy accent. "Oh, that would be a *shorty*. I must get *shorty* ticket from dispatcher. This way, I can come back. Can go to front of line. Please so kind as to wait." The driver started to get out of his cab.

"Hey, fella," Nichols barked. "Get in the goddamn car." He fished a fifty-dollar bill from his pocket and stuffed it through the plastic window that divided front and rear seats. "Here. Take this. Drive the fucking car. We don't have all day to fuck around here."

The man took the money and drove off. Without his *shorty* ticket. When they arrived at the International Terminal, Harper and Nichols jumped from the taxi and jogged to the entrance. The driver stepped from his cab and shouted, "There is being three twenty-five on the meter." They never turned to acknowledge his request for more cash.

Once inside the agents approached a television monitor listing departures.

"Fuck," Nichols moaned, "look at all these flights. What the hell is JAT, for Christ's sake? Can you believe all these piss-ant countries have their own fucking airline?"

"He could be going anywhere. This is useless. There's got to be a way to narrow this down."

"And the bastard knows what we look like. He could show up as anything. He could come in here dressed as Margaret Fucking Thatcher, and walk right by us."

Harper walked over to a phone bank. Nichols followed. He punched in a few numbers, and waited. "Let's see what the office has on our buddy Drew," he said to Nichols.

He studied the faces of passing passengers as he waited for the phone to be answered.

"Federal Bureau of Investigation."

"Yeah, Kate, it's Jack Harper. I need a rundown on an agent; can you throw it up for me? Thanks. Stevenson . . . Drew . . . Last three cases? . . . Vacations? . . . Family overseas? . . . Languages? . . . No, that'll do it. Thanks, Kate."

"What's up?"

"Well, his team never produced enough evidence to bring charges against the mob on that bakery deal. I guess he got a nice paycheck from the interested parties there, too. Other than that there wasn't much . . . Well, one thing . . ."

"What's that?"

"He doesn't have any sisters."

"Son of a bitch . . . What's he speak?"

"Fluent in Italian and Spanish."

"Well, he's not going to Spain and he's not going to Italy. My guess is we're now looking at the Mideast or South America. Venezuela more than likely. I'd still stay with an oil country if I were him."

"Yeah, well, Colombia's out. We've got too many people down there. They'd make him in a second. And Argentina and Chile don't throw out welcome mats. Too many skeletons in their closets."

"I'll bet you anything," Nichols said, smiling, recognizing his own genius, "the bastard's already checked a bag . . . We go over these airlines for early check-ins. Whatever name he's picked, I guarantee you, it's going to stick out like a sore fucking thumb. He's planned this out. He's not going to be walking around here with a goddamn suitcase this late in the game."

They narrowed their list to Mideastern and South American countries, split up, and started to work the terminal in alphabetical order, pushing first-class passengers aside and flashing their FBI IDs. Asking flight attendants for the identities of all early check-ins. They limited it to passengers who had checked baggage over three hours before flight departure. It went quicker than they'd expected. Many of the flights didn't leave until later in the evening. Each airline supplied them with only a handful of names.

Nichols started with Aerolineas Argentinas and would work through to Kuwait Airways. Harper picked up with Lan-Chile. He planned to go through to Yemen Airways, but he never got that far. At the Varig counter the attendant presented him with four names, Jamie Morales, Mr. and Mrs. Carlos Lenzi, and Dana Sizemore. "D.S.—Drew Stevenson—Varig flight 1123, five-fifteen p.m., gate thirteen," Harper said as he approached Nichols.

Nichols glanced at his watch and said, "He's cutting it close, but that's our boy."

Forty-seven

Harper phoned downtown for a backup, but was informed it would be highly unlikely they'd make it through the rush-hour traffic in time to be of any good. The Varig flight would start boarding in forty minutes, and even if they came out by chopper, it wouldn't guarantee a damn thing. Only make a lot of fucking noise and probably take just as long by the time they got the bird up. So they sat in the airport security officer's briefing room and explained the situation. Three airport guards had been diverted from their duties to help take Stevenson. The five men gathered around an oval table as the supervisor looked on. Harper made a gallant effort to speak in a friendly tone.

"First, I want to say that it is paramount we take this man alive. Under no circumstances is he to be harmed. He will have already passed through the metal detectors. There's no possible way he could be carrying a weapon. Agent Nichols and I will approach the suspect and lead him out of the terminal. You men are strictly here as a backup. If he somehow makes a break for it, wrestle him to the ground. Do not draw your weapons . . ." Harper took an overly long breath and pushed on. "He will be disguised. We have no idea what form that disguise will take. It could be a man, it could be a woman . . . The ticket reads Dana Sizemore.

"Until Agent Nichols and I feel we have the right person, I don't want any of you to make a move. The idea is to appear as if everything's the way it should be. Nothing's out of place."

Harper looked to Nichols, who picked it up from there. "This man knows what Agent Harper and I look like. He'll spot us long before we spot him, so keep your eyes peeled for any quick movements—anyone who may try to break from the pack and run. You men will take up positions outside the waiting area, while we mingle with the passengers. It's not a full flight. There should only be a hundred and fourteen passengers in the area. If all goes right, it will be a very simple exercise. It'll go smoothly. However, as Agent Harper said earlier, we must take this man alive." He glanced back to Harper, then said, "I think that's it. We won't be able to position you men personally, so find a spot where you can observe us without looking like you suspect anything's out of the ordinary. Any questions?"

They shook their heads.

"Good. We'll see you out there."

The three airport security guards shuffled out and Harper moved over to their supervisor. "How do you feel about these men? I don't want any gunslingers out there. I'd rather they turn and run for the hills before they start shooting at people."

"I just started here last week. I got promoted from the Port Authority bus terminal."

Nichols rolled his eyes and Harper said, "Well, let's hope for the best, shall we? My guess he's in the waiting area by now, so let's move."

The two agents stepped back into the main terminal and headed toward the departure corridor, and gate thirteen.

"What do you think we're looking for?" Nichols asked, already feeling somewhat exasperated and incredibly uneasy about his backup.

"Stevenson's got those high cheekbones. Those, he can't hide. Other than that . . . who knows. I wouldn't expect a beard, they're too hard to fake and make look good. And if he's shaved the mustache, there's no way he's putting on a new one. I would guess—wig. He could've darkened his skin down, too. Try to look a little more Spanish."

"Clothes?"

"He sure as hell isn't wearing a suit."

"What kind of a goddamn name is Dana?"

"Man, I guess . . . there was a Dana Andrews once."

"Shit . . . I forgot about him. What about Dana Delaney?"

"Who the hell is Dana Delaney?"

"Some broad."

"Great."

They continued down the passageway to the security checkpoint, where they displayed their IDs and passed without a word. After another forty feet they entered the waiting area of gate thirteen.

It appeared as if all one hundred and fourteen passengers were there, anxiously awaiting any possible preboarding announcement, so they could mob the flight attendant at the jetway. Almost everyone spoke in Spanish. They all chain-smoked cigarettes. They all seemed nervous. It was going to be tougher to pick Stevenson out of this crowd than they'd expected. Everyone was edgy. Everyone's eyes darted around the room like frightened mice. Everyone hated to fly.

And Harper and Nichols looked exactly like what they were—FBI agents. Immediately all passengers recognized they were being looked over. Examined.

It didn't take long for the travelers to put two and two together: Federal agents were searching for someone. Some terrorist, no doubt. Some mad bomber had wired their goddamn plane with tons of plastic explosives. They were all going to die a horrible death. The more Harper and Nichols hunted for Stevenson, the more uneasy people became.

"See him?" Harper asked Nichols.

"Nope . . . Fuck. I don't know what the hell I'm looking for."

"We're driving these people crazy. They're going to start asking to get off the plane if we don't watch ourselves. Come on . . ." Harper walked over to a flight attendant as she prepared to open the gangway for the early boarding of first-class passengers. He casually slipped his ID onto her podium. "Miss, we're looking for someone. He's not dangerous, so there's no need to be alarmed. But he's disguised. And we're not sure who or what we're looking for . . . We don't want this man leaving the country. We'd like to stand by the plane's entrance as people board. It should be very peaceful."

"If you give me the passenger's name I can locate his seat number for you, but I'll have to check with the captain first."

"No. The flight's not booked. He might take a different seat. Besides, I don't want him to get on the plane. I don't want to create a potential hostage situation."

"I thought you said he wasn't dangerous?"

"Can we talk to the captain, miss?" Harper voiced in a tone that easily said he'd had enough with her.

She turned without a word and led them down the gangway where they spoke with the captain and he reluctantly approved of Harper's strategy. The flight attendant returned to her post and started the boarding procedure.

Eventually people began to filter down the jetway. Nichols leaned into Harper and said, "He'll be flying up front. No way he's going to sit back with the peons."

"That doesn't mean he'll board early or sit in the right seat for takeoff. He knows we're here. He's going to have to look us in the eye as he passes."

Harper was hoping Stevenson's height would give him away as much as anything, but some of the passengers were surprisingly tall. Nonetheless, they were able to eliminate nearly fifty percent of the people quickly. Each passenger studied the agents with suspicion as they stepped onto the aircraft. Nichols was amazed at how many people genuflected as they passed, as though they were boarding the fucking *Titanic*.

Harper stopped a man with long hair, wearing torn khakis and a faded denim shirt.

The man said, *"Si?"*

Harper looked long and hard into the man's eyes, but released his arm after a moment. He said, "Sorry. I thought I knew you."

Next he stood directly in front of a statuesque woman with raven-black shoulder-length hair. Nichols moved alongside. She was easily Harper's height. She made no attempt to go around them.

Harper said, "Dana?"

She smiled at him and said, "I'm almost the last one. The waiting area's nearly empty . . . and I'm sorry to report, I'm not who you're looking for. I'm not Dana . . . It's too bad, really. I think the three of us could've had a good time together. I like men who carry handcuffs." She winked at Harper, then patted Nichols on the cheek.

Another passenger, decked out in a flowered print shirt, long brownish-blond hair, and sunglasses, attempted to pass them as they spoke to the woman. Nichols stepped aside to let the man by. He looked at the shirt, down at his ragged jeans, then further down at his shoes. He smiled and tapped Harper on the arm and whispered, "Fucking wing tips. What a dumb shit."

Nichols then grabbed the man's elbow and said, "You need a haircut, Drew."

Stevenson turned slightly to his left and then brought his free elbow swiftly up and in, to meet Nichols's chest dead center. Three of the agent's ribs, on the left side, snapped with the force of the blow, and all air immediately escaped from his lungs. As Nichols gasped for breath, Stevenson turned completely around and grabbed him by the lapels. He threw Nichols into the bulkhead with such force, the noise rang out like a cannon shot as it reverberated back into the waiting area. Nichols's head bounced off the corrugated steel wall. His knees deserted him, and he began to slide down to the deck, in a wholly unconscious state. Stevenson tore the pistol from Nichols's holster a second before the agent collapsed into a heap on the floor.

It happened in a blink of an eye, but Harper was able to push the tall raven-haired woman onto the aircraft and out of harm's way. The last thing he needed now was a hostage situation. The remaining passengers had panicked and retreated back into the terminal.

"You—fucking—guys . . . You—fucking—guys," Stevenson said as he leveled Nichols's pistol at Harper's face. "You left your fucking witness back there to die? Just to bust me? One of your own? I don't fucking believe you two. You toss procedure out the fucking window just to chase down one of your own. You—fucking—guys . . . Didn't you read the goddamn book?"

"It's over, Drew . . ." Harper glanced to his left as the copilot secured the aircraft hatch; the two ground technicians had already jumped on board behind the tall woman. Stevenson wasn't taking this plane anywhere.

"You fucks," he yelled as he slammed his foot into the side of the plane. Harper took a step toward him.

"Don't try it, Jack."

"It's all over . . . Look, Drew, you can waste me, if that's what you want. Go ahead . . . it's not going to do you any good. You've got the whole Bureau waiting for you out there." Harper pointed back toward the main terminal.

"I don't think so. I counted three rent-a-cops . . . Drop your piece."

"Look—"

"On the floor with it . . . move."

Harper reached for his pistol.

"Real easy, Jack. I like you. I don't want to have take you out."

Harper did as he was told.

"Now move. We're walking out of here . . . together."

"Listen to me for a second, Drew. You whacked the wrong guy back there. He was a fucking dupe. Preston's not going to make good on his end of your deal. Billy's still alive. You killed the wrong man."

"What're you talking about?"

"He was a double. We were setting Preston up . . . You didn't hear me call him *Joe* as he went down?"

Stevenson began to think about what Harper was saying.

"It's good, but it sounds like bullshit. Start walking."

Harper began walking down the gangway, back toward the waiting room. "It's no good, Drew . . . Let me take you in. You can cut a deal. It's Preston we're after. You testify for the government, and they'll go easy on you. Your position isn't as bad as you think. It's the train, Drew. Get on early. Get a good seat."

"Yeah? Aren't you forgetting I just killed someone? Whether it was Billy or some other dumb schmuck, it's murder-one. I went to the same school you did, remember, Jack? Nobody's cutting deals on murder-one these days."

"They will here." Harper stopped and turned to face Stevenson. "Give me the gun. It's the only way out."

Stevenson turned him back around.

"I'm running out of time. Where's your pickup car?"

"Back at the American terminal. You'll never make it."

"All right . . . Fuck. I've got to think here. I can't believe you guys fucking did this to me. One of your own."

They'd reached the end of the gangway. Stevenson opened the door and peered out to the waiting area. The three airport security officers had been briefed by the fleeing passengers on the situation. They'd cleared the entire area of civilians and were waiting with their supervisor in the main corridor, all four guns drawn.

"Fuck," Stevenson said again.

"What's up?"

"Those dickheads are out there making like it's the fucking O.K. Corral." Stevenson stuck his head out through the doorway and shouted to the guards, "Nobody come in here. I've got three hostages. Stay back. Any communication can be done by the flight-line telephone." He then said to Harper, "Let's go back. We'll take the stairs to the tarmac."

The pain in Nichols's chest was excruciating but he'd regained consciousness. He'd crawled across the gangway, picked up Harper's automatic, and chambered a round. Nichols felt more stable on his knees so he stayed there. Waiting. The Varig flight had pulled away from the jetway leaving him back-lit by the setting September sun. He gave off the appearance of a legless troll, guarding the entrance to the king's gold mine. He could now hear Harper and Stevenson talking. Louder. They were coming back his way.

Harper was the first to come back around the dogleg in the passageway. Stevenson behind him, pistol pressed into Harper's ribs. There was no way Nichols could take Stevenson down without losing Harper. He brought the pistol down to his lap.

"One question," Stevenson said to Nichols, "and no help from you, Jack. Who'd I nick back at the American terminal?"

Nichols looked to Harper who said, "Go ahead, tell him. He doesn't believe me."

"His name was Joe Bradlee. He was a dupe. We were setting up Preston."

"You—fucking—guys." Stevenson began to laugh. "How the fuck did you keep it quiet? Shit . . . son of a bitch, I like it. I really like it. It's got class. I can't believe you fuckers pulled this off. It makes me wish I'd been in on it."

Seven airport police cars sped up to the area surrounding gate thirteen and came to a sliding stop where the Varig jet had been a minute earlier. Gray smoke floated from their fat black tires. Men in blue piled from the cars and took up positions behind the vehicles. Several sported blue baseball caps and carried high-powered rifles with scopes. Nichols looked down at them from the gaping jetway and screamed, "It's over up here. We're working it out. Don't get itchy. He comes in alive . . . even if we don't. Everything's under control." It was all he could say. The pain in his chest was forcing his head to spin.

Stevenson continued to laugh. "That was beautiful, Nichols. I'm fucking touched. Who says altruism is dead?"

Harper began to sit on the carpet and Stevenson ducked down behind him as soon as he realized how exposed he was. "You fucker," he said when he was beside Harper.

"It's been a long day, Drew, let's call it quits. NYPD's here. All they can do is fuck it up. I wouldn't be surprised if they hose all three of us down."

Stevenson reached into his shirt pocket.

"Cigarette?"

Harper and Nichols shook their heads. Stevenson pulled a plastic lighter from his pants and lit up. "Man, this sucks the big one, I'll tell you . . ." He pulled a heavy wad of smoke into his lungs. "Nichols, why don't you hand me that other weapon? Just to be on the safe side. I don't want you to hurt yourself."

Nichols slid it over.

"You think I could get these fuckers to rustle me up a plane ride out of the country? Someplace exotic?"

Harper folded his legs in front of him and leaned back against the jetway wall. "Nope," he said.

They looked like three fraternity brothers talking Saturday-night dates. All they were missing were the beers and torn sweatshirts. Backward baseball caps.

"Why not?" Stevenson said. "They've done it in the past. I've got hostages."

"Yeah, but look who you're holding, ya dumb bastard," Harper said with a smile. "They're not going to negotiate for us. We're dead meat. Just like the sap back in the American terminal. You know the rules. No one negotiates for a Federal officer. Especially NYPD."

"It's over, Drew." Nichols coughed. "Let's go home.

We'll see what kind of deal we can cut for you. Preston's going down the tubes anyway. Billy'll have his day in court." He looked at his watch. "He's downtown and all tucked in by now. Give it up."

Stevenson took a long time to think it over, but eventually he chuckled, shook his head, handed the two pistols to Jack Harper, and said with a sigh that more resembled a demented laugh, "This really does suck the big one, you know that, don't you? I wish I could be more pissed off at you two, but I can't. It was smooth. It was really fucking smooth. I'm even beginning to feel a little sorry for the goofball back at the American terminal."

All three sat quietly while Stevenson finished his cigarette. When he was done he stood, stamped it out into the carpet, walked to the end of the jetway, and waved an "Okay" to the police cars. Nichols glanced at the sharpshooters. He sucked as much air into his chest as he could get and screamed, "Nooo . . ." He then reached up and grabbed Stevenson's belt at the back of his trousers in an attempt to pull him back into the corridor. As he did it, he felt one of his ribs slowly digging its way into the side of his left lung.

The first bullet smashed into Stevenson at the waist. It passed through his body, exploded out the back, and tore into Nichols's hand on the right side, completely removing his pinky finger and shattering his ring finger—along with his career in the FBI. Six more shells piled into Stevenson within the next two seconds. Three in the chest. Two in the head. The last one cut through his right thigh and continued down the jetway. He was dead long before what was left of his body fell to the deck.

"Jeeeesus . . ." Nichols bellowed as he jammed what remained of his hand into his crotch. "God fucking damn it."

Harper crawled over and kicked Stevenson's lifeless body out and down onto the tarmac so the sharpshooters would know they'd got their man. Only then did he stand. He ripped his jacket, tie, and shoulder holster off, then grasped at his shirt and pulled it straight out until all seven buttons flew off. He grabbed Nichols right hand and swiftly wound his shirt around the bloody mess. Harper secured the shirt as tightly as he could and went to the end of the jetway. He looked down. Police officers had already gathered around Stevenson's body. Two paramedics were bent over him as well.

"I've got a wounded man up here." Harper pointed down to Stevenson. "If you think you're going to save him, you've got your head up your ass. Get the fuck up here . . . *now*!"

The medics jumped from Stevenson and scrambled up the steel stairway.

"You didn't hear us say we wanted him alive, you fucks?"

A gray-haired man in a natty suit turned his head up to Harper. He said, "This is my airport, son. We handle all hostage situations the same way. I don't care who you work for." He looked back down at Stevenson and a job well done.

Harper shook his head and turned to watch the paramedics administer to Nichols. He then walked ten feet down the jetway, bent down, picked something up, came back, and handed the object to one of the men.

"Jesus," the man said, "what the hell is that?"

"It's his finger. Put it on ice, you dumb shit."

Forty-eight

"The only way to keep him alive, at this point, with this much upper body damage, is to remove both lungs. And, I'm sorry to say, there's no such thing as a lung transplant. The lungs collapse upon death and become useless to us. All of this means he'll be bed-ridden and connected to this machine for the rest of his life . . . which won't be long, I can tell you that. I'm sorry to have to be the one to pass this news onto you, Danielle. May I call you Danielle?"

"Oh yes, Doctor, please. But . . . is that our only alternative? Isn't there another way out?"

"We could always pull the plug . . . here and now. And that would be my advice; as a doctor. He was much too much of an active man for us to have to see him rot away this way, lonely, in an often unclean hospital bed. The most he could even hope to get out of it would be a year, and that's being generous. Can we bear to watch that? You and I . . . ? Danielle . . . ? But . . . I feel this decision is yours alone to make. I can only advise you. As a doctor, of course."

"Oh, Doctor . . ."

"Please, call me Fred."

"Oh Fred, I don't know what to say. We haven't

been together for very long. I don't know how well I really do know him. I'm much too young to have to make a decision like this . . . on my own. You're older. More mature than I am. You remind me so much of my father. Please tell me . . . What should I do?"

"Come. Come over to me. You can cry on my shoulder any time you feel you need to. I can help you get through this . . . I can be by your side . . . guide you. Shelter you. What should you do? I think you should pull the plug, Danielle. Let him pass away as the man he once was. Not what he is now. Useless . . . a disintegrating burden to society."

"Oh, thank you, Fred . . . You're so gentle, so kind. Which plug do I pull? Is it the green one?"

"*One Life To Live* will return . . . After these messages."

"What the fuck is going on here?" Joe said as he fought to regain his eyesight.

"Holy shit . . . I thought you were going to die on us. You're awake?"

It was all still very fuzzy.

"Who the hell are you?" he said. He squeezed his eyes together in three or four short flinching movements and his vision began to slowly clear.

She had short-cropped platinum blond hair and could have easily passed for the most beautiful woman he'd ever seen. Dark blue eyes that looked like Caribbean water at two hundred feet and blood-red lips. And she was no nurse, that was for damn sure. It was impossible for Joe to tell whether he'd landed in heaven or hell. The TV's soap opera made him suspect the latter.

She moved her mouth to his ear and whispered,

"Relax, Joey, I'm your sister . . . Nora. Remember . . . ? We were worried sick about you."

"Nora . . . ? I don't have a—"

"Just look at me. Everything will come back to you."

Joe looked at Nora long and hard as she held his face between her palms. He then deliberately and silently mouthed, "Andie . . . ? That's you?"

"Your friend Jack Harper is right outside. He'll be happy to see you've regained consciousness. He's been a prince throughout this whole thing. Should I call him in?"

"I don't think I'm ready for *The Prince* just yet. I'm still a little shocked at my *sister* being here . . . Nora?"

"I Just wanted to see you again before I faded into the woodwork. I wanted to be sure you were going to make it."

"How long have I been here? What day is it? How long have I been out?"

"About a week."

Andie moved over to the hospital door, opened it, and poked her head out. Then sweeter than sweet said, "Jack, I'm very hungry. Do you think you could be an absolute dear and run down to the commissary and pick me up a sandwich or something? Anything would be fine, a salad, maybe something green. Dressing on the side. Extra pepper. Oh, thanks, you're such a sweetheart."

"New hair . . . New eyes . . . But you haven't changed much," Joe said. A sharp pain raced through his chest. He coughed and the agony became unbearable. He was quickly aware of thirty or forty surgical stitches tugging at his flesh, inside and out, and the slightest torso movement made him feel as if he'd been put together like Frankenstein's monster.

"I like this look on you, Andie," he managed with a smile. "Harper didn't recognize you?"

"He's never seen me before, even as a redhead."

"What the hell is going on? Where am I?"

"Room six-six-six, Saint Vincent's intensive-care unit. We didn't think you were going to make it."

"Could you turn the TV off?"

"I'm waiting for Emma."

"Who the hell is Emma?"

"Dorian's long-suffering maid. I'm waiting to see if they have to sell the family jewels."

"Will you turn that shit off. Christ. What the hell happened? You've been watching that crap for a week?"

Andie reluctantly turned the TV off and sat on the edge of the bed. "It's good stuff once you get into it. You wouldn't believe how devious Emma is. She makes me look like a saint."

"Jesus . . . How did I get here? How did *you* get here? What's going on? God, I feel like shit."

"My brother shot you."

". . . At Kennedy . . . right . . . Jesus . . ." He winced as another sharp pain flew through his chest. "It's starting to come back to me . . . I thought it was bees. I was dreaming about bees."

"Bees?"

"Never mind. Where's your brother now?"

"They killed him."

"What . . . ? Who?"

Andie didn't seem terribly broken up, considering

her brother's funeral couldn't have been more than a couple of days ago.

"The airport police shot him . . . right after he shot you."

Andie walked to the window and gazed at the blue sky, snow white clouds, and Manhattan skyline as it trailed off toward the World Trade towers. She sighed. "Drew wasn't my brother . . ."

"Yeah, I figured that out . . . It only took one look into his eyes. Unfortunately I was sixty-five feet too late. Why'd you lie about him all these years?"

Andie took a moment to consider what she wanted to say. She pushed a strand of hair from her eyes and continued to look out the window as she spoke. "We were an item when he was going through Quantico, the FBI Academy. He was afraid of giving off the impression he was attached to someone. He thought it would hurt his chances for getting field work after graduation. He didn't want them to think he was going to end up married right from the start. We just kept the charade up for some reason . . . even after we split up. I don't know . . . I had too much on him—he had too much on me. I guess we were both paranoid about letting the other get too far away . . . or out of sight."

"I'm very fond of you, Andie, I really am, you have a way about you that I'm sure very few men could ever resist. But that story sounds like such an incredible load of bullshit . . ." He was smiling as best he could, but it hurt like a son of a bitch.

"That's tough. It's all you're going to get from me." She came over to him and sat back down on the bed. Then took his hand in hers. "I know more about you than you think and I'm sure you also know too much about me. That makes us even. Let's just leave it at that, okay? Life goes on. We don't have to tell anybody anything, do we? Like I said before, just a couple of sluts . . ."

"Thanks. I'm feeling better already . . . emotionally, that is."

Andie took a deep breath, let it out slowly, and looked back toward the window.

"Your *real* name?" he said. "Is that something you'd like to share with me?"

". . . Nora."

"Get out of here. Nora is not your real name."

"It is."

"Last name?"

"Well if I'm your sister, I guess it would have to be Bradlee, wouldn't it?"

"You're hopeless." He smiled.

"It's Lincoln." She then trembled slightly and whispered, "Oh . . . Jesus . . . this stinks."

"What? What stinks?"

Andie sighed again. ". . . I think she's in love with you."

"Who. . . ? What are you talking about?"

"Emma."

"Emma?"

"I mean Danielle."

"Danielle? Where the hell is she? Is she here? In New York?"

"She's been in and out. It's been nearly impossible to duck her. She'd recognize the new me in a second and I don't think that's in my best interest. She's gone on her lunch break."

They were quiet for almost a minute.

"Yeah, well, I wouldn't count on her being in love with me. She probably only feels sorry for me. I must pose a pretty pitiful sight . . . She'll get over it."

"It's more than that, you clod. She came all the way from Paris to be with you. Getting a visa couldn't have been easy, even with Jack's help."

Joe only groaned slightly as another wave of misery spread through his chest.

"The problem is . . ." She looked at Joe and then again out to the skyline. "I also fell in love with you." She found a tear slipping down her cheek. A bona fide one. Otherwise she could've held it back.

He tightened his grip on her hand and said, "Don't talk yourself into that . . . I'm a real bastard once you get to know me better . . . Not to mention the slut part."

"That's all I wanted to say. It's the only reason I stuck around. I wanted you to know I cared. And in the end . . . I didn't want to hurt you."

"Thanks . . ."

"I don't know what it is . . . but I always fall in love with the wrong damn people." She leaned in and placed her lips lightly on his, then stood. "I'm leaving . . . Take care of yourself."

"Where will you be?"

"I have to disappear . . . I can do it. I've done it before. I'd like to think that you wouldn't come after me once you're on your feet. You won't; I can see that in your eyes. But Preston sang like a bird when he saw Billy in that courtroom. He coughed up a list of names a mile long. He's running scared. It's only a matter of time before the FBI checks Drew's phone records and starts looking for Andie Stevenson. Then Nora Lincoln."

Joe squeezed her hand once more, ". . . I don't think I can help you, Andie."

"I wouldn't want you to. You're one of the good guys, remember?" She pushed another tear from her cheek. "If it makes any difference to you . . . I never hurt anyone who didn't have it coming. I've always rationalized what I've done as a form of vigilantism—another reason I couldn't do you, I guess. Why'd you have to be so damn clean?"

Joe watched as she crossed in front of the television set. He smiled at her and said, "Andie . . . ?"

"Yes?"

"We'll always have Paris."

Andie gave him a warm look, closed the door, and was gone.

Four minutes later Jack Harper walked in carrying a ham and cheese sandwich in a clear plastic box. No salad. No pepper. He had a broad smile on his face. "Welcome back to the living. What happened to your sister?"

"She had to go . . . Had a meeting in Tunisia."

Harper bent at the waist, let out with a colossal sneeze, and followed it with, "Goddamn these fucking roses. You mind if I stick them in the john? They stir up my allergies like a motherfucker."

"Go for it."

Harper picked up the three-dozen softball-size roses that had been neatly arranged in a silver champagne bucket, placed them on the toilet seat, and slammed the bathroom door. "Christ, I hate those fucking things."

"Where'd they come from?"

"Arthur Preston."

"You're shitting me."

"Junior. Junior. He somehow felt responsible for landing you here. I told him to forget it, but he sent the fucking roses anyway. He's in Palm Springs. Joined the PGA tour."

"Good for Arthur."

"Did Nora tell you we nailed his old man to the fucking wall?"

"Nora?"

"Your sister."

"Right." Joe shook his head slightly. "The painkillers must be kicking in. I'm getting fuzzy . . . Yeah, Nora told me that. She also said to tell you she was sorry about sending you all the way down for that sandwich and then disappearing."

"Fuck it . . . It's Monday. We can save it for tonight's Giants' game."